Surrender to a Wicked Spy

St. Martin's Titles
by Celeste Bradley

Surrender to a Wicked Spy

Book Two in The Royal Four series

Celeste Bradley

St. Martin's

Every ruler needs a few men he can count on to tell him the truth—whether he wants to hear it or not.

Created in the time of the Normans, when King William the Conqueror found himself overrun with "advisors" more concerned with their own agendas than with the good of the whole, the Quatre Royale were selected from the King's own boyhood friends. Lords all, and bound by loyalty rather than selfish motives, these four men took on the names of ruthless predators while acting as the Quatre, keeping their lives and identities separate from their true roles...

...to act as the shield of deceit and the sword of truth in the name of the King.

Courageous as the Lion
Deadly as the Cobra
Vigilant as the Falcon
Clever as the Fox

The appointment is for life—the commitment absolute. Bonds of family, friends and even love become as insubstantial as a dream when each hand-selected apprentice takes the seat of the master. All else is merely pretense, kept for the sake of secrecy and anonymity. For it is true that the iron bars of duty cage the hearts and soul of...

...THE ROYAL FOUR.

Prologue

ENGLAND, 1813

Lady Olivia Cheltenham fell into the Thames and was rescued by a Viking god. Rather, she was pushed in—by none other than her very own mother—and the Viking god saved her. In any case, he tried to. Sorry to say, she ended up saving him.

When Olivia felt her mother shove her over the railing of the Westminster Bridge, she had what seemed like a very long time on the way down to think upon the reason. Despite the fact that Olivia did not have her diary in hand—being in midair, after all—she was sure Mother had never shown signs of being homicidal before. Doubtful indeed that it was a sudden onset of madness.

Nor had Olivia done anything more offensive than ask repeatedly why she was being required to stand on a bridge and look at the Thames for hours on a chill, windy day. Therefore, the only explanation could be that there had been an eligible bachelor within sight.

As the icy water closed over Olivia's head, wrenching her bonnet from her head and taking her breath away, Olivia was forced to admit that perhaps she should be more charitable. Mother had been under such a strain lately.

Yet surely she wasn't mad enough to kill Olivia in the hunt for a husband?

The river was not deep here and Olivia felt her toes touch the soft, mucky bottom briefly before her natural buoyancy began to pull her upward again. Her head broke the surface and she took a much-needed breath. This not being the first time she had ever fallen into water in her life, she had begun to strip off her spencer immediately and now she was able to pull her arms free and toss the short jacket aside to float slowly away.

Fortunately, her gown would not weigh her down, for she was wearing a very light muslin without much in the way of petticoats. Mother had insisted she wear it this morning despite the weather—a fact made suddenly sinister in the light of recent events. Olivia put her mother's plotting out of her mind in favor of a more important matter—survival. She was an excellent swimmer, but the water was icy with autumn runoff. It was imperative that she get out immediately. She kicked her slippers away and examined her situation.

Above her, she heard her mother's horrified screams and the shouts of what seemed like a large crowd gathering, but Olivia did not waste time peering up at them. The water was so cold that it was already sending spikes of pain into her hands and feet. She ought to get out before she went numb. Turning easily with a sweep of her arms, she spotted a set of the slimy stone stairs that led from the bank down to the water every so often along the river's edge.

She was about to strike out for the spot when something large hit the water next to her, sending choking brown filth up her nose and into her open mouth. She sputtered in disgust and swiped at her face, clearing her vision in time to see a pair of great arms reaching for her.

With a kick, she avoided them easily and swam a short distance away. The arms belonged to a large, filthy stranger.

Of course, in his defense, he probably hadn't been filthy before he entered the water.

In fact, he'd probably looked very nice indeed a few moments ago. Olivia tread water easily as she considered him. If the chiseled cheekbones and firm chin visible beneath his streaming, dirty gold hair were any indication, he normally looked very fine indeed. His head remained very stably above water. Apparently he was large enough that he was able to stand firmly on the bottom. He looked like a very wet, very dirty Viking.

No, not descriptive enough. He looked like a large, wet, dirty Viking *god*.

There was only one man in London who matched that description—Dane Calwell, Viscount Greenleigh, official Catch of the Season. Olivia had never met him formally, but she had seen him at many of the events her mother had dragged her to in the search for a husband. Olivia hadn't bothered to dream of "the Dane's" attention—well, at least not that she would admit to, and midnight fancies of Viking . . . er, conquest notwithstanding, *she* was most definitely not the Catch of the Season.

As Mother never failed to remind her, she was a bit too tall for fashion and had never quite mastered the trick of wearing ball gowns with grace and her hair never seemed to stay in place and she never seemed to know quite what to do with her hands—or her unbecomingly large feet—in public and the gentlemen all seemed to be prettier than her, or at least seemed to pay more attention to their appearance.

Yet Mother had not given up. Cheltenham depended on Olivia. Hence the reason handsome, wealthy Lord Greenleigh had decided to go for a swim.

Enter the eligible bachelor.

He swiped long, previously golden hair from his face and blinked sky blue eyes at her in confusion. "Are—are you all right?"

Mother's game was working. He was dutifully going to rescue Olivia. How embarrassing. She grimly decided not to play. "Oh yes," she assured him. "No need to bother about me."

Obviously not understanding, he reached for her. Olivia evaded his grasp, swimming effortlessly aside. Unfortunately, this put him between her and the stairs and she was already starting to shiver.

He reached again. She evaded again. He stared at her in frustration. "Will you come here so I can help you?"

"No thank you," she replied primly. "If you'll simply move aside, I shall make my own way out."

He blinked, frowning. The river lapped at his chest much the way it did to the great immovable pillars of the bridge. "What?"

Olivia gave up. She had no time to make idle chatter with him. He was big enough to simply walk out, but she was growing colder by the moment. Striking out, she took a side tack that swept her a bit downstream of him. Of course, the great fellow reached for her again, but he seemed unwilling to take a single step, so she rounded him quickly and made for the stairs.

Halfway there, she glanced back. He still stood there, as immovable as a stone. "Aren't you coming?" she called. "The water is very cold."

He turned his head and upper body to look at her. "I—I can't."

Olivia was beginning to lose patience. Her teeth were chattering mightily now and she couldn't feel most of her body. "I'll make sure she apologizes," she snapped. "I know it was a terrible thing to do, but I do think you're being a bit mulish now."

He blinked at her. "I have no idea what you're talking about, miss, but the reason I can't move is that my boots have sunk into the mud."

"Oh." Olivia looked longingly at the stone stairs once more, then turned back.

"No," he protested when he saw her returning. "Go on! You must get out of this chill water!"

Olivia ignored him, stroking swiftly to his side. "Can you not pull your feet from them?"

He glanced away sheepishly. "They're very new and they fit quite tightly. It usually requires my valet's help to pull them off."

Olivia didn't bother to hide her opinion of that sort of vanity. He glanced at her expression and shrugged. "Everyone is wearing them that way these days."

Some Viking god he was. It was just her luck that the only man in London who attracted her was a vain and impractical dandy. As if he needed any help looking stunning!

Locking her jaw against the chattering that now verged on violent, Olivia reached for him. "You need to take the weight off the mud," she told him. "Let yourself lean back and try to float your weight on the water."

He frowned at her. "I think I'd prefer to stay firmly on my feet."

"I'm sure you would," she said patiently, though it cost her dearly. Still, she could hardly rail at the fellow when it was Mother who had caused the entire mess. "Trust that I know what I'm talking about," she urged him. "Livestock gets stuck in the mud at home in Durham all the time."

"Livestock?" He looked a bit miffed at that but began to lean back obediently. She caught his wide shoulders with her numb hands, kicking fiercely as his weight began to come on her. For a moment she thought he was going to sink like a stone, but then he began to float on the sluggish current.

"Now wiggle your feet from side to side," she instructed him. "You must break the suction of the mud."

He scowled at nothing in particular.

"Are you wiggling?" she persisted.

"I'm wiggling," he assured her gruffly.

Olivia was beginning to have trouble moving her limbs. She felt so heavy. . . .

"I've one free," he said exultantly, stretching out his arms for balance.

Olivia kicked too slowly and sank beneath his movement. It took all her strength to push back to the surface. She wasn't chattering anymore. Her brain felt sluggish, but somewhere she managed to dredge up the knowledge that that was a bad sign.

He lurched in her grip. "I'm free!" He pulled her close with one great arm, carefully treading water so his feet would not touch down again. "Miss?"

Olivia closed her eyes. Her lids were far too heavy to hold open any longer. She hung there in his grasp, too cold and numb to save herself now that she'd saved him.

"Miss!"

Being one of the most eligible bachelors in London Society, Dane Calwell, Viscount Greenleigh, was actually rather accustomed to saving damsels. In fact, they seemed to drop from the sky to land at his feet in various states of distress.

There was the time he'd rescued Miss Waverly from a near collision with a bog cart (although it was odd how she happened to be standing in the street just as he left his abode). He'd rescued Miss Morton when her hair ribbons had suddenly become mysteriously wound about a branch at the Teagardens' house party (they had been such unusually long ribbons). He'd swept Miss Hackerman from the saddle of a suddenly fractious horse when taking his daily ride through Hyde Park last week, although the horse had been perfectly docile until Dane had drawn near (but evidently he had a strange effect on young ladies' mounts, for that sort of rescue was becoming a regular event).

The Season was nearly over and Society's mamas were becoming desperate indeed. They might have been reassured had they known that Dane had every intention of marrying this year. After all, he was in his thirties and his wild days were long done. A man with his responsibilities required an appropriately demure, composed, well-bred hostess and mother for his heir. Therefore, Dane looked on all of this attempted entrapment with amused tolerance.

After all, it was not inconceivable that he might actually meet a suitable girl by plucking her from the path of a bog wagon. Unfortunately, the Misses Waverly, Morton, and Hackerman had all failed to impress him with their steadiness when they had indulged in outrageous fits of hysterics after being rescued. Still, Dane had hope that he'd find a young woman with a bit more substance before the Season ended.

So when a young lady fell into the Thames right before his eyes, Dane hadn't hesitated before leaping from his horse to dive into the water next to the struggling miss.

Except that this particular miss hadn't needed rescuing, at least not until she'd nearly frozen while rescuing *him.*

She lay in his arms now as he carried her up the grassy bank of the Thames. He didn't think it was precisely proper for him to be holding her so close, but the limp girl's mother—who only now had thought to run back down the bridge to the bank—was currently indulging in a rather overblown fit of panic and there didn't seem to be any servants with them.

Dane wrapped his sodden coat more closely about the pale, chilled form of his rescuer. He always did his best to see that his—er, damsels ended up properly taken care of after their ordeals, but there didn't seem to be anyone to take care of this one.

She wasn't quite unconscious, but her frozen state concerned him greatly. He was feeling deadly cold himself, and he was far larger than the young woman he held.

He glanced up at the gathering crowd—where had all these people been while the two of them had been floundering in the Thames?—and picked out a mild-looking young man at random.

"You there," Dane called. "Fetch a hackney coach here at once." The fellow nodded quickly and ran for the street. Dane glanced at the woman he was beginning to think of as "the mother from hell" and tried to smile at her reassuringly. This only sent her into a fresh bout of sobbing and carrying on as she clung to his side. She seemed to feel that she was to blame for some reason. Dane listened for a moment to see if the woman might let drop any hints as to her and her daughter's identity or what had happened or anything useful at all.

There was no sense coming from that quarter, so Dane tuned the woman out.

A shabby hack pulled up on the grass. It was a pretty poor specimen and small to boot, but Dane was in no mood to care. He ordered the mild young man to load the mother into the vehicle and carried the girl on himself. Seating himself in the cramped interior, he settled her into his lap, keeping a protective hold on her.

Perhaps he ought to be ashamed of noticing that she was a healthy armful and that she fitted rather nicely against him. Most young ladies seemed to aim for a sort of wispy daintiness. It was refreshing to be this close to such a sturdy female. She felt rather . . . unbreakable. He always felt somewhat uneasy when he came too close to some of the more petite women in Society. His common sense told him that he was not going to crush them during a dance, but his imagination supplied many an awful vision anyway.

She was attractive, as well, in a healthy country-bred sort of way. Not beautiful, but appealing enough . . . and vaguely familiar as well. He knew he'd seen her about, but he could not recall much more than the impression of quiet and stillness. Not a flash sort, then. Interesting. . . .

So when his coat briefly fell away from the young woman's bodice during the jostling carriage ride, Dane fell prey to his manly instincts rather than his gentlemanly ones and didn't precisely avert his eyes from what the thin, sodden muslin wasn't covering very well.

Well, well. Very nice. Very nice indeed. He could safely change his description from "sturdy" to "buxom."

Olivia wasn't unconscious, unless one counted being too cold and humiliated to be able to fend for oneself. Besides, her Viking lord was large and warm and strong and she found herself rather loathe to "wake," for then he'd surely set her aside.

However, when she felt the cold air wafting over her bared bodice, she could not resist taking a peek to see if he was taking a peek.

He was.

Then he promptly tucked his coat back around her. It had only been a tiny lapse, one she could hardly hold against him when she thought about how much she would like to see him nearly naked and soaking wet. . . .

Dane saw her open eyes and smiled at her, glad to see that she was alert once more. Her wry, assessing gaze told him she'd seen him peeking, but he certainly wasn't going to affirm her suspicions by appearing guilty. Besides, the brief glance at her full bosom capped with rosy points that pressed tightly to the translucent muslin had been the highlight of his rather trying day.

Her gaze left his, however, and slid to where her mother sat opposite them, now sobbing somewhat less vociferously.

"Mother," the girl said firmly through blue, chilled lips. "T-tell this nice gentleman that you're s-sorry."

The weeping woman uttered something unintelligible, which seemed to satisfy the girl in Dane's lap, for she then turned to look back up at him with a air of expectation. Dane hesitated, having the feeling that he was the only one who didn't know what they were talking about. "Ah . . . apology accepted?" he said finally.

The girl seemed to relax. "You're t—taking all of this very well, I must say," she told him as her shivers continued. "That bodes well f—for your character. You must be a man of g—great parts."

Perhaps it was the fact that he'd recently been peeking at her own rather "great parts" or perhaps it was the fact that his own "parts" were becoming more and more stimulated by the motion of a curvaceous bottom being jostled against them, but the commonplace saying struck Dane in quite a different way than it was intended to. He laughed involuntarily, then covered it with a cough. Smiling with bemusement at the very unusual creature nestled on his lap, he nodded. "Thank you. I might say the same about you." It was a pure delight to come across such a combination of robust voluptuousness and resilient poise.

The girl eyed him speculatively for a moment, then turned to her mother again. "Mama, you should allow this gentleman to introduce himself to you."

"Mama" nodded vigorously, then visibly repressed her sobs and dabbed at her eyes with a tiny scrap of lace that truly didn't look up to the task of drying all those tears.

"That's not necessary, my dear," the woman said, with a final sniffle. "The Viscount Greenleigh and I have already been introduced."

Dane sat there for a long moment with a smile frozen on his face while he racked his memory to place the red-eyed woman across from him. Finally, light dawned. Cheltenham. She was the wife of a destitute earl, but the family was of excellent lineage and spotless reputation. "Of course we have, Lady Cheltenham," he said smoothly, as if he'd recognized her all along.

Then he looked down at the self-possessed and voluptuous young woman in his arms. So this was Cheltenham's daughter. . . .

1

I shall be a willing and obedient wife. I shall be a willing and obedient—

Olivia—Lady Greenleigh now!—put down the boar-bristle brush that she had been absently drawing through her fair hair. There was that word again. *Obedient.* Drawing a deep breath, she placed both hands flat on her new mother-of-pearl-inlaid vanity and closed her eyes against her reflection in the fine gilded mirror.

The bedchamber in which Olivia waited shimmered with tasteful luxury, from the creamy silk brocade bed draperies, to the generously heaped coals in the hearth, to the very nightdress she wore, a floating confection of gauzy batiste that likely cost more than all her previous wardrobe combined.

The only thing it lacked was the presence of his lordship.

Men, Olivia decided, were rather like rain. If one needed it, it never seemed to come.

It is an honor to be chosen by such a gentleman. Her mother's voice echoed through her mind again and again. *You have little to recommend you but your bloodline. If your brother had managed to marry that awful Hackerman Shipping heiress, things would be very different for us all. If Walter had lived . . .*

If Walter had lived, Cheltenham would be saved, the family coffers would be full, her parents would be content, and Olivia would not be without her dear brother. She certainly would not have been constrained to accept the only offer of marriage that she had received.

Lord Greenleigh is a very handsome man. Lord Greenleigh is a very powerful man. Lord Greenleigh—

Lord Greenleigh was beginning to plague her off.

Enough. Olivia began to braid her hair for bed. She would get out of this silly, provocative nightdress as well. She may as well not have taken that second rosewater bath of the day, either. There was no point in waiting for the fellow—he obviously wasn't coming, just as he had not come to court her, just as he had not come to ask her if *she* wanted to marry *him.*

It wasn't as though she would have had the wherewithal to turn him down. She wasn't an idiot—she knew the family and all their dependents at Cheltenham had no other recourse but this marriage.

It simply would have been nice to have been asked.

Of course, Father had been no better, selling her off without the slightest thought to whether or not she even *liked* the man. No, Father had arranged the entire thing behind her back, like trading a recalcitrant horse.

Men were not like rain. Men were more like an outbreak of rodents. One never knew what they were doing out of sight. Just when one thought the cats were managing everything nicely, it turned out that the dratted things were plotting against one all the while.

Men were most definitely rats!

Feeling better having put that question to rest, Olivia removed her diaphanous wrapper—silly thing! It wouldn't serve a spider for its web!—and reached to untie the delicate tapes that held closed the neckline of her even more transparent nightgown.

A sound at the connecting door stopped her cold. Her indignation fled as she was forced to face anew the fears she'd been fighting for a month.

She was wife to a stranger. She was dependent on a man who could—well, who could do as he liked with her.

That could mean a great many things. She was not as sheltered as some of the young ladies she'd encountered during the last month of the Season. She'd not been governessed to bits, nor chaperoned by more than a lazy housemaid or two. As the years went by at Cheltenham, the servants had correctly assumed that Lord and Lady Cheltenham had no intentions of arranging a grand match for Lady Olivia.

Instead, her mother and father had pinned all their hopes on Walter, who was a year younger and a much better bet, being vastly more attractive and charming. Olivia could hardly blame them, for she'd been as dotty over Walt as any elder sister could be. He'd been full of life and humor yet not light-minded in the way of some spoiled young lords. She'd adored him, as had everyone who met him.

When Walt and her parents were gone from Cheltenham, which was much of the time, the entire estate seemed to go into a sort of hibernation. Most of the time, Olivia managed to occupy herself nicely with the cares and welfare of her family's dependents. The village of Cheltenham had suffered as much as the estate through the years of destitution, so Olivia did whatever she could to allay that suffering.

She was every bit as fond of her Cheltenham "family" as she was of her real one.

Which is why you wed Lord Greenleigh.

Right. Hopefully, pots of money would soon be on their way to Durham County in the north of England, earmarked for all the improvements that had been needed for so long.

Lord Greenleigh was a very generous man.

And he truly was a handsome giant. . . .

The fluttering in Olivia's middle was becoming a panicked beating of wings. She swallowed hard. *I shall be a willing and obedient wife.*

Unfortunately, obedience had never been one of Olivia's finest virtues. Not that she was intentionally rebellious or even especially contentious. She was more likely to be . . . *accidentally* disobedient.

Up until today, her mother's strictures had been the most difficult to obey: *Your hair must never fall from its place. You must keep your feet hidden beneath your hem or they will think you no better than a milkmaid. You must not laugh loudly or long. Better yet, do not laugh at all. Smile, but show no teeth—you smile much too widely. Do try not to loom over the gentlemen, but do not slouch!*

Her mother's rules did not matter now, she realized.

Alas, Olivia was fairly sure that her bridegroom—husband!—had rules of his own, likely even more strict than Lady Cheltenham's. Rules . . . and demands.

Demands. Oh heavens. Never one to give in to fear, Olivia decided to give in to pique instead. The beast hadn't even bothered to court her!

"Not a visit, not a single note! Nothing but jewels!"

The gifts had been frequent and costly and aloof. Olivia would have preferred a bit of actual conversation.

She'd only seen her bridegroom twice before today. The first had been that disastrous day on—or, rather, *under*—the bridge. From that encounter she'd gathered that he was inclined to rescue others, that he was as large as a bridge pillar, that he was vain—although perhaps deservedly so—and that he liked to look at bosoms.

This could be said of any number of men in Society.

The second time she'd seen him had been the following day when he'd asked her father for her hand in marriage. If she hadn't happened to come in at just that moment from another interminable afternoon of calls with Mother and seen the two conspirators shaking hands in the entrance hall as if they'd just concluded a horse trade, she'd likely not have found out until the wedding day itself!

Lord Greenleigh hadn't even been embarrassed. He'd simply bowed briefly over her hand and said he was happy to have received her father's consent, then had sailed out the door while she'd stared after him, openmouthed.

From that encounter and the following two weeks of

luxurious neglect she'd gathered that he was arrogant, managing, and thoughtless. Again, she could be describing any number of the gentlemen her mother had forced on her since she'd been brought to London and impressed into Society like a kidnapped sailor on a foreign ship.

Today she had been dressed and prepared for him like a veiled sacrifice. She had scarcely been able to see through the ornate lace and had spent most of the ceremony concentrating on not vomiting. At the wedding breakfast, the man at her side had been congenially indifferent, instead spending his attention on the man on his other hand, a fellow that Olivia vaguely recalled as being very nearly as handsome as Lord Greenleigh, in a darker, more pensive way.

From this she had learned that Lord Greenleigh was tidy in his manners, and that despite the fact that he smelled entirely wonderful, he was inclined to be very, very rude.

That was very little to go on. Yet here she was, wed to the man for the rest of her life. Her entire future rested in his hands alone. Of course, she had noticed during the meal, which she had scarcely been able to touch, that her new husband had large, shapely hands. In fact, despite his size, he possessed a leonine grace that made it difficult to take her gaze off him.

Now, however, her fascination was quickly dissolving into panicked exasperation. Could they not simply get it over with? Surely the dread was worse than the act itself! She wrapped both arms about herself despite the heat from the fire. She could not seem to get warm.

Olivia bent her head and paced before the hearth

once more. She could add another thing to her list—
Lord Greenleigh was rather inclined to be late!

Thankfully, Olivia felt her ire rise once more, drowning out her fear.

Men were rats.

Dane Calwell, Lord Greenleigh, had a problem. A very large problem. Even as he stood on the other side of his bride's door, he felt the problem growing. Damn, he hadn't even touched her yet!

There was nothing to be done about his problem. There was no one to discuss it with, for it was not the sort of thing one discussed with other men, and it was certainly not the sort of thing one discussed with a respectable woman—or even an unrespectable one, at that!

Dane had consulted a physician once—and only once. The man had laughed aloud and dismissed him with a clap on the back. "That's no problem, my lord—that's an asset!"

An asset? When even the most experienced courtesans drew back from him in alarm? When he was supposed to father an heir on an innocent, virtuous girl?

Some men would force her regardless. It was his right as her husband. The law was clear. Dane shuddered, appalled that he could even think it. There was much that he would do to protect the future of Greenleigh, but never that. If there was another heir, Dane would not even have attempted to wed, preferring to die forever celibate rather than beset a woman with his . . . problem.

Yet here he was, about to enter the bridal chamber, his problem growing unabated.

He had done his best to delay this moment, even to spending most of his wedding night working in his study. Then, when the clock had chimed eleven times, he had known he could not put it off any longer.

Across the desk from him, his best friend and protégé, Marcus Ramsay, Lord Dryden, caught his grimace and shook his head at Dane. "She's not unattractive, you know."

Dane shrugged carelessly, his expression carefully neutral. "She is precisely as I wished. A truly lovely woman would be far too distracting."

Marcus tilted his head. "So what is your difficulty? Why are you here working when you ought to be in the arms of your bride?"

Dane sighed and shoved himself out of his chair with both arms. "I'm off to her now. Are you satisfied?"

Marcus grinned, a flash of mischievous youth crossing his usually serious features. "I don't think I'm the one who is to be satisfied tonight."

Not likely, but he couldn't very well tell Marcus why. Dane frowned. "This is my lady wife we are discussing."

Marcus raised both hands against Dane's glare. "My apologies. Now, begone. I'll take these documents to the Prime Minister myself tonight. With Napoleon's spymaster still on the loose, I'd rather not trust these to a courier."

Dane nodded. The Chimera was not to be underestimated. The Royal Four had made that mistake already. For the better part of a year, the mysterious leader of the French espionage in London had avoided identification by the Liar's Club, the band of elite spies who acted at the command of the Royal Four. Only in the last weeks had it been discovered that the Chimera was a master of disguise who had walked among them as a petulant young servant they had all dismissed as harmless.

Denny—not his real name, surely, but all they knew to call him—had passed from Liar to Liar when his disagreeable attitude had made him impossible to keep around. Now Dane wondered if that had not been another part of the Chimera's plan. Passing through the households of several spies was bound to be more useful than remaining solely in the service of former spymaster Simon Raines, who had now retired.

The Chimera knew far too much about the Liar's Club—but how much did he know about the Royal Four? Only the Prime Minister and the Prince Regent himself knew the entire truth about the Four, and the current spymaster of the Liar's Club, Dalton Montmorency, Lord Etheridge, who had once been one of them.

Pondering the issue, Dane slowly climbed the stairs toward where his bride awaited him. If the Chimera learned the truth—if anyone on the other side knew of the power the Four wielded, power over the throne itself!—if the Four were exposed, the entire government of England would be ripped asunder. Especially when it was learned that it was the Royal Four who had declared King George mad and secreted him away, appointing Prince George IV as Regent of all Britain. The Cobra, the Lion, the Fox, and the Falcon had committed the highest treason, all in the deepest loyalty.

Although that particular decision had been made by Dane's predecessor and mentor, the previous Lion, as the current Lion, Dane upheld that decision with all his being. One man, king or no, could not be allowed to bring down England. Not even Dane himself, one of the four most powerful men in the land, could be permitted to put anyone or anything before his own duty.

Dane's own weak and traitorous father had taught him that lesson well. A woman had come between Henry Calwell and his duty, a beautiful Frenchwoman who had led Dane's father down a path of obsession and betrayal.

No breath of mistrust had ever reached Dane himself, but he knew perfectly well that if his father's betrayal had been known before Dane's appointment to the Lion's seat, Dane would never have been selected.

Blood will tell. No one so much as whispered the words, but Dane could feel the scrutiny of the other members of the Four like a breath on the back of his neck. He would always have to try harder—always be stricter in his observance of his vows—forever be prepared to sacrifice his own welfare for the sake of the Crown. Sometimes he almost envied what Nate Stonewell, the Cobra, had gone through when he'd been forced to take on the public role of traitor to hide a royal indiscretion. Dane had no such visible badge of honor to substantiate his loyalty. All he had was the shadow of his father's weakness.

Blood will tell.

Hence the selection of Lady Olivia for his bride. Not a woman to fall madly in love with. Not a woman to twist his thoughts and his soul into knots.

Not a woman to lead him to betrayal.

Now, Dane stood in his bedchamber and eyed the connecting doorway with disquiet. He had chosen

Cheltenham's daughter with utmost care. Her mother had assured Dane that Olivia was the soul of discretion and virtue, that she was well schooled in all things ladylike, and he had seen for himself that she possessed a surprising fortitude for one so sheltered in life.

Fortitude she was going to need if she was to be his wife in truth. He'd not been able to bear the thought that some other man might snatch up such a prize, and with his usual decisiveness, he'd acted to secure her.

It occurred to him now, too late, of course, that perhaps he ought to have courted the girl a bit. It was going to be difficult enough to win her affections. He knew from experience that if he was not very careful, he would never be able to secure her willingness long enough to gain an heir. He'd be damned if he would leave Greenleigh to some distant relation who'd never set foot on it.

Dane was forced to admit that he'd intentionally avoided his bride. *Coward.* Of course, he'd been occupied with much more important matters in the past two weeks, he told himself, but he could have sent a flowery, romantic note or three.

It was too late now. There was nothing left but to face her.

2

When her bedchamber door opened, Olivia's first thought was that she truly needed to stop making those ill-studied wishes.

Her second thought wasn't so much a thought as it was a wash of heat and astonishment that swept her entire being in a turbulent glow.

Lord Greenleigh's long golden hair hung loose over his wide, mountainous shoulders. He wore only a loose white shirt tucked into black trousers that hugged his muscled thighs and did rather nice things to his trim hips and flat stomach. He stood there, in all his great-cat fluidity and ease, one hand resting on the doorknob, one knee relaxed, one side of his perfect lips quirked up in greeting. . . .

Her husband was a god. There was an indisputable god in her bedchamber. Gods, she decided abruptly, truly ought to enter bedchambers more often.

If she was not vastly mistaken—and she'd lived in the country too long to be mistaken—he was rather glad to be here as well. She dragged her gaze from that daunting region below his waist, trying to take in the man as a whole.

The whole was entirely beyond compare. He looked wild and graceful and barbaric, a Norse chieftain from a less civilized time.

She'd thought him handsome in the river. She'd thought him truly superior looking in her front entrance hall. She'd barely seen him through her lace veil during the ceremony and she'd been a bit too nauseous to truly take him in during the wedding breakfast.

Now, here, alone with him, the full impact of his size and golden splendor quite took her breath away. His broad shoulders seemed to fill the room she'd previously thought spacious and his blue eyes seemed to lock her gaze to him like a magnet. In fact, her breath was still gone and it was beginning to make her dizzy.

She put a hand to her forehead. Very . . . very . . . dizzy. . . .

In a smooth motion, he was there to catch her even before her knees weakened. He plucked her from her feet as if she weighed no more than a cat—and Olivia was certain she weighed more than many well-fed cats—and carried her swiftly to the chair by the hearth.

"Are you ill?" His breath was soft and warm on her cheek. Olivia closed her eyes against his concern, too embarrassed by her display to answer. "Should I call for your maid?"

His arms were still about her, supporting her even though she was perfectly well. It was rather like being strapped between stone arches, as if nothing could ever induce him to let her go. Even the heat of his body surrounded her, and he still smelled exceptionally good.

Olivia flushed as she realized that she liked it very much. Unfortunately, she could not let it continue. She'd never been able to lie very well, so she was forced to blurt out the truth.

"You make it rather difficult for me to breathe."

He immediately loosened his grasp of her. Olivia was sorry at once and fought the impulse to fall upon his vast chest in a renewed swoon. She could, she realized, and it would not be at all improper. He belonged to her now.

As liberating and tempting as that thought was, she could not disturb him further. "That is not quite what I meant," she said, loathing the scarlet blush that she knew was flooding her face. She'd never been able to blush prettily like some women, with roses blooming in both cheeks. Her blushes looked rather more like blotches. "I did not eat today and I'm ever so slightly nervous and you're rather . . . overwhelming."

Dane gazed down at his new bride in deep disappointment. He'd guessed wrongly after all. She'd seemed nicely sturdy in his previous encounters, hardy and full of common sense. He released her rather reluctantly and stood. She had felt good in his arms and he'd so hoped . . .

She was obviously far more frail and timid than he'd thought her. She could scarcely bear to look at him. Never mind. What was done was done. She was now his wife. It was his duty to protect her, even if that meant protect her from himself. She could not help her lack of fortitude, no more than he could help his . . . problem.

"I shall ring for your maid," he told her gently,

concealing his disappointment. "Then I will leave you undisturbed."

His new bride gazed up at him in astonishment, her fiery blush fading. "Leave?"

Dane stiffened. "Of course. I am not the sort of man to force myself—"

"No!" She was on her feet in a flash. "I do not wish to go through this again!"

Dane flinched. "Of course not. I will make no demands—"

Incredibly, his demure new bride, a supposed paragon of propriety and self-control, stomped her foot and glared at him.

"Have you the faintest idea how hard it was to wait for you tonight? Or all fortnight, for that matter? I feel as though I've done nothing but sit by the window and twiddle my thumbs for weeks! And now, having spent only moments in my company—*again*—you are going to leave?" She crossed her arms beneath her breasts and glared at him. "Well, I won't have it. You're staying."

Dane could only gaze at her blankly for a moment. No one spoke to him in such a manner. Ever.

Since he'd reached his adult height at sixteen, standing freakishly tall over the other boys, he'd been treated with nothing but the most careful respect. He'd never tried to use his size to intimidate, but then he'd never had to. All he had to do was speak to ensure that his every word was heard and implemented.

He'd tried to lessen the threat by adopting an easygoing facade, quite the opposite of his naturally serious disposition, but the isolation caused by that wary deference had only worsened as he'd grown into his full strength and manhood. Even the Prince Regent kept his capriciousness to a minimum in Dane's presence, and Lord Liverpool, the Prime Minister, had been known to back down before Dane's opinions.

Yet here was this woman, not much more than a girl at that, who had just stomped her foot *at him*!

She was either mad or even more hardy than he'd originally thought. Either way, she obviously had no idea what her crossed arms did to her full bosom in that sheer nightdress. Dane found it difficult to keep his gaze high.

"You're demanding that I stay," he said without expression.

She cocked an irritated brow. "I am indeed."

In the spirit of research, Dane crossed his own arms and assumed a wider stance. He'd never yet met the man who didn't fail ever so slightly before that pose.

Incredibly, the spanking-new, still wet-behind-the-ears Lady Greenleigh did nothing but widen her own stance and increase the temperature of her glare. A heavy lock of fair hair slipped forward to drape over one plumped breast. She no longer looked like the faintly pretty, serenely demure daughter of Cheltenham. She looked like a fuming fertility goddess.

Dane would have smiled, but he suspected that it would only add fuel to her annoyance. Since in all fairness his neglected bride had every right to be annoyed with him, he finally spread his hands and smiled. "Then I suppose I shall stay."

She nodded crisply. "Good."

Dane endured a long awkward pause. His bride

shifted uneasily. Dane gave in to his curiosity. "Ah, do you mind telling me what I'm staying for?"

Her annoyed gaze faltered and her irritation shifted to sudden shyness. Dane watched the change with interest. Her face was a map of her emotions, to be sure. What was going through her mind now?

She cleared her throat awkwardly. "I thought we might discuss—that is, I would very much like to know your . . . your expectations of me."

Dane regarded her curiously. "I expect you to be my lady."

The shyness slipped long enough for her to shoot him a wryly disbelieving glance. *Don't be an idiot,* that glance said.

He ought to ease her anxiety, although he enjoyed watching the play of conflicting emotions across her face. It seemed there was only one area in which Lady Olivia did not feel easy in challenging him.

"I do not insist on consummating our vows at this very moment," he said easily. "Although I hope you'll consider receiving my affections soon."

Nibbling at her lip, she looked away. "Would you say that your . . . affections fall into the usual category of such things?" She turned a suddenly piercing gaze upon him. "I have heard of such things, you see."

He couldn't resist. She was too adorable. He made his gaze go blank. "I'm sorry, could you be more specific?"

She actually opened her mouth to answer, but something on his face must have given him away. Her eyes narrowed. "Not amusing. You know my intent."

Drat. Oh, well. He spread his hands, admitting fault.

"I do. And I can assure you, my lady, that my . . . er, affections are entirely of the norm." That wasn't strictly true, but now was not the time to bring up his problem. That wasn't what she was asking, at any rate.

She let out a long, silent breath, then smiled warmly at him. "Very well, then. Won't you sit down? We could converse for a while." She led him to the great chair by the fire.

As long as his bride remained in that wispy night rail with the top ribbons coming awry, Dane could quite happily sit across from her and converse for hours. She was far more enticing than he'd first realized, although if memory served, he'd noticed those amazing breasts at once.

He moved her dressing-table chair closer and seated her in it, then took the larger chair for himself. Not gentlemanly, but practical. He'd broken more than a few chairs in his life. He'd learned to judge what would hold him. Leaning forward, he rested his elbows on his knees and gazed with appreciation at his bride. Those really were the most astounding—

"My eyes sit somewhat higher, my lord."

Her tone was dry and her expression, when he pulled his gaze away from her bosom, was deadpan. Ah, she'd caught him again. He quirked one side of his mouth. "My deepest apologies, my lady. I intend only admiration, I assure you."

She tilted her head. "I hardly know whether to thank you or slap you. I suppose being my husband does release you from certain proprieties . . ."

He nodded with certainty. "Oh, yes."

She absently toyed with the top ribbon at her neckline.

The knot failed completely, giving Dane another inch of plump cleavage to enjoy. His groin throbbed in response and he shifted uncomfortably. This conversing business was going to be more difficult than he'd originally thought.

"I hardly know anything about you, my lord," she was saying. "For instance, have you any family for me to meet? I noticed there was no one at the ceremony this morning."

Family. The word took a long moment to worm its way through his distraction. "No—no, I have no immediate family living. My mother passed when I was a boy and my father—" What was he doing? He discussed Henry Calwell with *no one*.

She was gazing at him encouragingly. "Your father?"

Dane forced himself to shrug easily. "Gone two years past. Accident." He ought to elaborate, for she might hear something else entirely, although he'd done his best to keep it quiet. "While he was cleaning his pistol, you see."

She leaned forward and put her hand over his clasped ones. "It is hard, isn't it? I love my parents, of course, but when my brother Walter drowned last month—" She stopped and swallowed hard. "I think Walter was perhaps the best friend I had in this world," she said quietly.

Lord Walter had by all accounts been a decadent lout, but hardly worse than most of the other young lords occupying themselves in London these days. She had obviously loved the fellow, despite the reputation that had spread since his death. He liked that about her. "And yet your family did not strictly observe a mourning period," he said, careful to keep the judgment from his voice.

Olivia had been wondering when someone would ask her about that. She and her parents had donned the muted tones of half-mourning, and had not danced at any of the events they had attended, but those barest of observations did little to properly honor Walter.

"It was necessary that I make a good match this Season," she said slowly.

Dane covered her comforting hand with his large warm one. Her hand disappeared entirely. "Say no more, my lady. I deduced as much on my own."

Olivia liked his hand on hers. Experimentally, she slipped her other one beneath his. There was room for both and more. She felt absolutely tiny next to this man.

What a charming sensation.

Not to mention a stimulating one. She tilted her head up to study him, for even when seated on a lower chair, he loomed over her. "I think I should like to receive some of your affections now," she blurted.

He blinked, then looked about them. "Now? In the chair?"

In the chair? Oh, my—

That glint was back in his eye. "You're teasing me again," she accused.

He nodded slowly. "My apologies. I cannot resist, but now is not the time, is it?"

She pulled her hands away from his and stood, stepping away. She'd spoken impulsively again. Mother had never been able to rid her of that trait entirely. Still, it was too late to take it back now, and she did find him very appealing, and he had been most reassuring about his tastes . . .

Her face flamed, but she did not attempt to hide it.

"I thought perhaps we could get it over with."

The rate of Dane's heart increased immediately, as did something else. Perhaps she was the one. She certainly wasn't frightened of him, at least not while he was clothed, which was more than he could say for . . . well, everyone.

She huffed a breath at his hesitation. "Well, *I* cannot begin. I don't know how."

Her half-irritated, half-shy expression disarmed him. "Well," he said slowly as he stood. "We could begin with a kiss."

Olivia felt ice and flame flicker through her body as he began to move toward her. Despite her own insistence—and she'd meant every word—she found herself taking a step back for every forward step of his. Eventually, she backed directly into the solid bedpost and put her hands behind her to steady herself. He kept coming. He came so close that she had to tilt her head back to look into his face.

"I think you might be the tallest man I've ever seen," she heard herself say softly.

He pinned her with those winter-sky eyes. "Do I frighten you?"

A small gasping laugh burst from her. Fear was most emphatically *not* what she was feeling.

He blinked. "I take it that I don't."

She widened her eyes innocently, unable to resist plucking at his arrogance despite her breathlessness. "I could pretend to be frightened, if you like."

The corner of his sculpted lips twitched. "I could pretend to be shorter, if you like."

A healthy sense of the ridiculous! What a delightful

thing to add to the list of what she knew about him. She melted yet again and her nervousness eased yet more. "Are you never going to kiss me, my lord?" she whispered.

He lowered his mouth to her ear, letting his warm breath flutter into sensitive areas. "Are you never going to shut up, my lady?"

My lady. It struck Olivia anew that she was the Viking god's wife. *You belong to me now.*

She must have said it aloud, for she felt the Viking god smile against her neck.

"I suppose I do," he said, his deep voice rumbling into places within her that she hadn't known existed. Places deep, low in her belly, where she felt a hollow ache. Places like the tips of her breasts, where she felt a tingling tightness.

His warm lips progressed higher, up her throat and along her jaw, until she felt his breath against her lips. He paused, letting the moment stretch until Olivia could no longer bear it. She went up on tiptoe, catching his mouth with hers in an urgent peck. He went very still when she pressed her lips to his.

At first, she felt a stab of disappointment. His mouth did not feel unpleasant under hers, but neither did it feel as good as his breath on her neck. She had begun to drop back down to her heels when he caught her to his chest and brought his mouth down on hers.

Dane hadn't intended to assault her thus. It was only that she was suddenly *there,* touching her soft lips to his, with her firm, lovely bosom pressed to his chest.

It had been so damn long. . . .

The parched, cold years of deprivation suddenly dropped away and a wave of heat and longing overwhelmed his scrupulous self-control. For a brief, eternal moment, he clutched the virtuous, virginal daughter of Cheltenham to him as if she were his only hope—as though he feared drowning in that wave. For a brief sweep of the hands of the clock, he kissed her like a starving barbarian suddenly presented with a feast.

It was only a second or two—or ten. Then Dane came back to himself abruptly, shock at his own barbarism rippling through him—only to find his innocent bride gripping the front of his shirt in both fists, making the tiniest of whimpering sounds beneath his mouth.

Dane quickly slammed the door on his mystifying outburst of lust, pulling his lips away from hers with difficulty. He pulled her close, tucking her head beneath his chin as he fought to regain his composure. This was not the way to gain his objective. If his new bride was to be properly cultivated to bear his invasion, he could not begin by frightening her with uncontrolled lust.

Control was paramount to this undertaking. Due to his impediment, he would never be able to abandon strict control with her, even if he somehow convinced her to allow him in. His baser nature was not something he could ever burden her with. It would only terrify her. He only hoped he had not ruined everything already.

As he drew a last deep breath, he realized that Olivia did not seem irreparably terrified. In fact, the girl in his arms continued to clutch at him, clumsily attempting to kiss his neck while still constrained in his grasp.

Relief swept him as he gripped her shoulders in both hands and set her gently away from him, keeping a tight rein on his self-control.

Olivia blinked in surprise as she was firmly but gently detached from her new husband. "Did—did I not do well?" she asked breathlessly as she struggled to focus her vision. "I tried to do what you did. Should I try again?"

She stepped forward to do just that, for she longed to be drawn back into that whirling, passionate moment once more. She'd never, ever, *ever* in her life— well, of course she hadn't. No virtuous girl would.

He'd not released her shoulders. Now, he pressed her back, keeping her at arm's length. Olivia gazed up at him, her brows drawn together. His lack of expression confused her. "Why—"

No virtuous girl would.

Mother was constantly telling Olivia she was too unrestrained, too prone to disgraceful behavior. Why, she'd not only kissed him, she'd *licked* him! She backed a step from his hold, her hands covering her hot cheeks. "Oh heavens! What you must think of me—"

First she'd berated him for his neglect, then shamelessly demanded that he stay and consummate the marriage—how mad that was!—then she'd thrown herself at him!

It had been heated and wild and more than she'd ever dreamed. His lips had felt hot and hungry—and the scorching wetness of his mouth and the way his tongue had invaded her—*inside* her! The way he'd pulled her forcefully against his big, hard body, making her feel small and helpless and utterly in his power, the way his lips had covered hers—*owned* hers!—sparking a hunger of her own that had nearly overwhelmed her.

Even as she stood there, racked by embarrassment, she felt a hot shudder of hunger ripple through her at the memory. Oh, she was irredeemable!

"Olivia."

He'd never called her by name before, she realized. She liked the way he said it, especially the way the second syllable deepened his voice slightly. Large, warm hands covered her shoulders and pulled her back against the solid wall of his chest.

"Olivia, do not be distressed."

She shook her head quickly. "I was too brazen. I was too—"

He gave her a tiny shake. "No. Look at me, my dear," he ordered gently.

She did so. He was gazing down at her, his blue eyes serious. She'd never seen him thus. He'd always seemed rather jovial, yet somehow the sober expression suited him.

"I am your husband," he told her. "It is my charge to lead the way in matters of physical love. You were simply responding to my own lack of restraint."

She bit her lip. "I was?"

He raised his hands to cradle her jaw tenderly. The heat of his palms sank through her and began to inflame the banked coals inside her once more.

"My dear, your honest responsiveness was delightful in every way. It is my fault that you were led astray."

"It was?" Olivia frowned slightly. Somehow that didn't seem quite right, but then, what did she know on the topic? "So the way you kissed me wasn't correct?"

The corner of his mouth twitched slightly. "No, it was not. Between a man and his lady wife, there should never be such an assault."

Oh dear. She truly was shameless, for she felt deep disappointment that he might never kiss her that way again. Still, it was the only kiss she'd ever had. It could be that other sorts of kisses were even better. Unlikely but possible.

Encouraged, she placed her own hands softly on his face, mirroring his on hers. She watched his eyes, prepared to stop if she saw disapproval there. He held very still, allowing her to slip her fingertips into the golden hair at his temples. "Then, perhaps . . ."

He lifted a brow. She felt the movement under his soft skin. "Perhaps?" he inquired.

Quite without thought, the tip of Olivia's tongue slipped out to wet her lips. His eyes went dark as his gaze riveted to her mouth.

"Perhaps you could show me—" Her voice sounded husky and unfamiliar to her own ears. She swallowed hard, feeling poised on the threshold of a world unknown. "Show me the proper way to kiss you?"

Dane knew he needed to make a better beginning this time. She seemed shaken and unsure now—and it was all his fault. Damning his lack of restraint, he vowed to make this kiss count in his favor.

Slowly, he brought his lips down to hers. She began to go up on tiptoe to meet him. When he went still, she stopped, settling back down to wait for him. Hope began to spring within him that she had been the perfect choice. She seemed imminently teachable and astonishingly willing to please him.

That willingness could also be dangerous, he suddenly realized, for her complete submission to him fair to enraged his lust once more. His animal nature beat at the bars of the cage he'd built about it.

The things he could convince such a woman to do— the things he could convince her to allow him to do! Dark, erotic visions darted through his mind, fleeting and tantalizing and entirely wicked.

He banished them by force of will and bent once more to the task at hand.

Olivia let her eyes drift shut as he neared, tiny shivers of expectation running up her spine.

Warm lips touched hers, so carefully that for a moment she was not sure it wasn't simply his soft breath she was feeling. Touch, retreat, touch—like the lighting of a butterfly on a blossom. The shivers increased, vibrating through her to set her lower belly trembling anew. Her lips parted instinctively, blooming for him.

His mouth settled gently on hers, the tip of his warm tongue slipping briefly in to trace the sensitive inner lining of her lips.

At that sweet invasion, the strength in her knees vanished. She sagged against him. He wrapped one mighty arm about her waist, supporting her while his other hand continued to cradle her face. His lips awoke hers with firm, gentle pressure and, to her surprise, the tiniest, teasing suction. He pressed his large thumb to her jaw, encouraging to open her mouth further for his slow, sweet penetration. She turned herself over to him entirely, letting him easily guide and maneuver her.

The luxurious room around them vanished, as did Olivia's embarrassment. Even her mother's critical voice faded to nothing in the seductive glow of her husband's tender kiss.

3

When he lifted his mouth from hers, Olivia continued to sink into him. She had no choice, for her knees were still weak.

"I was quite right," she sighed. "That was lovely, too."

His arm tightened about her. "I'm glad you think so."

She drew a long breath. "I'm dizzy again."

"Are you often thus?" A thread of concern tightened his husky whisper against her lips.

She shook her head. "Never in my life. I'm beginning to think it is your doing. You make my heart beat so."

Something shivered through him. She could feel his tension. For a moment, his grip tightened fiercely. It was only an instant, passing almost before she noticed.

She opened her eyes to gaze into his Viking-god face. His eyes were twilight dark and narrowed as he fixed them on her. "When we kiss, does the room disappear for you as well?"

His jaw worked. "No."

She frowned slightly in disappointment. "That is too bad. It's rather lovely. I like it."

He closed his eyes and touched his forehead to hers. "Olivia . . ."

"Yes . . . Dane?" She'd never called him by name before.

"Shut it."

She closed her eyes and smiled. "Yes, Dane."

After that, there was no more talking. She held still, allowing his large hands to rove over her freely. First he slid his palms over her shoulders and down her arms, then he raised her hands to clasp loosely behind his neck. Then she felt him stroke down her arms again and down her body to her waist.

His hands didn't linger there for long. She felt him bend slightly, then jerked in surprise as his hot palms slid down and cupped her bottom. The thin fabric of her nightdress might as well not have been there at all, for she could feel the heat of his palms burn directly into her flesh.

"Shh." His whisper across her neck sent another shiver through her. "I only wish to get to know you."

"Oh," she said breathlessly. "I like dogs."

He went still, his palms still pressing her to him. "What does that mean, precisely?"

"It means that if you want to know me better, you might be interested in the fact that I like dogs." She cracked one eye open. "What did you think I meant?"

She saw him shake his head slightly, as if dislodging something stubborn.

"You don't want to know." He sounded slightly breathless himself.

She closed her eyes and took a breath, deciding to enjoy the way his hands grasped her softness. It made her feel as though her figure was not as bovine as her mother had so often insinuated. "You may continue."

He did just that. He pulled her body into his, until his groin pressed to her belly . . . but only for the briefest moment. Then he pulled his lower body away. That was unfortunate, for Olivia was mightily curious about that lower body, but she didn't think he would appreciate any more interruptions. There was time, after all. They had the rest of their lives to discover each other.

Forever. What a lovely thought when one's husband was a Viking god.

His hands were moving again. They moved down the backs of her thighs a bit, then smoothed around them to the front. Olivia tensed slightly, for he was about to head into delicate territory—but he only moved upward and wrapped his hands around her hips, thumbs nearly touching her navel.

He cradled her thus for a moment, his breath still coming warm on her neck. "You are my wife," he whispered.

"Yes," she replied uncertainly. "I thought we'd established that."

"You are mine."

Oh heavens. A shiver of anticipation went through her at the faint possessive growl behind those words. "I am," she whispered.

"All of you."

Her knees threatened to weaken again. "All of me," she breathed.

He slowly slid his hands up her waist until his thumbs rested against the undersides of her full bosom.

"Mine," he said softly as he slowly swept his fingers and palms up over her breasts, until he was hefting their weight fully in his hands.

When his fingers rubbed across her, jolts of wicked pleasure shot from her rigid nipples to places best left unmentioned. Olivia gasped, nearly pulling her hands down to fend him off. She'd never—it wasn't—

"No," he ordered softly. "Stay just as you are."

His sensually commanding tone made her shiver anew and she reclasped her fingers behind his neck, leaving her helplessly awakened flesh undefended before him. He caressed her breasts in a slow circle, his hands at once hard and gentle. "Open your eyes," he said. "Look down."

She did so, and the sight of his large tanned hands covering the bodice of her nightdress sent new heat below. Her nipples—they were large and always such a burden to hide in chill weather—pressed out from between his fingers, their rosy color showing through the filmy fabric.

"Your breasts are lovely," he said huskily. "I want to see them."

Olivia closed her eyes again, a tiny sound escaping from her lips. He must have taken it for acquiescence—and truly, what else could it have been?—for his hands left her flesh. She felt his touch at her neckline, felt the ribbon ties give way and the bodice of the nightdress part, and felt the cooler air of the room waft over her skin.

The candles still burned, the room was still bright, and she was bare before him. It was wicked. It was delicious.

He covered her breasts with his hands again.

Olivia gasped. She'd been wrong. It was nothing like being touched through the thin batiste fabric. His hands were a thousand times hotter, and the slight roughness of his palms and fingers on her softer skin was exquisitely arousing.

"Look down, my lady," he urged.

She opened her eyes and gazed down to see. The sight of his darker hands covering her white breasts, the way her flesh welled between his fingers, the way her ruby nipples thrust eagerly outward as if awaiting something—

He lowered his head to her, taking that waiting tip into his mouth—oh, dear heavens, *hot*!—his hot mouth, and suckled her deeply. Wicked, violent pleasure jolted through her like lightning and Olivia threw her head back, unable to watch, unable to do anything but try to breathe in sharp gasps as he drew on her.

Her knees buckled and she clung to his shoulders as he followed her down, laying her to the mattress without letting up the suction for an instant. The bed— she'd forgotten the bed. . . .

His tongue flicked roughly across her nipple and she forgot the bed again as she shuddered at the new pleasure. He wrapped one big arm behind her back to lift her breasts to his mouth and slid the other hand down her body to her knee. He went from one nipple to the other, suckling and flicking and even—oh my—gently biting. Helpless under the wicked assault, Olivia was barely aware of his other, roving hand until she felt the heat of his palm crossing the sensitive skin of her inner thigh.

Then he cupped her center and began rotating the heel of his hand gently, just where she wanted it the most, his fingers dipping lower to trace the crease of her. Then they slipped inside.

She convulsed in his grasp, gasping and digging her fingers into the thick muscles of his shoulders. "Oh! *Oh!*" After that, there were no words. She was lost in the sea of new sensations washing over her, into her, through her. . . .

His hot, hungry mouth suckled and nibbled. His hand moved faster, sliding up and down now, his long fingers tracing through the dampness that she was much too far gone to be embarrassed by, slicking past and around her most sensitive place again and again and again—

Something inside of her reached its highest point and then detonated. Piercing tremors racked her body and she was vaguely and indifferently aware that she was making the oddest noises, soft and gasping and not at all like her.

"Shh." He held her close now, having pulled her into his lap with her head on his shoulder, almost rocking her in his iron-banded arms. "You're all right now."

She became aware that she was gasping open-mouthed like a fish. She shut her mouth and swallowed drily. "Oh . . . my." She blinked her gaze back into focus. "Was . . . was that supposed to happen to me?"

Dane nodded, his own mouth a bit dry at the moment. His own arousal thundered in his blood as he fought for control. This was unexpected. She was liquid heat in his hands, so responsive to every touch and so eager for every sensation. He'd thought it would take several nights to work a sheltered virgin into her first orgasm. It had taken Olivia less than an hour.

That did bode well for his ultimate purpose, but it also played bloody hell with his self-restraint. Even now, as she lay limply and trustingly against his chest, he knew he could work her into another frenzy with his hands, for he could feel the tiny tremors still shimmering through her lower body, making her quiver slightly in his lap. Torture . . . and temptation. He wanted to release his throbbing erection, ached to lay her back down on the bed and push himself into her wetted body, her tight, slick, virginal opening—

Impossible.

He reached behind him to pull the coverlet down and released his hold on her, letting her slip down to the waiting sheets. She went softly and sleepily, apparently unaware that her nightdress still gaped and that her luscious breasts made him want to throw back his head and howl.

He fought back that instinct with alarm. He wasn't an animal. It was only basic lust, male for female. It was because of the way his hands still smelt of her and his mouth still felt the rough strawberry texture of her nipples on his tongue.

He covered her succulent flesh with the counterpane, beating down the beast once more, but the fight was exhausting. As Olivia closed her eyes, still smiling sleepily at him, he felt weariness weigh down his shoulders. He pulled off his shirt, for her room was too warm—or at least, something was too warm.

The bed called to him. He ought to go back to his room. He ought not to get into the habit of sleeping the night with her. That smacked too much of intimacy and dependence.

He moved, and her hand slipped from the covers to touch his. "Don't go," she whispered, her eyes still shut.

He gazed down on her curled alone in that big bed. He ought to think of her. This was her first night in a strange house. It was only . . . well, *polite* didn't seem like the right word. It was only *considerate* of him to watch over her for a while until she was deeply asleep. He moved to the other side of the bed and leaned his tired shoulders against the headboard. He stretched his legs out and let his head fall back against the wood. He could use this time to think about the Prince Regent. Something must be done to keep the man under control. . . .

Dane's head slipped to one side and he slowly slid down the headboard until he rested fully on the pillows. He was completely unaware when a soft hand slid from beneath the covers to entwine its fingers with his.

Milady's bedchamber looked out over the gardens. Past the gardens there was a high wall keeping the mews and its attendant manure and other noisome smells from interfering with that of the last fading roses.

On that wall, kept in indistinct shadow by climbing ivy and the shedding leaves of a young elm, perched a watcher who had particular interest in milady's bedchamber. He'd seen the lord and the lady come together near the grand bed, he'd seen them topple together out of his sight, and he'd seen the candle die by neglected flickering hours later.

Mission completed.

It was a good match. They were two of a kind, after all. And after all, as everyone knew, blood would tell.

And such lovely, traitorous blood it was, too.

The watcher smiled. Henry Calwell had been a pleasure to suborn—stalwart and self-righteous until that pretty little French girl had been planted in his path. Then all that passion and loyalty had belonged to France, or at least to a woman who was sworn to France, which amounted to the same thing with these English sods. Really, they were so impractical about the game of love.

Losing Henry had been costly to the grand mission. Only shame before his own son could have made Henry revert, that was certain. How satisfying now, to watch the son fall beside the father. A fitting replay of history, in addition to being precisely what the circumstances called for.

There had been several losses of late, mostly due to those bloody Liars—

The hands planted on the top of the wall curled into fists, fingernails gritting against the stone. The Liars were nothing but gutter-rats or inbred aristocrats. How could they have destroyed the best of his ring so easily?

Lavinia Winchell had been a prize indeed. Lovely and heartlessly sexual, she'd had such a way of luring those English spies to their fates—until the Liars had turned one of Lavinia's own operatives, Jackham, against her.

Wadsworth, the arms maker, had belonged to France from boyhood—a man with vision, unlike his greedy son. Still, both had been useful, until those glorified pickpockets had destroyed them as well.

Then the Liars had snatched the codemaster's daughter up before she could be captured, leaving the emperor without leverage to force her father to work for France—an embarrassing failure indeed.

To have such victory yanked from him just when he was about to take down the Liars themselves . . . he burned for vengeance, but he needed a new cell of operatives. He'd set everything aside to pursue Dane Calwell without end.

His current minions, a mealy handful of worthless younger sons and devious servants, could bring him nothing but more of the same. Sneak thieves and perverts would not ultimately serve his cause. He needed Lord Greenleigh, a man of impeccable reputation— aside from the secret of his father's treason. Yet he was rather lazy and non-political for one who could wield such power in the government.

Well, if England could not win his devotion, then France would.

And to ensnare the king, he would use the queen.

Carefully, for limbs tended to stiffen while crouching on cold stone, the watcher uncurled and dropped back behind the wall. In the wooden stable building, a few horses stirred, nickering softly in hopes of an early breakfast.

The watcher moved quickly down the alley before a groom could investigate the horses' unrest, fading into the shadows with the ease of long practice.

. . .

When Olivia woke, the room was dark and the coals were only a glow in the hearth. She stretched out languorously, preparing to turn over and go back to sleep, when her toes touched a hard, cloth-covered surface.

A leg. A man's leg. A husband's leg.

A husband who still wore his trousers while she slept nearly naked. How embarrassing. Except that the thought sent a startling ripple through her body. What would it be like to be naked before him, like a . . . a slave princess before the barbarian king?

The ripple increased to a tremor of arousal. If he should wake to find her bare to his touch, would he finish what he had begun earlier this night? There was more to come, she was sure of it. She'd seen stallions breeding mares and hounds breeding bitches—although she suspected that humans didn't do it quite like four-legged creatures.

She closed her eyes against the dimness and tried to imagine Dane mounting her like a stallion. Him behind her, golden muscles rippling and gleaming in the sun—

A violent shudder went through her at the thought. *Oh my.*

Her movement must have wakened Dane, for he rolled toward her. "Are you all right?" he asked, his deep voice husky with sleep. "Did you have a nightmare?"

Olivia pulled her mind from her depraved imagination with violent speed. "Ah, no. It was not a bad dream." *No, not bad at all.*

He wrapped a big arm around her midriff and tugged her closer. His large hand was hot on her skin and she shivered at the contact. "Are you cold?" he murmured.

No, she was quite the opposite. Before she could answer or kiss him or do any other of the twenty-odd things she would have liked to do to her brand-new Viking-god husband, her stomach gave a ferocious growl. Olivia clapped one hand over her mouth in stark mortification. Her mother would be so shocked. Her mother would go completely ashen with horror. Her mother would—

Dane chuckled, a gentle rumble in the dark intimacy of their draped bed. "That is my fault, is it not? I never rang for your dinner."

He rolled away from her to reach for the cord at the head of the bed to ring for a servant.

Olivia put her hand on his bare shoulder. "Must we wake them? They worked so hard today."

He turned to look at her quizzically. "It is their job to come when I call. That is what I pay them well to do."

Olivia frowned. "Servants are human beings, my lord. Human beings who need rest in order to 'come when you call.' I feel the urge to foment a rebellion."

He rolled back toward her, rising up to rest his chin on his raised fist. His broad outline looked like a mountain range in the dimness. "What do you propose I do, my Lady Greenleigh—service you myself?"

Olivia decided that once she got her breath back, she would like precisely that—

She shook her head sharply. Her imagination was beginning to interfere with her thinking. "No, of course not. I'm perfectly able to go down to the kitchens and sort out something to eat."

"Alone?"

She shrugged. "Why should I not?"

"In that?" His tone reminded her that the ties were undone on her gown.

She pursed her lips. "Well, no. I would dress, of course."

He chuckled. "Absolutely not. I forbid it."

Being ordered to remain nearly naked ought to have bothered Olivia at least a little. The fact that it didn't should have bothered her a lot. Mother had never touched on this particular topic, but Olivia was fairly certain that undress on command was not something a lady should tolerate.

This was not her mother's house. It was *her* house, hers and her lord's. And if her handsome, astounding lord husband wanted her barely dressed, then barely dressed she would willingly be!

"I can wait until breakfast," she amended.

Dane rose from the bed. "Then I believe I'll return to my room now."

Olivia really wished he wouldn't, but she could hardly beg him to sleep with her. Although she doubted she'd be able to go back to sleep with him there within reach. Begging was beginning to look better and better.

So, purely in the spirit of good manners, of course, she spoke. "You're welcome to stay if you like."

He didn't turn to look at her. "I think not."

On his way from the room, he took a fresh candle from the decorative box on the mantel and lit it in the glowing coals. After he affixed it in the silver candlestick, the flame stabilized and filled the room with a golden glow.

Olivia caught her breath as the light revealed him in all his bare-chested magnificence. The glimpses she'd caught of his body when he'd . . . taught . . . her had only hinted at the rippling breadth of his torso. The candle glow highlighted every hill and valley of his muscled chest and all the lean power of his rippling abdomen.

He turned at her faint gasp, raising the candle in order to see her better. Olivia realized that she had sat upright at the sight. She had also forgotten to pull her nightdress closed to cover herself. Suddenly shy, which was ridiculous considering what he had done to her—and what she wanted to do to him—she grabbed her neckline.

She thought she saw his jaw clench and she was sure his eyes could scorch steel. It looked as though his lordship might not be leaving after all.

Then he blinked and took a breath, and the flash of male ferocity left his features. He smiled easily in the way he had, as if he were just an ordinary fellow, easygoing and congenial.

What a ridiculous notion! As if a man like him was ever ordinary!

He wagged one finger at her. "Tut-tut. Play fair."

Hiding her disappointment, she tugged the nightdress closed and tilted her head at him. "Did you actually say 'tut-tut,' my lord?" she asked him teasingly. "I thought only ladies of a certain age used that phrase."

His jaw dropped and he stared at her for a long moment. "You truly aren't afraid of me, are you?" he asked, shaking his head in bemusement.

Olivia drew her knees up under the covers and rested her arms across them. "You keep asking me that.

Why would I be afraid of you? Are you a bad man?"

The question caught him up for some reason. He stood there, a half-naked god of a man, and actually seemed to ponder his answer. She frowned at him. "It was not meant to be a poser, my lord."

"I do not like to think of myself as less than honorable," he said slowly. "I do have rather high standards of behavior for myself and others."

"Of course." She nodded easily. "You are a gentleman."

He gazed at her soberly. "And for you, as my wife."

An uneasy tremor went through Olivia. His tone was suddenly severe. She nodded again, slowly. "Of course. I am a lady." She truly tried to be, anyway. She must take care to prove it to both of them.

He seemed to relax then, for he smiled slightly.

"Then I bid my lady good eve." He bowed and strode from the room, taking the light and Olivia's previous contentment with him.

4

The next time Olivia awoke, pearly daylight streamed in through the high arched window, turning what had been dark and intimate now quite commonplace, if luxurious.

A flutter of cloth drew Olivia's attention toward the dressing-area door where she saw a maid shaking out one of the gowns from Olivia's trousseau.

"Good morning," Olivia said brightly, expecting a smile and a comment on the day, the way the Cheltenham servants would have responded.

The maid stood and turned, bobbing warily. "Good morning, milady."

She was a nice-looking girl of perhaps seventeen. Olivia smiled to put her at her ease. "What is your name, please?"

The girl went entirely still. "I am called Petty, milady." Her voice was flat and her gaze was anything but friendly. "The housekeeper presented me to you yesterday."

Olivia faltered. "Well . . . thank you for the fresh coals, Petty." She gestured toward the now-blazing fire.

"My room turned quite chilly overnight and I'm glad for a fire."

If possible, Petty became even more stiff. "That was the chambermaid, milady. We was instructed not to wake you any earlier. If you want your fire freshened before ten, milady, you must speak to Mrs. Huff, the housekeeper."

"Oh no." Olivia blinked. "I didn't mean . . ." She'd bungled it now. The girl would take anything she said as a criticism, it was clear. She gave up. "Ten will be fine. Er, carry on."

Olivia watched Petty from the corner of her eye as the maid briskly finished her task and left the room. It seemed Olivia's lord husband kept an entirely different class of help. Even Petty's black gabardine maid uniform was of fine quality—better, in fact, than much of what Olivia had worn in the past.

Walt would have managed to tease a smile from the girl, Olivia had no doubt, but she'd never had that knack for ease in all company.

Olivia could have used a bit of that talent during her excruciating debut. It wasn't so much that she was shy. It was more that she simply didn't seem to speak the language. In the last month of this Season, she'd watched in mystification as the other young women rendered the young men speechless with one coy flick of their fan or employed an adoring gaze to make a suitor plump up like a proud rooster.

She'd tried it a few times herself, but her flick of her fan had nearly put out one fellow's eye and her adoring gaze had prompted her dance partner to inquire if she was feeling the need to vomit.

Alone again, Olivia flopped back onto her mounded pillows in relief. She'd not needed any such devices to attach her own magnificent husband after all, had she? Why, that day in the river, she'd forgotten to employ even the slightest flirtation—and he'd asked for her anyway.

Yet if she hadn't flirted, nor truly even conversed with Dane before they wed, how was it that he had come to ask for her hand? He could have had one of any number of prettier, wealthier, more stylish young ladies. She sat up with a surprising thought.

Had he loved her from afar?

She quickly slipped from the cozy covers and padded across the room barefoot to the mirror over her vanity. Seating herself on the stool, she tucked her chilled toes beneath her hem and examined her own reflection.

Hmm. To her surprise, for she'd not so much as brushed her hair this morning, she was looking rather fine. Her cheeks were flushed becomingly and her tousled locks were messy but somehow suited her better than a sleek, restrained style. She smiled at herself, for she was justly proud of her good teeth. Dane must have liked her looks. He'd certainly approved of her bosom.

Perhaps . . . just perhaps . . . he'd admired her even as she'd admired him! It was a vain and outrageous thought, but what else could it be? Her life had taken on a dreamlike quality of late. Who was to say that dream might not include true love? That might be why he wed her so abruptly and why he'd spent so much time carefully wooing her—seducing her—last night.

The avid gleam that came into her gray eyes at the

thought of last night only made her look better, she decided. Better than she'd ever looked in her life. But then, why not?

Love became her.

Joy rose in her. She stood and spun her way back across the room with arms outstretched. How fortunate she was! Lucky, lucky girl!

Smiling widely, she set about dressing herself rather than call upon the sour-faced maid. In the course of finding where Petty had placed her things, she found the locked box that had previously lived under her bed in her parents' house.

There wasn't anything of value in it, unless her private thoughts were counted. As far as Olivia was concerned, she'd sooner lose her clothes than lose her diary.

She opened the lock with the key that she'd hidden in her cloak pocket before leaving home yesterday. Inside was a small, unimpressive book.

She was a married woman now. Keeping a diary would undoubtedly seem childish to a man like Dane.

It was only that making note of the world helped Olivia keep her true feelings to herself. When she didn't keep a written record, things tended to bottle up and she never knew when the worst possible thing would burst out.

So she put it all on paper, in the book Walt had given her, keeping her writing tiny and cramped and using her own playful abbreviations so that she wouldn't use up the paper too soon.

There was a lovely, dainty writing desk in the corner of the room, but Olivia brought the inkwell and pen back to the bed and drew the curtains about her. It was dim within, but at least she'd have a moment to hide the book beneath her pillow if Petty came back into the room.

Olivia closed her eyes and let her feelings about the previous night well up within her. *Dane* . . . heavens, were there even words?

She blushed. There probably were, but she didn't think she ought to write them down! Nor would vulgar descriptions do to capture the spell she'd been under. His hands, so large and strong, yet so gentle on her . . .

The scent of him, sandalwood and heat and man . . . the way his hard body felt to her touch . . . his mouth . . .

Goodness, the minute she was done she was going to finish dressing and seek him out! Her breath coming more quickly, she bent to write, the pen nib scratching madly as she filled the page.

Dane scowled over the pages from the file before him. "What do you mean, Liverpool opposes this plan?"

Marcus was pacing before Dane's great desk. "I mean, he opposes it!" He threw out his hands. "I informed him that we were preparing to employ a member of the Liar's Club to engage the Prince Regent in a close friendship that would help us keep better tabs on his moods and whims and to influence him away from behavior such as he has previously embarked on."

It was a good plan. Prince George IV had led the government on many a merry chase over the years, not the least of which was his recent disappearance in the company of two young spy trainees.

Dane slapped both palms down on his desk. The oak trembled. "Did you explain to Liverpool that the Chimera is still at large and that we must keep George under constant supervision? No more unauthorized jaunts!"

Marcus threw himself into the chair by the fire. "Oh, Liverpool wants the Prince Regent controlled all right. Preferably with iron chains. It's the companion we chose that the Prime Minister objects to."

Dane looked down at the name written in the file. "What's wrong with the Phoenix? He's entirely suitable, wholeheartedly loyal, and His Highness has already shown a marked preference for his company."

Marcus shrugged. "Apparently there is something we don't know about Collis Tremayne. Or it could be his wife, Rose. She's lowborn, and you know what a snob Liverpool is."

Dane grunted. "Unless she's deucedly pretty, I don't think we need to worry about George wanting to spend time with her."

Marcus shook his head. "I happen to think she's quite lovely, but you know George's taste runs to an earthier sort."

Dane nodded absently. *Earthier,* in regards to George, meant endowed with a great deal of bosom and a hearty appreciation for bed-play. . . .

A thought began to trace its way across Dane's frustration. He leaned back in his chair and contemplated the ceiling as the idea began to grow. *George's taste runs to an earthier sort.*

"Liverpool was right," Dane said slowly. "Using Tremayne is not the answer. What we need . . ." He sat up and regarded Marcus with a grim smile. "What we need is the right woman."

"What sort of woman do you need? Will I do?"

The playful question from the doorway made both men start and spin toward the voice. There, smiling brightly, stood Lady Greenleigh.

Dane blinked. Damn, he'd forgotten all about her. It was clear he'd have to get into the habit of locking his study door while he and Marcus were working. The servants never entered without invitation. It had never occurred to Dane that his new wife would traipse in unasked.

Marcus shot Dane a worried glance. Dane agreed completely with his concern. It wouldn't do to have their plans overheard. If one didn't know who they were— hell, even if one did know—their discussions would occasionally resemble darkest treason.

Dane stood smoothly and approached her. "I'm sorry, my dear. Did you need something?"

His tone must have been cooler than he'd intended, for her bright smile faded. "No." She glanced past him at Marcus, her brow beginning to knit with worry. "I apologize for the interruption. I—I only wanted to tell you good morning."

Dane hid his irritation with a smile. She'd obviously meant nothing by her intrusion. "And a good morning to you, Olivia." He waved a hand toward Marcus. "You recall my investment partner, Lord Dryden, do you not?"

She dipped a quick curtsy at Marcus, who bowed warily in return. "My lady."

Dane took her elbow and turned her gently toward

the door. "Now, if you'll excuse us, we have many business matters to work through this morning."

He propelled her through the door and shut it on her bemused expression. However, when he turned back to Marcus, his friend still seemed concerned.

"Shouldn't we have tried to explain away what we were talking about? She's an intelligent girl. She might begin putting bits and pieces together."

Dane shrugged casually. "If it will make you feel better." He stepped back into the hall to find Olivia still outside, regarding the study door with her brow still furrowed. Marcus had been quite correct. That intense concentration on matters that did not concern her did not bode well for any of them.

The fact that she looked completely delectable with her gray eyes so serious and her arms folded beneath her bosom—

Dane battered down his distracting libido with iron control. Still, the rising of his interest did give him an idea.

He approached her slowly, purposely reminding her of how he'd moved toward her last night. The reminder worked, for he saw her eyes begin to gleam and the tip of her tongue come out to wet her lips. She began to back up as well, until she encountered the wall at her back. Dane moved in close, reliving every moment of last night's seduction with intent. When he got through with her—

He looked both ways down the hall, but there were no servants in sight. Gazing down at her, he saw that her eyes were wide and her breath was coming fast. Dane wrapped one hand behind her neck and one about her waist and dipped his head to almost touch his lips to hers. He hovered there for a long moment. She began to quiver in his grasp. Finally, a tiny, hungry sound broke from her lips.

"Olivia," he whispered almost against her mouth. "When I come to you tonight . . ."

"Y—yes?" Her whisper broke with breathlessness.

"Do you know how I would like to find you?"

She made that sound once more. Dane found that he liked that sound very much.

"H-how?"

Dane slid his hand from her neck down her shoulder and traced her neckline with one finger. She quivered when his touch passed over the full hill of one breast and dipped lightly into the valley between.

"I want you entirely bare," he whispered into her parted lips. "No wrapper, no nightdress. Not even a ribbon in your hair."

Her breath left her in a gust and she sagged in his grip. "Yes. . . ."

"Do I have your word, Olivia? Will you wait naked for me, with nothing but the candlelight touching your skin?"

She could only nod frantically. Dane eased her from his hold, propping her gently against the wall. She leaned there, her impressive bosom heaving, her wide gaze locked on his.

Dane straightened with a smile. "Thank you, my dear. I shall look forward to it." With a swift, impersonal peck to her dampened brow, he turned away and strode back to the study and the more important issues at hand.

That had taken care of matters nicely. He doubted if Olivia could even remember the conversation she'd overheard.

Now all he had to do was diminish his towering erection before he got back to business.

5

Dane needn't have worried, for it was several long moments before Olivia could even recall her own name, much less anything that had happened before that devastating, marvelous, extraordinary moment of public arousal.

He hadn't even kissed her, not really. He'd scarcely touched her, although she could still feel that line of fire leading to her cleavage. Yet here she was, breath short, pulse pounding, knees weak, having given her word that she would wait for him in the altogether—well, frankly it was a relief that he hadn't asked for something more scandalous. She'd likely have promised him anything! It was quite obvious that she became a complete fool at his touch.

She smiled shakily, wrapping her arms tightly about herself. She liked it very much. She shook her head briskly, taking a deep breath to quiet her panting. Goodness, how was she to think on anything else for the rest of the day?

If she'd thought her husband mad for her—well,

she rather thought she was becoming mad for him as well!

Olivia spent the afternoon getting to know the house, at least the parts she was permitted to enter. The housekeeper, Mrs. Huff, a ferociously elegant figure in widow's black, made it quite clear that her ladyship needn't bother with belowstairs or the servants' quarters and the cook had nearly popped a vein when Olivia had thrust her head through the kitchen door with a bright "Good afternoon!"

So Olivia wandered the three floors she was allowed, from the entrance hall to the guest rooms, searching out morning rooms and withdrawing rooms and music rooms—she hoped Dane played, for she most certainly did not—finding every room lovely and perfectly furnished, every surface spotless, and every passing servant far too busy and far too proper to chat.

For the first time, Olivia understood why a lady might employ a companion, although it did seem tremendously wasteful to pay someone to listen. If a listener had to be paid, it rather reduced the joy of speaking, did it not?

Finally, Olivia wandered back to her bedchamber. Petty was turning the covers on the bed.

"Good afternoon, Petty." Olivia was determined to be cheerful.

The girl turned and bobbed. "Pardon me, my lady, but I'm Letty."

Olivia blinked at her. Same height, same coloring, same spray of freckles across her nose, same resentfully furrowed brow. Olivia folded her arms. Petty was having a bit of "wind up the new mistress" fun. "I was sure you said your name was Petty."

"No, milady," a voice came from behind her. "I'm Petty."

Olivia turned to see Petty—again—in the doorway to her dressing area. "Oh." She turned back to see Letty concealing a smirk.

"Mrs. Huff presented us to you yesterday, milady."

Mrs. Huff had rattled off the names of a line of servants that could have gone round Cheltenham's front drive at breathtaking speed. Apparently, Olivia was now expected to remember them all.

Oops.

"Well, yes, of course she did. How very nice to see you again, Letty."

"Letty's the chambermaid, milady," Petty pointed out.

Hence the tending of bed linens. Olivia should have noticed. Things at Cheltenham were a bit more loosely organized. The elderly remaining servants did what they were capable of and hired out the rest to the work-hungry village.

"But you must be related, then." She was positive on that point. She might be confused, but she wasn't blind.

"Sisters, milady," Letty volunteered, then hushed abruptly.

Olivia turned to catch an admonishing glare retreating from Petty's expression. Petty must be the elder. That made sense, for a lady's maid ranked higher than a chambermaid in any house. Olivia made determined note of it all. She would be the viscountess that Dane wanted. All she needed to do was keep her eyes and ears open.

For the first time, she noticed the gown that Petty held. It was the second-best evening gown from Olivia's hurried trousseau, a gray satin that matched her eyes. "Is there a problem with my dress?" She rather hoped there was. She didn't much care for the gown, thinking it dull and severe, but Mother had chosen the fabric and cut.

Petty stiffened. "Of course not, milady!"

Olivia hid a sigh. The girl was determined to take everything wrongly.

Petty went on. "It will be ready for tonight."

"Tonight?" The only plans Olivia had for tonight were to obey Dane's command and await him in the altogether. Her skin heated at the thought and her mind spun off into imagining all the various and sundry things that might ensue. . . .

". . . Cheltenham, my lady."

Olivia's attention snapped back to Petty. "What?"

Petty's lack of expression spoke volumes. "This evening you are to dine with Lord and Lady Cheltenham, my lady." She enunciated slowly, as if to an idiot. It was just this side of insulting, but Olivia scarcely cared.

They were having dinner with her parents? Dane had said nothing of the kind earlier. Olivia was wounded and dismayed to be less informed than the insolent Petty.

"Oh . . . yes, of course. How silly of me to forget."

Petty truly was a master of the snide glance. "Yes, milady."

Olivia closed her eyes briefly. "Carry on then, Petty, Letty." She left her own room, grateful for the emptiness of the hall outside. She'd found a library earlier. She could spend what remained of the afternoon there, away from chilly servants and Dane's busy indifference.

She tilted her head back and heaved the sigh that had been brimming for several minutes. Dinner with her parents.

Oh dear. And she'd only just managed to leave them.

Another thought brightened her mood, however. At least she would be alone with Dane in the carriage on the way.

"I do hope you don't mind me tagging along, Lady Greenleigh."

Dane turned his gaze to where Marcus was smiling engagingly at Olivia across the roomy carriage. "Nonsense," he said. "Why shouldn't you ride with us?"

Olivia shot an indecipherable glance in his direction, then turned back to Marcus. "Yes, you are most welcome, Lord Dryden," she said quietly.

She seemed a bit tired this evening. He'd likely kept her up too late last night. She'd perk up once they reached her family home, at any rate.

He gazed back out the window to the grim, blurry London streets passing outside. The weather was always unpleasant now, with the air gone to soot and fog. Most of Society had already left for Scotland or their home estates. Dane looked forward to showing Greenleigh to Olivia, but that would have to wait until the Four had settled the matter of George's "companion."

Tonight's excursion was merely an excuse to hold an impromptu meeting. He'd asked Lady Cheltenham to invite the Cobra, Lord Reardon, and the Falcon,

Lord Wyndham, along with a few other benign ac-
quaintances for camouflage. Just a casual evening with
friends and family, at least to the outside world.

In addition, it would surely please Olivia to see her
mother again. New brides pined for their mothers, did
they not?

Not that he intended to concern himself too deeply
with Olivia's needs. It wouldn't do to coddle her too
much but there was no reason to mistreat her by keeping her from her loved ones. They would be leaving for
Kirkall Hall in Scotland in a few days' time and Olivia
wouldn't see her family again until Christmas at the
soonest.

He was merely being considerate.

Olivia, on the other hand, was being anything but.
Her answers to Marcus's friendly ventures were short
and quiet—not rude but not forthcoming, either. Dane
hoped he wouldn't have to speak to her on the topic.

Perhaps she would warm up once she'd arrived in
her old home.

Olivia hadn't been in her family's London abode for
more than a moment when she was made to feel as
though she had never left.

Alas.

"Olivia dear, you've soiled your hem already!"

Lady Cheltenham had likely never soiled a hem in
her life, not even as an infant. As her slender, imperious mother in her ruthlessly stylish gown came down
the entrance hall, Olivia flashed on a tiny, imperious
baby in ruthlessly stylish nappies.

Olivia sighed. The family butler, Huxley, hadn't

even completely removed her cloak yet! "Good evening to you, too, Mother."

"What a pity. You needn't be such a hoyden,
Olivia—"

Dane stepped smoothly between them. "I defy
Princess Charlotte herself not to take on a bit of soot
on an evening like this." He smiled indulgently at
Olivia. She could have kissed him right there. "Besides, Lady Greenleigh need not concern herself with
such things, eh?"

"Of course not." Lord Dryden stepped out of the wet
and loomed alongside Dane like her own personal
brick wall against her mother's criticisms. Lady Cheltenham made a few flustered noises, then hurriedly
turned away to greet newly arriving guests.

Olivia caught Dane's hand at his side and squeezed
it. "Thank you," she whispered.

Dane turned to look down at her and went still,
caught by her grateful gaze. One might have thought
he'd saved her from a charging bull for the thankful-
ness that shone from her eyes. He had to wonder what
sort of woman Lady Cheltenham was, to cause such
distress with a single comment.

He felt a tug of commiseration. His father had been
a hard taskmaster, demanding and critical even when
approving. Lady Cheltenham didn't seem as though
she handed out much approval of any kind. It must
have been very difficult for Olivia to remain as fearless
as she was. His father would have liked her—

Dane clenched his jaw. His father had been a traitor,
turned by a seductress, who had probably pinned him
with such a grateful gaze at some time or another.

He banished the tug of sympathy and chuckled genially as he handed Huxley his greatcoat. "No trouble at all," Dane said lightly. He and Lord Dryden began to move away from her down the entrance hall, already absorbed in their conversation.

Olivia watched Dane go, a slight frown creasing her brow. For a moment, she'd felt the most astonishing sensation, as though he'd looked into her eyes and understood every single little thing about her.

Then it was gone, like footprints from beach sand after a wave.

"Lord Greenleigh is already inside?" Her mother's peevish tone let Olivia know who this evening was really for.

Olivia turned to see her mother enter the hall accompanied by a very handsome gentleman and his plump, pretty wife. He was prettier than her by far, until she smiled. Then dimples deepened and blue eyes shone with friendliness. Olivia adored her at once.

Astonishingly, Olivia's mother led them over and presented *them* to *her*. "This is the Earl of Reardon and Lady Reardon."

Reardon bowed and Olivia and Lady Reardon curtsied. When Olivia straightened she saw that her mother was off again, greeting more guests. "Heavens, this is turning out to be quite the party."

Lady Reardon grinned. "It looks like she's invited everyone who is left in town. Look, Nathaniel, isn't that Wallingford?"

Olivia looked toward the door to see her mother greeting a bored-looking young man. She turned back just in time to glimpse the expression of distaste that crossed Lord Reardon's face.

Lord Reardon . . . Reardon . . . "Oh!" she blurted. "You're Lord Treason!"

He grimaced. "Not anymore, I hope."

Olivia clapped a hand over her wayward mouth. "Oh dear. Oh no. I'm so sorry. Of course you aren't. I mean, you couldn't be anymore, could you? Not that I ever thought you were. I mean to say, I never even heard of you until a month ago, but . . ." She gave up and let her hands fall to her side. "Oh, bother."

Lady Reardon was gazing at her, both brows high. "You do carry on."

"I know," Olivia said miserably. Now the obviously interesting Lady Reardon would suddenly decide to be elsewhere. "I can't help it."

Lady Reardon tilted her head. "Me, neither. Want to go off somewhere and carry on?"

"Oh my," Lord Reardon said faintly. "What a harrowing thought."

Lady Reardon tucked her arm into Olivia's and waved a hand at her husband. "Go on and play with the other boys while I get to know my new partner in crime."

6

When everyone was gathered in the parlor, Olivia had only moments to attach names to faces before her mother pulled her aside.

"Olivia, dear, I must beg your opinion of our new music room draperies."

Olivia threw a regretful smile Lady Reardon's way but went willingly enough, although she knew perfectly well there were no new draperies. She'd only left home yesterday morning, for pity's sake! Still, it was doubtful she was going to be able to avoid her mother's censure for the entire party. Best to have it done without witnesses.

Olivia let her mother guide her to the never-used music room. "You wished to speak to me privately on some matter, Mother?"

Mother turned to her with an odd expression on her face. Was she actually *nervous*? Whatever for?

"Olivia, dear, please sit down for a moment." She led Olivia to the aged sofa that still looked good enough but was best sat on carefully. Olivia perched on the edge of the cushion so as not to tempt fate with the elderly springs.

She folded her hands in her lap and prepared herself. What had she done now? True, her hair had lost several pins already—she was fairly certain she'd left a few in the carriage—and her hem was still undeniably soiled, although the soot mark was barely visible on the gray satin. So what more fault could her mother possibly find?

"Olivia, I ought to have had this talk with you yesterday. It plagued me sleepless all night that I had sent you into his house without—well, *motherly* preparation, you see, for the . . . the *act.*"

Olivia went very still. Oh dear. If her mother asked her what had happened last night, what was she to say? *You could say you had a marvelous time and cannot wait for it to happen again, and more.*

Hmm. Perhaps not.

Lady Cheltenham took Olivia's hand in her own. It was an odd and slightly alarming show of affection, since Olivia could not remember her mother ever touching her except to correct some malfunctioning hair ornament or an askew bodice.

"Livvie . . ."

Eek. Past alarming and directly to appalling! No one called her Livvie except for Walt. This bode no good.

"Livvie," her mother began again, "I ought to have made sure that you understood the importance of what you were about to undertake." She sighed. "As you likely already have discovered . . . men are rather basic creatures, dear, capable of the most disgusting demands. Why, even your own esteemed father—"

Father? Oh, *ack!* Olivia's ears rang and she fought

the violent impulse to leap up and flee. With all the will she possessed, she tuned her attention to her own breathing and heartbeat and to the faint murmur of the guests down the hall. She finally resorted to humming very softly to herself.

At last, it seemed to be over.

". . . well, that was the last and only time he ever dared ask to leave the candles lighted, I can assure you!"

"Mmm-mm." Olivia would never be able to look her father in the eye again. Ever.

"So you see what you must tolerate, dear. Of course, for you it will be doubly difficult."

Doubly? "Why is that, Mother?"

Her mother shook her head and patted Olivia's hand sorrowfully. "Because you must pretend to enjoy it, you poor creature. I was merely forced to tolerate. You must draw upon all your will and convince him that not only do you enjoy it, but that you want *more!*"

She fixed Olivia with pale-eyed intensity. "It is a terrible prospect, I know, but you must tie him to you tightly, my dear, and I fear that you have little to use for rope."

She must? She did? *Rope?*

Olivia brushed aside that intriguing mental picture. "Mother, I don't understand. Are you saying that he won't love me if I don't please him in the bedroom?" As generally icky as this conversation was, it warmed her that her mother so desperately wanted her and Dane to be happy.

Mother blinked. "Love? Who said anything about love? I'm talking about Cheltenham! Cheltenham *needs* you. You *must* do this!"

No longer quite so warm, Olivia withdrew her

hand from her mother's grasp. "Cheltenham."

Mother blinked at her. "Of course Cheltenham. Goodness, would you lay yourself down for a man for anything less?"

No, but perhaps for something more.

"So you wish me to seduce my husband for the good of Cheltenham?"

Her mother tilted her head and smiled. "Thank you, dear. How lovely it was to have this little chat with you." She patted Olivia's hand and stood. "Well, I must get back to our guests." And she was gone.

Olivia remained in the room for a moment, staring at the gleaming piano that hadn't been tuned in years. "All for the good of Cheltenham. . . ."

"What?"

Olivia turned toward the door to see Walter's fiancée . . . well, previous fiancée . . . standing in the doorway.

"May I join you, Lady Greenleigh?" Miss Absentia Hackerman asked. Most people had difficulty saying the name of the country's wealthiest heiress with a straight face.

Olivia absolutely pined to ask Sir and Lady Hackerman what they had been thinking. Apparently, extreme wealth did not always go hand in hand with a thorough education. Even Walter, who had always been a good sport about marrying for money, had made more than one reference to liking his fiancée's company best "in absentia."

"Of course." Olivia made room on the sofa, caring little if Miss Hackerman sank deep into the tired horsehair. "How may I be of service?"

Miss Hackerman eyed the sofa with distaste—although perhaps that was because she eyed nearly everything that way—and elected to stand. With a sigh, Olivia began to stand as well when she realized that not only was she not the hostess, she was the guest of honor.

With a smile she smoothed her skirts and folded her hands on her lap. She didn't have far to look up into Miss Hackerman's face. "Yes, Abbie?"

Miss Hackerman smiled, but her eyes were narrowed. "I wished to say how happy I am that you have *finally* wed. You must be so relieved."

Vile little cat. "I am entirely blissful, thank you, Abbie," Olivia said serenely.

"I imagine so. After all, you managed to capture none other than 'the Dane' himself." Olivia knew Miss Hackerman had moved Dane up her list after Walter had died. The girl smiled spitefully. "Someday you must tell me how you did it."

Implying any number of nasty maneuverings, of course. Outwardly, Miss Hackerman was quite attractive, and no expense had been spared to make her the most stylish young lady about.

Outwardly only. The girl had never been friend to her, for she'd known there was nothing Olivia could do about her cutting remarks and snide jests. Sir Hackerman had bought his knighthood as surely has he had bought Lord Walter Cheltenham for his daughter. Cheltenham had needed Hackerman money too badly to be lost over something as insignificant as Olivia's feelings.

Olivia smiled. "Runaway horses are rather old hat, are they not? Nothing shows a man that you care like leaping into the Thames." It was worth every moment of Mother's excruciating admonishments to realize that Cheltenham could get along quite nicely without the Hackermans.

Miss Hackerman hesitated, obviously needing to re-group. She'd doubtlessly expected Olivia to blush horribly and fade away, as she had done before.

Olivia tilted her head and assumed a faintly bored expression. "You must have wanted something else, Abbie."

Her opponent glanced away, conceding the field. "Well . . . yes. I was hoping I could arrange an introduction to Lord Wallingford."

"I'm sure Mother could easily manage that."

"Hmm. Yes." Miss Hackerman paused, waiting for Olivia to twig. Olivia had already twigged, thank you. Apparently, Miss Hackerman wasn't satisfied to be introduced by Lady Cheltenham, eminently respectable but hardly the highest of the high in Society. Miss Hackerman wished for the implied approval of Greenleigh.

It was an interesting sensation, this possession of social currency. Olivia doubted she was much in the way of using it—except perhaps this once. She stood gracefully, suddenly completely comfortable with how she towered over the petite heiress.

"Well, I suppose you'll be on your way to Mother, then."

Storm clouds darkened that pretty brow. Miss Hackerman positively twitched with fury, but there was nothing she could do.

It was a delicious moment indeed.

"Well, then I suppose I shall." In a whirl of expensive skirts, Miss Hackerman was gone.

Pity it wasn't forever.

Olivia sighed. Dinner was going to be grim, she simply knew it.

Dane eyed his table companions with a furrowed brow. An unlikelier bunch he'd never seen.

Lord Cheltenham sat at the head of the table, of course, with Dane at his right. Olivia sat next to Dane, while on her other side lounged Lord Wallingford, who was bloody drunk already. After him sat Lady Reardon, then Marcus, then Lady Cheltenham at the foot of the table, with a pained-looking Nate at her right. After him sat Miss Hackerman, the very one who'd needed rescuing from her fractious horse—now that he'd spent the evening with the girl, he understood the mount's objections—and then there was Stanton Horne, the Marquis of Wyndham, at Lord Cheltenham's left.

Four spies, a monosyllabic earl, an annoying heiress, an obnoxious young sot, two very pleasing ladies— although Olivia had scarcely spoken this evening—and the mother from hell.

Dane found himself listening eagerly for the chiming of the clock in the hall. Soon the ladies would excuse themselves and the gentlemen would take out their cigars. Dane had arranged this evening in order to hold an impromptu session of the Royal Four. If they could rid themselves of Cheltenham and Wallingford, then the Cobra, the Lion, and the Falcon could discuss Dane's plan for Prince George.

If Dane could persuade the others, he could declare a quorum—they had little choice, with the Fox on his deathbed. Lord Barrowby had named no successor yet, and their reconnaissance had reported no apparent candidate lingering about. If Barrowby had neglected his duty, there was going to be hell to pay in the Four.

The Prime Minister of England, who had formerly served as Cobra, would likely fight to have his own candidate take the spot. Frankly, Dane was weary of Liverpool's constant maneuverings within the Four. Nate had been Liverpool's successor, after Lord Etheridge had stepped down to take over the Liar's Club, but thankfully Nate wasn't inclined to kowtow to his former master.

The last thing Dane or the others wanted was to allow Liverpool to install someone who still retained loyalty to him.

Dane looked down the table to where Marcus was valiantly trying to maintain an attentive facade to Miss Hackerman's complaints and objections. Marcus would make a good Fox, although the duties were slightly different from the Lion's. Marcus was brilliant and deathly loyal to England. He deserved more than to live out his days as only Dane's protégé.

Unfortunately, that meant Dane would have to begin all over again selecting his second—and a poor crop of candidates there was, too. Most of the young lords about these days resembled Wallingford, drunken, stupid, and useless.

If Dane could be allowed to choose from the gentry, it would at least widen the pool, but for seven hundred years the Four had been carefully selected from the peerage. Dane would not like to be the first to break tradition thus.

Dane's attention was caught by his wife's rather delectable bosom. From his seat he had an excellent view.

He'd told her to wait for him naked. What an in-spired thought that had been. To have her before him, bared and aroused, the candlelight flickering on her skin like a molten glow . . .

He rubbed the back of his neck. He was becoming a bit molten himself. By God, he wished this inter-minable dinner over with so he could carry her off to her bedchamber and watch her undress herself—

With a jerk he realized that he was contemplating leaving before he and the others had their meeting. Dismay jolted the last of his arousal away.

Duty first. First, last, and always.

Of course, making his heir was one of his duties— then again, making his heir did not necessarily include mentally undressing his wife during a dinner party.

He turned his gaze away from her bosom with deter-mination.

Duty.

The watcher kept an eye on the proceedings from out-side the window. He missed nothing, from the amount of wine young Lord Wallingford downed to the way Lord Greenleigh's gaze kept traveling back to his wife's bosom.

Everything was going as planned, although it itched at him to see Lord Reardon and his bride at the table. What were they doing there?

It could be happenstance—most men of that rank knew each other well enough to sit down to dinner. Reardon's wife could be there on behalf of Lady Green-leigh, for that matter.

Greenleigh might scarcely know Reardon. The watcher

certainly had seen no sign of companionship at the table, although that would be hard with the seating arrangement.

Yet Reardon had been part of the downfall of Wadsworth . . . and there had been those rumors about Lady Reardon and that mysterious group called the Quatre Royal . . .

If Reardon was working for the Crown, then he could be here tonight for much the same reason as the watcher.

Recruitment.

Well, then, perhaps it was time to advance the queen. A spot of danger always heated the blood, did it not?

In the meantime, it bothered him no end that he'd never seen the fifth gentleman before. The fellow sat with his back to the window now, but he'd seen him clearly when the party had entered the dining room.

Something was going on, something beneath the surface.

As if he felt the watcher's gaze, the fifth man turned his head and glanced over his shoulder, his sharply cut features in profile against the well-lit room.

The watcher stepped back quickly, although it was unlikely the man saw anything but himself and the other guests reflected in the glass.

The fifth man gestured to a servant, who rounded the table to close the draperies.

Never mind. Despite the stranger at the table, there was no reason why the evening's entertainment could not go on as planned.

7

Olivia fidgeted. She and the other ladies sat in the drawing room, the most presentable room in Cheltenham House. The draperies were hardly shabby at all, and the stuffed sofas scarcely sank under one's weight. Dinner was finally over and the gentlemen would join them soon.

"Is there something the matter?" Lady Reardon—Willa, she'd insisted—gazed at Olivia with amused concern. "Or is it just a newlywed affliction?"

Olivia pressed her lips together. There was something she was dying to ask someone—something her mother evidently didn't have the answer to—and Willa seemed just the person. Looking about to see if the other two ladies were nearby, Olivia leaned closer to Willa.

"You're recently wed, yes?"

Willa nodded, her dimples deepening. "Mere weeks."

Olivia took a breath. "May I ask you a very improper question?"

Willa leaned closer as well. "Those are my favorite kind," she whispered back.

"Is it . . . is it wonderful?"

Willa leaned back slightly and gazed at her. "Not yet?"

Olivia shook her head. Willa gazed thoughtfully at the door through which the men would enter. "Well, bully for him."

Olivia sighed. "I know it's terribly wicked to be so eager, but—"

Willa put her hand over Olivia's. It was a warm, friendly gesture, nothing like her mother's. "Olivia, someday I must tell you how I repeatedly tried to attack Nathaniel. He would have none of it. It nearly drove me mad at the time, but in retrospect, I believe it was good that we grew to know each other a bit first."

"Oh dear. How long did it take?" She hadn't much wait in her, she feared.

Willa gave a tiny, secret smile. "A week. I'm irresistible."

Having seen Lord Reardon's moonstruck gaze when he looked at his bride, Olivia could well believe it. "How do I do that—be irresistible?"

Willa bit her lip and gazed at the ceiling for a moment. "I hadn't considered it, but . . . I think the most irresistible thing is that I find *him* irresistible. I believe men like a woman who likes them."

"I like him," Olivia said, her voice low. "Enormously."

Willa smiled and patted her hand again. "Well, then it's only a matter of time."

"Hmm." Olivia narrowed her eyes at her new friend. "I notice that you never answered my first question. Is it wonderful?"

Willa widened her eyes and shook her head emphatically. "Oh no."

The door opened and the gentlemen entered at last. Willa smiled across the room at her husband, her gaze every bit as moonstruck as his. "It's not wonderful," she said dreamily. "It's *divine*."

It had taken most of the evening, but the Lion, the Cobra, and the Falcon were finally alone. They'd had to hint broadly to their host that the semiconscious Wallingford had required Cheltenham's personal attention to see that he was sent home safely.

When Olivia's father left the room at last, Dane leaned his elbows on the table. "Meeting called to order. Prince George must be controlled."

The Cobra nodded thoughtfully, but the Falcon only raised a brow. "What manner of check have you to offer, then?"

"A mistress, chosen by Prince George himself from an array of ladies we present to him. . . ."

It didn't take long to convince them, although the Cobra expressed reservations about the Hunt Ball proposition. "His Majesty hates Scotland. You know he'd rather spend time in Brighton with his pet soldiers."

The Falcon slid a cool glance in his direction. "Leave that to me. He'll be there."

The Cobra narrowed his eyes. "Perhaps we all ought to be there."

Dane shook his head. "The ladies invited will be a carefully chosen selection. All married to loyal men, all having borne their husband's heir, all women who feel free to dally outside their vows."

Marcus made a noise at that. Dane shot him a quelling glance. Then he tilted his head at the Cobra. "Your lady does not qualify."

The Cobra blinked. "I should hope not!" Then he shrugged. "Yet I could bring her. His Majesty won't cross that line, I can assure you."

The Falcon frowned. "Why not?"

The Cobra held up his hand. "My lady's business and not relevant anyway. Suffice it to say that His Majesty's bond to Willa is . . . avuncular, at most."

Dane shrugged. "That is yours to judge. I could use the reinforcement. You know how he can be when he feels hard-pressed."

"I shall join you after the ball to review the results," the Falcon said. "I'm staying close to Derbyshire in case Barrowby passes. In the meantime, I have decided it is time to review the utility of the Liar's Club."

Dane leaned back and grinned, his point won. "I like that lot. Bunch of rowdies, but I like them."

The Falcon twisted one side of his lips. "I'd like them better if the Chimera had not hidden in their midst for the last year."

The Cobra held up a hand. "That isn't quite true. As Denny the valet, he was never made privy to the inner workings of the club. He knew more than a servant should have, I'll grant you that, but he never knew everything, and he certainly never learned about us."

The Falcon didn't look pacified. "I'm none too sure about that. I know you think those attempts on your life a few weeks ago had more to do with your involvement with that ring of French spies—"

The Cobra shook his head. "He knows nothing but a few decades-old stories about a mythical group known as the Quatre Royale. Old business and long-dead men."

Dane shook his head. "There's no way to know in any case, unless we had the fellow here in a pair of thumbscrews."

The Falcon obviously found that a pleasant thought indeed, for he very nearly smiled. Nearly.

Bloodthirsty bloke. Of course, the Falcon was due his grimness, for keeping an eye on the wayward prince's antics would sour a clown.

The door opened, revealing a harassed-looking Cheltenham. "Bloody piker. Falls drunk on my tablecloth, then tries to hit me up for a loan after he vomits on my front steps."

Dane shook his head with a commiserating smile, glad to see that Olivia's father had a properly disdainful opinion of sots like Wallingford. Lady Cheltenham had indicated that Wallingford had been a friend to her deceased son, but Dane found that hard to believe. Wallingford didn't have friends—he had creditors who daren't let him out of their sight.

Duty was concluded. Dane pushed back from the table. Not eagerly, of course. Not at all. "Shall we go join the ladies then?"

The rest of the evening passed in a blur for Olivia. Once Dane entered the drawing room, she had no thought but what awaited her at home.

Surely he would complete her education tonight. Willa had admired his restraint, but frankly, Olivia could do without it. She was dying of curiosity and half-satisfied arousal.

Oh, hang it. She was dying of lust. Lust for her magnificent golden husband.

He'd sent her a single volcanic glance when he'd come in the room and she'd been able to think of nothing else since.

This was not a problem, since she was currently conversing with Miss Hackerman. The girl had nothing to say but complaints that young Lord Wallingford had left early. Frankly, Olivia was surprised the fellow had been able to find the door. She wouldn't have given a useless idiot like him a moment's thought, but apparently Wallingford had something Abbie wanted.

A title, any title.

As the daughter of the shipping merchant who had supposedly single-handedly financed the military excesses of the now-mad King George, Abbie Hackerman had a great deal to offer. She could afford to be choosier.

Olivia glanced at the girl. Abbie responded with a sunny smile, the very picture of amiability. Of course. Multigenerational social climbing tended to produce a rather professional grasp of who was to be mocked and who was to be manipulated.

Olivia was quite aware that wedding Dane had taken her from the first category to the second with blinding speed. Miss Hackerman had abandoned her previous scorn and now fixed on Olivia the expectant gaze of a long-beloved best friend.

Oh dear.

Olivia couldn't wait to leave with Dane, to ride home in the carriage only inches away from him—oh, hang it—and Lord Dryden.

Oh dear.

At last, Dane thanked her parents and called for their carriage. Olivia stepped outside to await him, drinking in the cool and quiet after the endless, stuffy evening indoors. Dane and Marcus were in the entrance hall taking their leave of that sternly handsome Lord Wyndham, so Olivia wandered politely a few yards down the walk.

How could Dane bear to stand there talking when such wickedly delicious plans awaited them at home?

Home. How easily she'd transferred her loyalties. Then again, with Walt gone, there really was nothing tying her to her family but duty.

She had a new family now. Dane was her family and someday soon they would have children of their own and she would never, *ever* turn them away when they cried or reached out to her—

Thundering hoofbeats rang down the cobbled street toward them. Olivia absently turned her back and wrapped her cloak about her gown to keep it from splashes when the rider passed. Someone was taking a chance riding so fast in the dark.

How many children did Dane wish to have? Personally, she'd like to have as many as she could fit in the time she had left. She was nearly thirty, after all—

"Olivia!"

Something hit her hard, knocking her from her feet and whirling her away.

. . .

When the speeding horse struck him—a glancing blow, equine chest to his shoulder—Dane hit the cobbles hard, unable to break his fall with his arms wrapped about Olivia.

His head cracked on the street with a sickening thud. For a moment his vision blackened. His senses awry, all he could think was, *Protect her.* He held on, keeping her tight to his chest, wrapped in his arms.

He felt hands tugging at him, pulling at his wrist, trying to take her from him. Dane resisted foggily, flinging them away with an uncoordinated shove.

"Greenleigh, ease your grip, man. You're squeezing the life out of her!"

That sounded like Marcus. Dane blinked hard, clearing his vision to see Marcus, Wyndham, and Reardon bent over them.

"Dane . . . you can let me . . . go now." Olivia lay sprawled on his chest, breathless, trapped in his fierce embrace.

He was crushing her. "Oh God!" Dane threw his arms wide, releasing her to slide limply to the cobbles at his side. "Are you—"

He tried to sit up to see to her, but someone swung an anvil inside his head. He pressed the heel of one hand to his skull, fighting the gray creeping around the edges of his vision. "Olivia—"

It took two of them to pull him to his feet, where he wavered, trying to see Olivia.

She stood shakily in Marcus's grip. "I'm quite all right." She shook Marcus off with a half smile. "See?

All in one piece." She turned to Dane. "Bring him inside," she ordered crisply.

Dane blinked bemusedly as three of the most powerful men in England obeyed his bride without a thought. What an excellent choice he'd made. Fortitude, indeed.

As the party re-entered Cheltenham House, Dane was dimly aware of Olivia's mother fluttering in the background as her father huffed indignantly about "rowdies." He was deposited on a sofa in the now-empty drawing room. Olivia knelt before him with a candle in her hand.

"Open your eyes," she instructed. "I want to see if your pupils match."

Dane had seen physicians do that before while serving out his commission in the army. "I'm surprised you know what to do." His voice worked anyway, although he found himself speaking a bit slowly.

"I am the closest thing to a doctor that Cheltenham has, barring the local midwife. I know a few useful things."

She was confidently examining him, pushing his hair aside as she gently probed the lump on his head. "As big as you are," she said drily, "could you not have found a better portion of your anatomy to land on?"

Dane heard Reardon choke back a laugh, and Marcus openly chuckled. Was this the same woman who had scarcely spoken a word during dinner, who had allowed her mother to berate her in front of others?

Dane liked her this way, he decided muzzily. Just like that day in the Thames—competent and self-assured. A true viscountess.

He gently caught her hand away from his sore head. "I'm fine." His voice was stronger as well.

She pulled reluctantly away from him and stood. "Well, that rider ought to be shot," she declared.

Dane didn't answer, but the gaze he shared with the other three assured him that the incident would most definitely be looked into. Accident? Perhaps or perhaps not.

His vision had cleared and he stood without help this time, although his head still pounded. "I think we had better get you home," he said to her.

She crossed her arms. "Get me home? I'm not the one leaning like last year's Maypole."

Dane fought back a grin and raised one hand to point to the door. "Go."

She heaved a sigh and dropped her arms. "You first."

Marcus laughed. "I'll break this battle of wills. *I'll* go first."

In the carriage, Olivia insisted on sitting next to Dane. When he begged off her nursing, she denied it. "If you fall over, I'd rather you land on him." She gestured at Marcus seated across from them. "I've already had the pleasure of being squashed tonight."

Dane smiled at her. "You hold up nicely, nonetheless."

She blushed. "Oh, pish. My hair looks a sight, I'm sure."

It was true. Her hair, apparently disinclined to stay pinned in any circumstances, now stuck out in ludicrous disarray. She looked like a tangled skein of blond yarn.

Her gray silk gown was entirely done for, smeared with street muck and torn at the shoulder where he'd grabbed her.

Then again, Dane hadn't been talking about her appearance. He'd meant something more, something inside. She possessed a surprising resiliency.

Out of the corner of his eye, he noticed Marcus nonchalantly turn his gaze to the window, raptly watching the dark streets go by.

With one hand, Dane tipped her chin up. "You look lovely."

She bit her lip, gazing up into his eyes. "I do not. I—"

He dipped his head to kiss the protest away. Only a quick stolen touch of his lips to hers, but it stopped her cold.

When he released her, Olivia dipped her head to hide the burning in her eyes. The sound of his head cracking on the cobbles had struck deeply, a lance of icy fear. She'd been terrified that he'd been seriously injured, her insides aquiver with panic even as she'd taken charge and barked orders.

They'd only been wed two days, and already she could not imagine what she would do without him.

8

"You'll not spend the night without me," Olivia insisted, her arms crossed and her feet braced like a sergeant major. Dane couldn't get over how she found it so easy to stand up to him. "I insist on staying with you," she said. "Head injuries can be very dodgy. If you sleep too deeply, you might not wake up!"

Dane tied the belt of his dressing gown and jerked his head to send his fluttering valet away. Proffit went with a sniff and a glare toward her ladyship. The servants were taking their time warming up to Olivia, for some reason.

Dane's head hurt and he had larger things to worry about than a discontented staff. If Olivia had issue with any of them, she ought to know what to do. Her mother had assured him that Olivia was well acquainted with the running of a large household.

The lady's maid he'd hired for her tapped on the open connecting door of their chambers. "Your bath is ready, milady."

Olivia tugged at her destroyed gown in irritation.

"I have to get this muck off me. Will you promise not to lock me out while I'm gone?"

Dane couldn't help smiling. "Isn't it usually the lady who locks the gentleman out?"

She narrowed her eyes at him. "I wouldn't put anything past you, my lord. You seem to have an allergy to being taken care of."

Dane waved her on. "Go take your bath and get the horse manure out of your hair. I'll take to my bed like a good boy. You can check up on me when you're done."

"Hmm." To ensure he didn't close her out, she dragged a footstool to block the door from shutting entirely. "So I can hear you if you call."

Dane nodded wordlessly. His head hurt and he had many things to think about—the incident tonight at the top of his list.

He lay on his bed, a vast construction made to his specifications, with the covers pulled to his waist. The tester above him enclosed a mural on the ceiling, a depiction of the Siren on the rocks, calling the sailors to their deaths. The artist had grinned at Dane's request, undoubtedly thinking Dane wanted the erotic image of the bare-breasted woman to entertain his nights.

On the contrary, Dane had wanted the nightly reminder—never let temptation decide your course for you.

Tonight, however, he closed his eyes against the image above him. He had not let Olivia distract him from his duty this evening, nor could he regret his preoccupation with her afterward. If he had not been so aware of her on the street tonight, he never would have made it to her in time to save her from being trampled.

All in all, he had to grant that he'd balanced duty and marriage quite nicely.

It was too bad she'd forgotten about their plans for tonight. He'd been looking forward to furthering her education.

For the sake of his heir, of course.

With his eyes closed and his own room gone quiet, he could now hear the faint splashing sounds of Olivia in the bath. She must have sent Petty on to bed, for there were no voices, only the sound of water lapping at the sides of the tub.

She'd be close to the hearth for warmth. The fire would lick her skin with golden lights, gleaming off the soapy water.

After she dunked and sat up, her hair would slick down her back like a dark gold stream, exposing her long neck and white shoulders . . . and those magnificent breasts would float slightly in the water, buoyed by their own lush abundance. She would wash them, lifting them and soaping them until the bubbles ran from her skin and drops fell from her nipples like diamonds in the firelight. . . .

He'd never actually seen a woman in the bath, he realized.

He also suddenly realized that he was completely aroused—surprising considering the condition of his head. Yet there was no help for it. The thought of a wet, soapy Olivia was as erotic a fantasy as he'd ever known.

He shouldn't have sent her away.

That was ridiculous. She'd had a trying evening, in more ways than one. They both needed their rest.

Yet he must continue his tutoring of her. He must train her well in her own sexuality. He must draw all her deepest responses out and make her open to nearly anything.

Do I have your word, Olivia? Will you wait naked for me, with nothing but the candlelight touching your skin?

Ah, well, there you had it. He couldn't very well be the cause of her breaking her word, could he?

He threw back the covers and stood. His headache was easing, likely because all the throbbing had been diverted to other areas.

He pushed the footstool aside and entered her room, looking eagerly toward the fire. The tub was there, but the used toweling and the wetted floor meant he'd missed his chance.

"Dane? Is your head worse?"

Her concerned voice came from behind him and he heard a rustle as if she moved his way. He held up a hand to stop her without turning.

"Do you recall what you promised me this morning, Olivia?"

He heard her draw a breath. "Y—yes. But your head—"

"You gave me your word, Olivia."

A pause. "Yes, Dane," she said quietly. He heard a heavy rustle, the sound of damp toweling hitting the carpet.

He turned.

She stood there, bare and glowing from the heat of her bath and the blush beneath her skin. Her chin was high, but her gaze slid away from him and her fingers twitched nervously at her sides.

A pagan goddess indeed. Her heavy breasts rose and fell with each broken breath, her nipples crinkled with chill and . . . arousal? Dane moved toward her, desperately curious. She wouldn't look at him.

He reached out one hand and slowly drew his fingertip lightly up her belly and between her breasts. She shuddered spasmodically, her flesh twitching beneath his touch. He felt her breath on his chest where the dressing gown had parted slightly, a small, hot gust on his skin.

He drew his finger up between her collarbones and up her throat until he could tip her chin back and see her eyes. She shut them as her head tilted.

"Look at me." The words were soft, but he wasn't asking.

Her eyes fluttered open and his question was answered. Her gray eyes were dark and hot with excitement.

Dane thoughtfully stroked one thumb down her cheek. She was so many women in one, it seemed. Sometimes shy and diffident, sometimes confident, and sometimes, like now, she was a keg of gunpowder that begged to be ignited.

"Do you like this, sweet Olivia, this obedience to me in our bed play? Does it arouse you to be mastered?"

He felt her swallow, her throat convulsing against his hand. She nodded, a tiny movement.

"Do you trust me?"

She nodded again, her gaze never leaving his. She felt wordless and acquiescent before his virility and strength. She was under a spell, as if he held her will in the palm of his hand. It was his instrument, and she was merely the music it played.

"Lay on the bed then," he ordered softly.

She did so, aware that he watched her bend and crawl up onto the counterpane. Even her natural shyness could not compete with the thrilling command in his deep voice.

She lay down on her back. He moved to stand at the foot of the bed, a blond giant framed by the bed curtains. "I want to see you hold your breasts in your hands."

Olivia shivered, but she obeyed, covering her breasts with her hands.

"No." His voice was soft steel. "I want you to heft them, as if you are proud of them. Hold them high."

She hesitated.

He tilted his head. "Do you wish me to leave?"

She shook her head sharply. No, she wanted him to be here. She wanted him to stay. She lifted her full breasts in her hands, pressing them high until her rigid nipples pointed proudly to the ceiling.

"Do you remember my mouth on them last night?" His husky tone proved that he certainly did. Olivia nodded, closing her eyes to recall the wet roughness of his tongue and the sharp pleasure of his teeth.

"Touch your sweet nipples. Pinch and roll them between your fingers, as if my mouth is on you."

With a quiver, she wondered dreamily how far this would go. He would never hurt her. That she believed with all her heart. This . . . play . . . was about pleasing them both, but she knew so little. The yawning void of her knowledge only served to titillate instead of frighten. He had much to teach her.

She couldn't wait.

She did as he commanded, rolling her hard nipples between her fingers. It felt pleasant, but it was the thought that he was watching her that sent hot jolts of fire deep into her belly. Her head fell back and she surrendered to his gaze, all shyness gone, excited beyond belief.

"Open your thighs, my lady," he said, his voice tight.

She parted her knees slightly.

She sensed him putting his weight on the foot of the bed and felt his large, hot hands on her inner thighs. "Open," he said.

Her eyes flew open. Did he mean for her to expose her sex, with the candles lighted and him leaning over her? He pressed her knees open wide until she felt the cool air on her dampness.

Evidently so. Mortification threatened to drown out her arousal and she clenched her eyes shut once more.

"You're beautiful, my lady. You're like the petals of a rose, still yet to bloom entirely." His hands slid up her thighs to caress those petals, leaving trails of warmth behind.

Olivia slowly released her embarrassment, realizing that he meant to stroke her there again, as he had the night before. How lovely. She'd been so hoping—

He lowered his mouth to her.

Hot shock rippled through her. Outrageous! Shocking—

Oh, the *pleasure*!

Sweet, liquid, fiery, *wicked* pleasure!

She forgot the candles. She forgot the shyness. She forgot the very world itself. Nothing existed but the wild, primal ecstasy provided by his hot mouth.

Her hands flew to the side and she gripped fistfuls of linens, seeking any handhold to keep her from flying into the night and losing herself in the stars.

His hands pressed her open, pinning her thighs, his fingertips still parting her for his sinuous invasion. She was grateful for that solid mooring as his lips, tongue, and teeth drove her higher.

Slick and probing, his tongue entered her, stabbing deep, then flicking up to where her sensitive nub awaited. He kept moving, lips and tongue on her nub, then below, then back, slippery with her wetness, all heat and sensation and delightful circling tongue until she thought she'd die of it—

Her body convulsed, the explosion dimming that of the night before. Pleasure swept in rollicking waves from the center of her body out to her fingertips, stealing her breath on its way.

On and on it went, rocketing through her until sheer exhaustion brought her sliding down from that high plane. She lay panting, slowly becoming aware of her surroundings once more.

Dane rose from her and leaned one shoulder on the bedpost, watching his lady wife come back from the most violent orgasm he'd ever witnessed.

How could it be that such a proper young woman was so responsive to his merest touch? Even now, she lay sprawled shamelessly on the bed, her thighs wide, her breasts heaving with her panting, her damp hair wild on the pillow.

She was an erotic picture to be sure and he couldn't deny some pride in making her thus. His own ignored arousal beat at the walls of his will like a caged beast, his erection twitching mightily beneath his dressing gown.

It would take the merest parting of the heavy silk to expose him. She was as ready as he could wish, plumped and slippery and waiting for—

For someone normal.

Slamming the iron bars on temptation, he rose from her bed. The maid had left out her gown on the foot. He lifted it, stroking the filmy stuff between his fingers.

"Put this on, Olivia," he said softly. "You need to cover yourself—" *so I won't ravage you senseless.* "For warmth."

She stretched, finally closing those tempting thighs. Blinking wearily, she gave him a soft smile.

"Did I do that right?"

The infinite rightness of her could not be denied. He placed the gown into her hands and pressed a kiss to her forehead. "I shall see you tomorrow, my lady. Sleep well."

It was a damned sure thing he would not.

"Dane."

He stopped automatically at the tone of command in her voice, obeying her much the way the other men had earlier tonight. Then he shook off that reaction and turned to face her. "Olivia, I would prefer that you use that only in emergency situations."

"Use what, pray tell?" She blinked innocently at him, her face still flushed from his lovemaking. She

began to push back the covers. "I only wished to remind you that I intend to stay with you tonight."

"No." He held up a hand when she began to rise. If
he spent one more moment with her thus, with the firelight flickering on her skin, his control would shatter.
"You must rest as well. I shall have Proffit check in on
me." He shook his head against her protest. "My lady,
Proffit makes an obscene salary to look after me. Let
him earn it. I beg of you, let me be tonight."

She nodded, obviously curious in a sleepy way, until
he turned and left her chamber, blowing out the candle
on the way.

9

When Olivia awoke the next morning, she rolled over with a smile on her face before she even opened her eyes. Things would be different today. She was sure that she and Dane had crossed a boundary the night before. He'd saved her life. She'd taken care of him.

He'd done that *thing*.

She bit her lip, her smile turning naughty, wondering if she could convince him to do that thing again.

At any rate, he would be properly glad to see her this morning. Perhaps he might even steal a quick kiss when the servants weren't looking.

She rose and dressed, too cheerful for even Petty's sour presence to oppress. She danced downstairs, feeling as though she could bear any number of Petty with Dane's presence to bolster her.

But Dane was nowhere to be found.

Instead, his study contained only Lord Dryden sitting behind Dane's massive oak desk. He looked very much at home in the deep green, masculine room. He smiled at her when she entered, although she noticed he slid the pages he was viewing beneath the blotter before he stood to greet her with a bow.

"Good morning, Lady Greenleigh. Did you rest well? No ill effects from last night's incident, I hope."

Last night. The only ill effect Olivia felt was a slight weakness in the knees, but she didn't think that was what he meant.

She bobbed an absentminded curtsy. "I-am-very-well-thank-you. Have you seen his lordship?"

He smiled slightly. "Himself is out, I'm afraid. I believe he said he'd be back before lunch."

Olivia sat in the chair opposite the desk, her enthusiasm deflated. "Oh."

Lord Dryden sat as well, a grin creeping across his face. "I take it that there's nothing I can help you with in his stead?"

Olivia jerked her head up at his teasing tone. Yes, he did mean what she thought he'd meant. She ought to be insulted. She ought to fling herself about in a fit of offense.

The look on his face was puckish and the gleam in his eyes was friendly, not lecherous.

She couldn't help it. She snickered.

His grin widened. "You're quite a surprise, I must say." He leaned back in his chair and regarded her. "I thought you'd be more of a Miss Hackerman sort."

Olivia rolled her eyes. "What, all style and no substance? Spare me the Misses Hackermans of the world, do please."

Lord Dryden made a moue. "Oh, I don't know. I like her well enough—"

"*In absentia,*" they said together, and laughed.

Olivia regarded him with a smile. "I think you ought to call me by my given name. It ought to save hours out of your life, since you always seem to be here."

He bowed his head. "It would be my honor, Olivia. You must call me Marcus." He quirked one side of his mouth. "I do have a home of my own, you know." He shrugged. "Dane's cook is better."

She laughed again, shaking her head. "Men and their stomachs. My brother was just the same." She smiled fondly at Marcus. "You are very much like him."

Since it was intended to be nothing less than a compliment, she was surprised to see a flash of distaste cross his face.

She recalled last night, when Lord Reardon had much the same reaction to young Lord Wallingford—supposedly Walter's closest friend in London.

She gazed at Marcus with confusion. "Did you know my brother?"

He looked down at his hands. "I can't say that I did. We . . . ah, ran in different circles, you might say." His tone said he didn't approve of Walter's circle.

"What do you mean?"

Marcus looked away. "My apologies. One shouldn't speak ill of the dead."

She folded her arms and glared at him. "People only say that when they truly want to speak ill of the dead."

His gaze slid back toward her. "Ah. Well . . ."

She let her breath out in a sigh. "Marcus, I only want to know what happened to my brother. I loved him, but I realize that no one is perfect."

Marcus's gaze softened. "I never heard anything ill

of your brother himself . . . only of the company he kept."

Olivia leaned forward. "What company was that?"

Marcus frowned. "They're a useless lot, all in all. A bunch of well-dressed ruffians living on their expectations. More stupid than dangerous most of the time, but they've been known to do harm to . . ." He hesitated.

"Do harm to whom?" Walt would never harm anyone—well, that wasn't entirely true. There was the time he'd caught the blacksmith's son torturing a stray dog with a freshly heated poker. A broken nose and some cracked ribs—yes, what had happened to the other, much larger boy might be termed harm.

Yet Olivia didn't think Marcus was talking about boyhood fights. "Do harm to whom?"

"The ringleader, young Lord Wallingford—well, suffice it to say that his family tends to go through housemaids rather quickly. And his second, Lord Ashby, is rumored to have raped his younger sister's governess, although the woman disappeared before any charges were brought. Lord Connor isn't as bad, although he won't lift a finger to halt the excesses of the others. Too drunk, most likely."

Olivia listened with growing horror. "No! Walt wasn't like that at all! He wouldn't consort with that sort of fellow, ever! He was honorable and fine and—"

Marcus only gazed at her sadly. "And drowned when he drunkenly fell off a pleasure barge fully stocked with prostitutes and opium."

Olivia sat back, her jaw set. "I don't believe you."

Marcus raised a brow. "You asked me what I heard.

If you don't like it, I'm sorry." His eyes took on a steely glint. "You might want to rethink calling me a liar, however."

Olivia slumped. "I'm sorry. I know you are only telling me what I wanted to know. I know you aren't lying." But someone was. Walt might have been boisterous and occasionally careless, the natural result of being spoiled by their parents, but he would never, ever—

She stood. "Thank you for your time, Marcus, and your patience. I shall leave you to wait for his lordship now." She turned to leave.

"My lady—"

She turned back. "Yes?"

Marcus was gazing at her soberly, his eyes shaded and unreadable. "Stay away from Wallingford and his lot. I'm not sure they'd stop at dishonoring a lady."

Olivia pursed her lips. "Yes, well . . . good day, Marcus."

She turned to leave the study only to find Dane standing in the doorway watching them. "Oh, good morning, Dane!" Blast Marcus for ruining her mood. She smiled at Dane, confident he would smile back.

He didn't. He merely nodded and walked past her to seat himself in the chair Marcus had promptly vacated. "I'm glad you're up, Olivia. I want to speak to you on a matter."

He was being sly, the naughty fellow, just because Marcus was there. When the other man left, she'd get her kiss and then some, she'd wager. She smiled serenely and seated herself in the chair she'd had before. "Yes, Dane?"

First Dane pushed one of the papers in his hand over

to Marcus, then he leaned back and regarded her seriously. "We're leaving in a few days for my—our— hunting house in Scotland. Once there, we will host our own Hunt Ball to, er, celebrate the opening of the season."

Olivia blinked. "I was under the impression we would be going to Greenleigh. I assumed that was the reason we had no honeymoon."

Dane frowned at her. "Of course not. My . . . business affairs precluded our honeymoon. Everyone goes to Scotland at this time of year. It is grouse season."

She frowned back at him. "You're going to hunt grouse? Why? You don't even like chicken."

He didn't care for chicken, although he was surprised she'd realized it. "Hunting grouse is for sport, not necessarily for food."

"But why?" she persisted. "You could shoot at clay targets, or run horse races, or very nearly anything! What did those poor birds ever do to you?"

"Because . . ." He sputtered for a moment. "Because that is what we do!"

" 'We.' I do not see anything compelling in your logic." She crossed her arms. Dane willed himself to keep his gaze level.

"Olivia." He gazed at her warningly. "Back to my topic, I would like for you to take on the planning for the Hunt Ball in four days. Cost is not an object, of course, but I should like sophisticated fare and entertainment. Plan for forty guests."

She blinked. "Oh. Ah . . . yes, of course. You do realize that four days is not much time."

He smiled at her confidently. "You can do it. Your

mother assured me that you've planned many such events."

Oh dear. Mother had sold Dane a pig in a poke, for Olivia hadn't even *attended* many such events in her life. She fought down panic. She might not have, but she knew Mother lived for such things. All she had to do was get Lady Cheltenham's help in this.

She nodded regally. "Of course." She held out one hand. "Is that the guest list? I must send the invitations as soon as possible."

Dane put the paper facedown on his desk. "No need. I sent the invitations yesterday."

Marcus, who had been watching them without expression, jerked his head to look at Dane. Olivia was surprised to see a brief flash of astonishment and anger cross Marcus's face.

It was gone so fast she must have imagined it. Besides, she had her own astonishment to deal with. "I am not privy to the guest list?"

Dane's mouth twisted up at one corner. "Don't worry. I've only invited the best sort." He clasped his hands on his desk and gazed at her, apparently waiting for something.

He wanted her to leave, without a kiss or even a real hello. She'd been given her assignment, just as if she were one of the servants.

She stood. Marcus and Dane stood with her. "I . . . I suppose I had best begin, then."

Dane nodded, clearly dismissing her. "I expect to hear all about your plans tonight at dinner, my dear."

By *dinner*? "Yes . . . yes, of course."

She left the room, dizzy with confusion. Who was

that man? Where had admiring-when-she'd-nursed-his-head Dane gone? What had happened to endlessly-willing-to-give-her-pleasure Dane?

How many men was she wed to, anyway?

The clock in the hall chimed. It was nearly noon. Her mother would be rising soon.

For the first time in a very long while, Olivia couldn't wait to see her mother.

Dane watched Olivia leave the study, then turned back to the sheaf of papers in his hand. "We need to—"

"You sent the invitations *yesterday?*" Marcus was clearly stunned. "Yesterday, the plan was merely a proposal. You hadn't yet secured the approval of the Four!"

Dane sat, regarding Marcus levelly. "I don't need the approval of the Four to host a ball. If they'd not agreed, I would have held an interesting evening and Olivia would have made the acquaintance of some important people." He shrugged. "There was no reason not to move on it instantly."

"Without telling me. And what about Olivia? How do you expect her to pull this off in four days?"

Dane turned his attention to his work, but his jaw tightened. "Since when," he said without looking at Marcus, "do you refer to my wife as Olivia?"

Marcus threw out his hands. "Since this morning when she asked me to. You're changing the subject."

"No." Dane's voice was flat. "I've closed the subject."

"You know I don't agree with this plan."

"I know. You're not the Lion yet, Marcus."

"That horse should have hit you harder. Perhaps it would have knocked some sense into your thick skull."

"Don't be dramatic. This is a solid plan. If His Majesty chooses a lady, we're set. If he doesn't, we've all had some wine and dancing and no harm done."

"I suppose."

"No supposing about it. Now, may we please finish this other matter, Marcus?"

Marcus scowled, but took up the sheet that Dane had handed him when he'd entered.

"So this is the Chimera?" He tilted the drawing this way and that. "Not a very prepossessing fellow, is he?"

"That is his 'Denny' persona. According to Lady Jane Damont, he can seem entirely different at a moment's notice. A face so ordinary and so forgettable—"

A face flashed across Dane's mind. *A mild-looking young man at the edge of a crowd.* He reached for the drawing and held it nearer the light. "I feel as though I've seen him somewhere . . ."

Marcus brightened. "Excellent. Where?"

Dane searched his mind, but the image slipped away again. The fact that his head still pounded from last night's encounter with the cobbles didn't help. He shook his head. "I cannot bring it to mind at the moment."

"Well, let me know when you do." Marcus swore. "I want this bloke strapped down tight with a bright light shining in his eyes."

Dane sighed and rubbed at his aching head. "As do we all." Proffit had taken his obligations most seriously last night. Dane didn't think he'd slept more than a few hours all told.

Marcus sighed and took his place at the desk. They worked through three stacks of reports before Dane looked up. "Are you staying for dinner? You can hear

Olivia's preparations and eat my food, which for some reason you prefer to your own."

"I'll stay. Do you really think she can pull it off?"

Dane shrugged. "According to her mother, she's an extremely experienced hostess."

10

Olivia controlled her panic until the Greenleigh carriage pulled up outside Cheltenham House. She would not have thought she would return so soon, especially not voluntarily.

Mother was going to pay for this. How could she lie to Dane thus? Nervously Olivia wondered in what other ways Mother had misled Dane.

Mother had better get her out of this one, before the entire house of cards fell down on them both. Dane was not the sort of man who enjoyed being lied to.

She hopped out of the carriage on the Greenleigh footman's hand, too intent on her mission to look at him. It was only as she was turning away that she caught the insolent gleam of disdain in his eyes.

What was that about? Good Lord, were they all a bunch of Pettys?

No time. *Four days.* The panic began to well up once more. Blast Petty and the footman and all the other sullen Greenleigh servants. Olivia was about to be tested and she was very much afraid she would not pass.

Mother was still in her morning gown, having a cup of tea in the sunny, comfortably shabby back parlor. "Oh, good morning, Olivia. Why on earth did you wear a green spencer with an orange gown?"

Why on earth did you insist I buy an orange gown? Olivia hated the thing. It made her sallow and it matched nothing. "Mother, I have no time to discuss my wardrobe choices. I'm here to discuss the ball."

Mother perked up at that, of course. "Ball? What ball? The Season is well over, dear." She patted the pile of opened invitations she'd been perusing. "All I have here are readings and musicales and dinners, none of which will be any fun at all, now that everyone who matters is off to Scotland." She sighed. "I suppose your father and I will go on back to Cheltenham, though I dread another winter there. Do have Greenleigh send that cheque soon, will you, dear? I'll be wanting to fill every hearth with coal this year." She smiled at Olivia. "Isn't it lovely? We'll never have to worry about money again."

"You wouldn't have to worry about money now if Father had implemented even half of Walt's ideas on Cheltenham," Olivia said absently. Mother hadn't received an invitation to Dane's Hunt Ball.

How could that be? Why wouldn't he invite her parents?

Her mouth continued without her mind. "The restoration of the flour mill alone—"

"Olivia!" Her mother's shocked tone brought her out of her musings with a jolt. "How dare you criticize your father! And to remind me of Walter when you know how terribly I grieve!"

Oh dear. She'd actually said that out loud.

Olivia finally sighed. "Mother, why not simply ask Dane for the funds?"

Her mother gaped at her, appalled. "*Tell* him? Expose our delicate matters to a man of such standing in Society? I'd sooner tell the Prince Regent himself!" Her voice began to rise shrilly once more. "Why not pin a beggar's badge to my bodice right now? Should I smear soot on my face and crawl on the cobbles? I'd as soon do that than speak one word of this outside the family!"

"But Dane is my husband," Olivia said soothingly. "He is family now."

"Hmph." Mother turned away in a snit. "Thanks to my efforts. Nevertheless, do you think he would have given you a second glance if he'd known we were beneath such a cloud of possible scandal?"

Olivia frowned. "What scandal? Many people have financial troubles. Most of Society is living in debt."

Mother looked at her hands. "There is debt and there is debt. Cheltenham had been in severe debt for several generations. Eventually, those one owes stop waiting for a good crop that never grows or a rash of new tenants that never come."

Olivia patted her mother's shoulder awkwardly. "No one can actually take Cheltenham. It is entailed and Papa is the last of his line now that Walter is gone."

Mother made a damp, exasperated sound. "No one *wants* Cheltenham, Olivia. It is a heap of rubble amid weed-choked fields. The danger we are in is much greater than that." Mother took a deep breath. "*Ruin.*"

"Ruin?" Olivia drew back. "I don't understand."

Mother managed a glance of vast irritation even through her tears and theatrics. "Debtors' prison, for pity's sake! I realize you haven't much experience of these things, Olivia, but for people of our stature to declare bankruptcy is—is—well, let us just say that it is disastrous enough that not even Lord Greenleigh's stature could save your children from the stain of it!"

Bankruptcy. Olivia's blood went cold. What would Dane think of such news?

I do have rather high standards of behavior for myself and others.

Mother wailed once more and Olivia turned her attention back again.

"Mother, that cannot happen now! Dane will help you. I know he will."

She only wished she could be as sure as she sounded.

It took several minutes to reassure Mother, but all the time Olivia's mind was racing furiously.

She was going to have to do the ball on her own. She couldn't very well ask Mother for help when she hadn't been invited! That would be cruel—not to mention the fact that she'd never hear the end of it for the rest of her life.

Then something else occurred to her. Marcus's story about Walter must be untrue. It was only gossip, after all. Unfortunately, Olivia knew that much gossip contained a grain of truth within.

"Mother, I know it pains you to talk about Walter, but there is something I must know."

Mother heaved a great impatient sigh and dropped her hands to her lap, sodden handkerchief still clutched tightly. "Oh, very well. What is it?"

"Do you know precisely how Walter drowned?"

Mother sniffed. "He fell off a boat his friends had rented. That's all there is to it."

"What sort of boat was it?"

Mother blinked. "I have no idea."

Olivia longed to discuss the gossip with someone. Mother was not that someone. "How do you know that was what killed him?"

Mother grimaced. "Goodness, I had no idea you were so morbid, Olivia. It's most unbecoming."

Olivia opened her mouth to answer that one, but Mother only fluttered her handkerchief at her. "All I know is what Walter's valet told us. He saw the entire thing, you know. Walter had a bit too much wine and fell off the boat into the Thames. It must have been awful for him. The Thames is so filthy!"

"I wouldn't know, I'm sure," Olivia said drily, but the irony was—as always—lost on Mother. "Where is this valet now? Do you remember his name?"

"No." Mother blinked at her oddly. "Why would I?" She stood, wringing her handkerchief again. Olivia expected it to release a puddle on the floor, but apparently Mother was rather dry-eyed under the histrionics. "I don't want to talk about Walter anymore. I want to talk about your husband. Did you take my advice?"

Time to exit, before this became a repeat of last night's toe-curling discussion. "Heavens, is that the time? I must go, Mother. Give Father my love."

She was on her own. For a moment, Olivia considered asking that lovely Lady Reardon for help. Yet surely she and her husband would be invited, being Dane's friends. And to be truthful, Olivia would rather have the opportunity to impress Lady Reardon.

She could do it. How hard could it be, anyway? Featherbrained Society women did it all the time.

The food she could put off on Cook. Like Dane said, that's what the servants were paid for.

All she had to do was come up with "sophisticated entertainment."

A walk in the park.

Hopefully.

The watcher scowled when milady came down the steps of her parents' home. Up and about already? She ought to be lying artistically draped over a fainting couch or perhaps fawning over her hero. It must take a great deal to put her down.

Still, milord had rescued her nicely. The watcher had been afraid for a moment that the fellow was too indifferent to notice. It had been all he could do to slow the damned horse enough so the man could get to his wife in time.

He had no intention of killing her, at least not at this time. He needed her, as distasteful as it was to need a woman for anything.

He watched as she paused for a moment, dithering on the walk. What was afoot? Something he was not aware of—and he hated that.

The watcher decided to keep a constant watch on her. He wasn't fond of surprises.

Olivia entered her bedchamber, intent on her plans and the writing desk in the corner. She'd spent the last half hour with Cook, who was none too pleased with her assignment and made no bones about it. Olivia had quailed before the woman's fury—and her gleaming knives flashing through the evening's meat—and had left the menu entirely up to her.

Olivia had never had this sort of trouble with the Cheltenham servants—then again, the elderly lot at Cheltenham had raised her and loved her dearly.

A maid was cleaning the grate in Olivia's bedchamber. When she entered, the girl stood and curtsied. "My lady."

There it was again, that nearly undetectable thread of contempt beneath the respect. Olivia shook her head, trying to convince herself she was imagining it.

The girl straightened and Olivia understood. It was either Petty or Letty standing before her. She could ask, but she ought to know by now. A real viscountess would.

She looked closely at the girl. Dark hair, freckles . . . her face was a bit round and young.

"You're Letty," she stated with surety.

The girl twitched slightly. "No, milady."

Enough was enough. "Yes, you are!" The girl started to shake her head. Olivia stamped her foot. "You're having me on again and I won't permit it!"

The girl paled. "No, milady! I'm—"

Olivia clapped her hands, hard. "Admit that you're Letty right this instant or I'll have you sacked, just see if I won't!"

"I'm Letty, milady." The words came from behind her. Olivia whirled, determined to give Petty a swift kick to the street for taking the joke too far—

Behind Olivia stood a girl who was clearly Letty,

not Petty. As Olivia gaped, Petty came up to stand with Letty in the doorway.

Olivia jerked her head back around to stare at the third girl. Letty. She turned back to the pair at the door. Letty again.

She gazed sourly at Petty. "Twins."

Petty didn't sneer . . . quite. "Yes, milady."

Olivia nodded. Of course. "And her name?"

"Hetty, milady. She's one of the housemaids."

Olivia threw up her hands. "What else?" She turned back to the owl-eyed Hetty, who gazed at her as if she were poisonous and covered in scales. "Hello, Hetty," she said gently. "It's very nice to make your acquaintance."

"You already met her, milady," Petty offered. "When Mrs. Huff—"

"Introduced the staff to me, yes, Petty, thank you." Olivia sighed. She'd made a complete fool of herself— again—a fact that she had no doubt Petty relished greatly. Not to mention she'd terrorized a perfectly innocent young girl.

"I apologize for my outburst, Hetty. I believed—" *your sister was being an obnoxious snot.* Ah. That probably wouldn't play well with young Hetty, either. The poor thing was practically cringing as it was. Olivia gave up. "Carry on," she said wearily. "Just . . . carry on."

She turned toward the writing desk, but her former bravado was gone. She couldn't even remember the names of the servants or earn their respect despite her rank. How was she supposed to throw a suitable event for forty presumably worldly and *au fait* members of Society?

Sophisticated. What precisely did Dane mean by that? Refined? Clever?

Fashionable?

Oh, dear God. Don't let him mean *fashionable*!

Dane sat at the table, his fork raised and his mouth open. Olivia had just finished outlining her plans for the entertainment at the Hunt Ball.

He looked at Marcus, who appeared confused. Then Dane put down his fork and gazed disbelievingly at his bride, his supposedly well-trained hostess.

"Dancing *dogs*?"

Her face fell. She looked away. "They're very appealing," she murmured faintly.

Marcus blinked and turned toward Dane. "Don't they wear little dresses and such?" He was obviously fighting back a grin.

Dane leaned back in his chair and laughed until his eyes teared. "And hats . . . I believe." He caught his breath, still chuckling. "Little, tiny dog hats."

Olivia bit her lip, obviously hurt by their amusement. "I like dogs," she said quietly.

Dane beat down his hilarity with an effort. "Oh, come now, Olivia. You weren't serious."

She said nothing, staring at the tablecloth. Oh hell. She'd been completely serious.

An uncomfortable pall settled over the table. Dane frowned at his bride. Could it be that she had no idea how to hostess a ball?

"Well, I'm sure you'll come up with something better tomorrow," he said uneasily. She better had. "What about the menu for the weeklong house party afterward?"

Her eyes became slate moons. "The house party . . . yes . . ." She cleared her throat and raised her chin. "Cook has already received her instructions."

Dane nodded and smiled at her, relieved. "Good! The rest of the week's entertainments will be easy enough. Most of the gentlemen will want to go shooting."

She crossed her arms and gazed at him sourly. "Shooting grouse no one will eat."

He was going to lose this one, he could feel it. Whenever she crossed her arms, he lost his will to argue against her. The hell of it was, he was quite sure she had no idea she had such a power over him. He planned on keeping it that way, so he forced himself to continue even though the twin swells of her breasts were beginning to make him forget his point.

"I intend to shoot grouse in Scotland," he stated firmly. "You may do as you wish, shoot at targets and sponsor horse races and anything else you wish."

She looked pensive. "Anything?"

A distant part of Dane's mind flashed a warning, but he'd let down his guard now that he'd made his point and was now dreamily regarding her bosom. "Hmm." He was going to watch her bathe tonight, he decided. The thought of those luxurious breasts covered in soapsuds threatened to cause his trouser buttons to fly across the room and break the window glass. With difficulty, he turned his gaze back down to his plate. He refrained from reaching for his fork, however, because he was quite sure his hand would be shaking with lust.

Olivia finished her dinner cheerfully enough, exchanging sweetly barbed comments with Marcus and being far too inclined to wrap her lips sensuously around her fork.

He really must speak to her about that . . . later.

11

Olivia paced her bedchamber, trying desperately to think of something for the Hunt Ball. She'd been so sure of the dancing-dog idea. Who didn't love a curly-haired little dog in a dress?

Dane, apparently. He'd found the idea amusing enough, however. Their laughter still smarted.

By the fire, Petty had just poured Olivia's bath and was preparing to drop rose water into the steaming water.

"Petty, I think I should like to select a different scent tonight." She liked rose water well enough, but she was peevishly tired of being told what to do. She would pick her own blasted bath scent, at the very least!

Petty gazed at her without expression, the bottle still tilted above the great copper tub. "The master bought rose scent for you, my lady."

This was going to be another issue with Petty, Olivia could see. She nearly gave in, simply out of exhaustion with the maid, but didn't think that would set a very good precedent. "Petty, did the master purchase any other bath scent?"

"Yes, my lady." The bottle didn't waver. Would it work to argue the point until the girl tired of holding the rose water in midair? As tempting as the prospect was, Olivia didn't have time to debate with Petty.

"Fetch the other scent, Petty."

Petty hesitated for a long moment. Just when Olivia thought she was going to pour the rose scent into the bath anyway, Petty lowered the bottle. "Yes, my lady."

Olivia didn't relax until the girl had left the room. Was Petty angry? Dane wouldn't care if a servant was angry, of course. Neither should she.

Unfortunately, she did care. If she was forced to make do with an angry, reluctant servant, life could become rather unpleasant. Yet she couldn't bear to fire the girl, even if Dane allowed it. She was Lady Greenleigh now, with all the attendant responsibilities. Dependents were just that—dependents. It was up to her to win Petty over.

The maid returned with another scent bottle. It was much larger and rather square in shape. Petty began to tilt it over the bath.

"Wait!" Olivia stepped toward her. "That bottle—is that a lady's scent?"

Petty seemed to consider pouring anyway. It was probably only the thought that she might have to draw a fresh bath that stopped her. She dropped her hand once more. "No, my lady. It is his lordship's sandalwood."

Olivia gaped at her. "You were going to let me bathe in *sandalwood*? And then what—were you going to dress me in trousers and a cravat?" She threw out her hands. "Why stop there? Why not simply christen me Lord Oliver and get it over with?"

Petty's eyes widened and she took a step back. Oh, drat. Olivia had lost her temper again and now the girl would never—

Petty laughed, a short, surprised gasp. Olivia watched in astonishment as the girl raised a hand to her mouth to cover her smile. Petty had a sense of humor? Impossible. Petty was the devil's handmaiden. Devil's handmaidens had no sense of humor. It was a matter of biblical record. Olivia was very nearly sure of that.

She folded her arms and gazed at Petty suspiciously. "You aren't actually evil, are you?"

Petty tried to restore her expression to its former stolidity but failed miserably as another giggle bubbled up.

Olivia shook a finger at her. "That won't work on me any longer, my girl. I know your secret now."

Petty drew a deep breath and shrugged. "I were getting tired of it anyway."

Olivia frowned at her. "But why—"

The connecting door opened and Dane entered. "Good evening, my dear."

Petty bobbed smartly to him, then fled the room.

Olivia watched the girl go. Petty probably believed she'd merely bowed to her master, but Olivia had caught a glimpse of something else in the girl's eyes when she'd looked at Dane.

Petty was in love with him.

It was impossible and very unfortunate. Poor Petty. Yet what else could be expected when a young, handsome lord employed impressionable girls in his household? It likely happened rather often. Hearts didn't care a jot about place and standing. Hearts were wild, not domesticated.

And Petty's wild, young, hopeful heart was bound to be broken.

Olivia turned to gaze at Dane. Men were rats. She'd been quite right all along.

Here she was, trying to be the perfect viscountess, when Dane wouldn't even allow her to be an actual wife!

When Dane entered his bride's bedchamber that night, he didn't find her lounging naked on the bed as he'd expected.

Instead, she was clad in a wrapper, standing by a ready tub on the hearth.

The Fates were with him. He was finally going to see her breasts all slippery with soap. All in all, he was having a very good day.

She looked up at him, her gaze unusually somber. "Dane, I think we ought to talk."

We ought to talk. Had four words ever put more fear into the heart of men around the world? He'd not heard them before himself, but ancient gender memory recognized them well.

He was in for it now.

Then he shook off the pall of a thousand years of conditioning. What a ridiculous thought. Olivia probably wanted to redecorate the parlor or some such. Dane resolved to give her full rein and a fat purse to do it with.

"What can I do for you, my dear?" Dear God, please let it be a matter of decor.

She hesitated, biting on her lip. It didn't look good for him, not at all.

"Why . . ." She took a breath and fixed her gaze on his with determination. "Why have we not consummated our union?"

He opened his mouth. Nothing came out.

Hell. He ought to have had some explanation prepared, some smooth and easy delivery of why it made sense to wait a little longer—but he had nothing. He could only gaze at her mutely, the words caught in his throat.

Then it was too late. She saw in his expression that something was wrong. Her brow creased with sudden concern.

"Dane?"

It was too soon. If only he'd had a little more time he could have made sure of her passion for him. He could have gently broached the subject. He could have—

He'd never really had much of a plan, had he? He'd lied to himself as surely as he'd lied to her, letting her believe that someday the two of them would have a normal marriage. He'd only been stalling, staving off the night when he would have to tell her she'd married into a hopeless situation.

"I shouldn't have done this to you, Olivia." He couldn't look at her, at the way her sweet expression became alarmed. "You were my only hope, but now I—" Words failed him.

He turned away, feeling clumsy and out of place in her chamber. He was a freak of nature—and now he would have to explain to her that she was tied to a freak for the rest of her life.

He felt her come to him, felt her press herself to his back and wrap her arms about him.

"Dane? What is it? What distresses you so?"

There was only one answer. For a long, last moment he enjoyed her concerned affection. Then he took her hands from where they hugged his torso and gently pushed them down his body.

Even that simple touch spurred his starving senses. He began to grow even before her hands slid past his waistline. He felt her inhale sharply when he pressed her fingers over the ridge of his growing erection. Her fingers tightened involuntarily over him, only for an instant, but his body responded with all the hunger of long celibate years. He felt himself throb against her hands.

She began to pull away from him, but he held her hands where they were. She had to know, and the truth was not finished yet, not by a long shot. He continued to swell until her two hands didn't cover him any longer, and then yet more.

"Oh my god." Her voice was no more than a whisper. A whisper of horror? Of revulsion?

Her fingers began to move, sliding up and down the length of him and back and forth the width of him, blindly measuring him through his tightened trousers.

Dane threw his head back with a great gusting breath. Her tentative touch wasn't even the caress of a lover, yet he grew still more rigid beneath her exploration. He took his hands away from hers, releasing her at last to express her repugnance for his monstrosity, to flee him and his unnatural needs.

She didn't run.

Olivia stayed where she was, pressed to Dane's broad, hard back. Her eyes were closed as she took the measure of her man.

The thick—oh, dear god, was it even possible for him to be that thick?—rigid rod of Dane's . . . um . . . instrument filled her two hands, slanting from his groin to his hipbone. She spread her fingers wide upon him, then traced the outline of him with her fingertips. He pulsed against her touch. She let her fingers continue to stroke curiously while she pondered what this meant to them both.

She wasn't entirely ignorant of the proceedings, after all. She knew what went where, in a general mammalian sense. The trouble was, she didn't think *that* was going to go *there*. No. Not. Absolutely—

Dane's hands came down over hers once more. "I cannot allow you to continue that, I fear." His voice was tight with tension.

Olivia pulled her hands away, embarrassed. She'd been absently fondling him.

"Not that I don't enjoy your touch, my dear, but—"

"May I see it?"

The question surprised her as much as it apparently did him. He turned quickly to stare at her in surprise. Drat. She'd been brazen again. Ladies didn't ask to see a gentleman's member! She truly needed to paste her lips together these days!

She folded her arms defensively and looked away. "I'm sorry. I shouldn't have asked."

Dane turned from her and strode to the mantel. He braced himself there on both arms and gazed into the fire. "Olivia, I cannot tell you how sorry I am."

Sorry? He was sorry? There was something still quite wrong here, but she couldn't decipher it. She sank down on the chair near him and waited.

He continued to avoid her gaze for a long moment, then he took a deep breath and pushed away from the mantel to face her. "I lied to you."

"Oh." She waited a bit more, but he didn't continue. "Precisely which lie do you mean?"

"I mean I lied when I pretended to be a normal man—" He halted, blinking at her. "What do you mean, 'which lie'?"

"Ah . . . nothing. I misspoke." She waved a hand. "Please continue."

He took a breath. "I promised you a normal life as my lady. I should never have wed you without letting you know . . . I should never have tied you to me when you could have married someone . . . someone not flawed as I am."

"Oh." She waited some more. Nothing. Must she pull it from him with a pair of fire tongs? She took a few breaths of her own and reached for her patience. "Which particular flaw do you mean?"

This time he was quicker. "What do you mean, 'which flaw'?" he bellowed.

She smiled. "Oh, there you are. I'm glad you're back." She smoothed her wrapper over her knees and primly clasped her hands in her lap. "Now, would you care to speak plainly in the manner to which you have led me to be accustomed?"

He passed both hands over his face, then chuckled weakly. "My lady, you are entirely unexpected."

She nodded. "I do tend to hear that on occasion.

Now, pray, explain—and try to lessen the dramatic pauses."

"Very well." He leaned one elbow on the mantel and gazed at her soberly. "You experienced my flaw yourself. You must see that a natural relationship—that we cannot—that it is impossible!"

Oh. She'd been so hoping he knew more than she did. "So you are saying that you never intend to consummate our marriage?"

He ran a hand through his hair. "That is precisely what I'm saying."

"I see." Her heart was beginning to feel the effects of all this plain speaking. Olivia gazed at her own clasped hands for a moment. "Are you quite positive about this?"

He nodded. "Yes. I allowed myself to hope, but deep down I knew there was none. I cannot do such a thing to you."

Olivia closed her eyes for a long moment. "Do you think that you might have brought this up sooner? Say, *before* our wedding day?" She heard him sigh.

"I avoided you so that I would not."

She opened her eyes and frowned up at him. "Were you afraid I would not marry you?"

He blinked. "Of course."

Despite her heartbreak, she had to laugh at him. "Turn you down? The mighty, wealthy, generous, handsome Lord Greenleigh?" She shook her head at him. "How many offers do you think I received that I should be so particular?"

"Oh." He rubbed the back of his neck sheepishly. "I didn't see it like that."

Olivia closed her eyes for a long moment, then took a deep breath. "So what do we do now? Shall we go to bed?"

He hesitated. "Olivia . . ."

"No, we are not going to go to bed?"

His jaw tightened. "Is there any point?"

No point? What about being close? What about reassurance and touch and warmth?

He bowed briefly. "Good night, my dear." Then he turned and left her chamber as she gazed after him in surprise and loss.

What about not being alone?

12

The next morning dawned as gray as Olivia's mood. Although she took pains to rise earlier to breakfast with her husband, Dane merely nodded to her over his news sheet. Then he polished off his eggs and left her alone with another distant nod.

At least he left the news sheet for her. Sadly, she couldn't seem to focus on anything heavier than the gossip column.

Someone known as "The Voice of Society" was in fine form today.

"Turn and turn again, Darling Readers, it is time for us all to quiet our ballrooms and our mews and return to the country. Here is a winsome thought to hold you all through the long winter—who will our dear Prinny choose to be his new lady-love? There are widows and wives abounding, but His Highness had better be quick about it, before all the plump grouse fly away to Scotland!

What of London's most notorious hostess, Mrs. Blythe? Prinny noticed her fine feathers once upon a time. Is she in the running for Prinny's new caged bird? Wouldn't that put a bit of steam in the teakettle, your Voice asks with glee!"

Apparently, the entire world was being romanced, except for her.

Frustrated, Olivia poked at her own breakfast, stabbing at her eggs with great energy.

"I hope that isn't me on your plate."

She looked up to see Marcus lounging in the doorway to the breakfast room. She scowled at his conciliatory smile. "Perhaps it is and perhaps it isn't."

He crossed his arms over his chest. "Meaning you can't decide who needs forking more, me or Dane."

"You're very perceptive . . . now."

He stepped closer and braced his hands on the back of the chair opposite her. "My lady, I apologize for our insensitivity last evening. But you must admit—dogs?" He shrugged. "This is an event of the ton, not a child's birthday celebration."

Olivia didn't answer him, for how could she explain that she had no idea how to hostess an "event of the ton"? *Mother, you've truly done it now.*

Unfortunately, Marcus was continuing his spate of uncharacteristic perceptiveness. "You've never done this before, have you?"

Olivia tossed her head with a smile. "Don't be silly. My mother is a renowned hostess." Of course, Olivia had been forgotten back in Cheltenham, unable to see her mother in action.

Marcus threw out his hands. "There you go, then! Call your mother in for a bit of assistance."

She shook her head. "My mother isn't . . . available

to assist just now." However, an idea began to bloom from the seed of Marcus's suggestion.

Who was it who found her name in all the gossip sheets as a well-known hostess? Who was hinted at having entertained the Prince Regent himself?

Olivia smiled cheerfully at Marcus. She could kiss him for giving her such an idea! "I know precisely who to ask for help."

After all, who would know more about throwing a grand Hunt Ball than the most celebrated hostess in London, a certain Mrs. Blythe?

Olivia took Petty with her, counting on Petty's general reluctance to keep her sullenly in the carriage while Olivia tended to business. Olivia needed no more disrespect from the Greenleigh staff, and she knew they'd love to carry tales about how she had to get help to throw a simple ball.

True to nature, Petty slumped dispiritedly on her tufted velvet seat, not protesting when Olivia left her there, despite her duty to accompany her mistress.

The brass knocker of Mrs. Blythe's house was curiously shaped, but Olivia's business was far too urgent for her to ponder why the vaguely floral design seemed a bit disturbing. She rapped briskly, then waited with her gloved hands clasped before her.

The door was opened by stout lady in a housekeeper's white lace cap instead of the customary butler or footman. Olivia smiled at the woman and handed her one of her new engraved calling cards. "Good morning. Is Mrs. Blythe receiving callers today?"

The woman gazed at her curiously for a moment,

then took the card. She peered closely at the florid script, then jerked her gaze back up to Olivia, her faded blue eyes wide. "My . . . my lady? You wish to call on Mrs. Blythe?"

Taken aback, Olivia cast another glance at the odd door knocker. Then she shook off such an unworthy thought and smiled to ease her discomfort. "Please, simply tell Mrs. Blythe that I would like to speak to her if she has the time."

The woman nodded faintly and stepped back, still staring at Olivia. When Olivia crossed the threshold, she was a little surprised to see how dark the interior of the house was.

"Come this way, my lady."

A man stood across the park, oblivious to the rain in his alarm. What was her ladyship doing in that house?

True, she was trying to win his lordship's affections— and it was certain she could learn a few things in the most notorious bordello in London—but a woman of Quality should not even know such a house existed or at least should pretend not to know!

Dismayed, the man slammed a lid on his worry. This was merely an unexpected development. He knew what to do.

Yes, she was where she most certainly didn't belong. Yes, if his lordship found out, he would likely reject her entirely.

What a marvelous idea.

Olivia found herself situated in a parlor where the overbearing theme seemed to be purple velvet. Everywhere.

After handing her hat and gloves to the house-keeper, Olivia sat on a violently violet sofa and gazed at the velvet-draped ceiling in bemusement. No wonder Mrs. Blythe kept the draperies drawn. When one preferred her colors so . . . opulent, one probably ought to consider the dangers of fading.

Olivia let her gaze roam the room. Was there anything here that wasn't deeply, severely purple, other than herself?

No. Even the mantel was carved of a purplish veined marble.

"Too much is never enough," she murmured as she gazed about the room. She was beginning to have the feeling that she didn't belong here.

"My sentiments exactly" came a low, melodious voice from the doorway.

Olivia turned to see a stately woman of middle years gowned in, of course, purple. Even her unnaturally black hair gleamed with a purple tint. Olivia stood. "Mrs. Blythe, I am Lady Greenleigh."

Mrs. Blythe sailed gracefully into the room and curtsied with just the proper hint of serene pride. Olivia decided to practice that particular flowing motion.

"My lady, I am honored by your visit," Mrs. Blythe said as she seated them both on the sofa. "To what do I owe this pleasure?"

Olivia smiled and tilted her head. "I am here to beg your assistance."

Mrs. Blythe blinked, obviously surprised. "I do not know that I can help you, my lady. I have never—ah, your husband, his lordship, is not a personal acquaintance, you see."

Olivia blinked. "But the Prince Regent is, is he not?"

Mrs. Blythe choked a bit. "Ah. Well." She cleared her throat. "My lady, perhaps you ought to explain how you require my help?"

Olivia nodded briskly. "Yes, we must not waste time." She folded her hands in her lap. "Mrs. Blythe, I need your help to throw a Hunt Ball that Society will never forget!"

She outlined the specifications for Mrs. Blythe—the location, the number of guests, Dane's ridiculous timetable . . .

Mrs. Blythe was staring at her in shock. Olivia tsked. "Yes, I know. Isn't it just like a man to set such an impossible task?"

The woman folded her hands in her lap. "My lady, are you sure about this? Does Lord Greenleigh know what you are planning?"

"Of course." Olivia raised her chin. "My lord husband trusts me to deliver his guests an exceptionally *sophisticated* entertainment. Tastefully, of course. Can you help me? Your events are famous for their originality. I wish to make sure that all of London is talking about my Hunt Ball."

Mrs. Blythe narrowed her eyes. "Lord Greenleigh is an adventurous sort, then? He seems rather . . . well, tame. I mean no offense—"

Olivia would hardly term a man like Dane as "tame." She frowned. Who was this woman, really? This curious house . . . the housekeeper's reaction . . .

Olivia had gambled on a name in a gossip column,

but now she feared she was out of her depth.

Yet, she was already out of her depth with the planning of the Hunt Ball. Mrs. Blythe might not be quite what Olivia had thought, but she seemed kind and she was certainly experienced—

And Olivia was running out of options and time.

Desperate times. Olivia leaned forward. "So will you help me?"

Mrs. Blythe shook her head. "It is not the strangest request I've ever had, but it comes close." She gazed at Olivia for a long moment. "I think I should very much like to help you, my lady. *Tastefully*, of course."

Olivia smiled brightly. "Wonderful! What will you need from me to arrange this?"

Mrs. Blythe waved her hand. "I will be pleased to arrange everything personally. Do not fear, Lady Greenleigh. No one who attends this ball will ever forget it."

Olivia bent forward and gave her a spontaneous hug. "Thank you! You have no idea what this means to me."

Mrs. Blythe seemed staggered by the affection. "I . . . well, my lady, you certainly are an unusual sort. A true Original. Lord Greenleigh is a very lucky man, my lady. He must be very satisfied with you."

Satisfied with you. Olivia's glee faded abruptly. She looked away. "I . . . I'm sure I wouldn't know. . . ."

"Ah." Mrs. Blythe regarded her steadily for a moment. "It's true then, isn't it? What I've heard about Lord Greenleigh is true."

Olivia blinked back her sudden sadness and gazed at Mrs. Blythe in alarm. "What have you heard?"

Mrs. Blythe took Olivia's hand in hers. "My lady, it is

not common knowledge. It is only that I once knew someone who—well, what I heard is that your husband is . . . ah . . . shall we say, more than mortal woman can bear?"

Olivia slumped. She ought not to discuss something so personal—Dane would hate it if he knew—but where else could she turn? And Mrs. Blythe was a widow. She knew a few things about men, it was clear. "You've heard correctly," Olivia whispered miserably. "I am a wife of four days and a virgin still."

"Hmm."

The woman's pensive tone drew Olivia's attention. "What are you thinking?"

Mrs. Blythe tilted her head and regarded Olivia closely for a long moment. "Normally I wouldn't think of suggesting such a thing, but you are obviously made of sterner stuff than most ladies. Tell me, do you truly care for him?"

"I am his lady," Olivia said. "I would do anything for him."

Mrs. Blythe shook her head. "But do you wish this as much as he does? Do you *want* him?"

Want Dane? Want him to cover her, to claim her, to enter her and feed that endless ache? Want to love and satisfy him and be his wife in truth? "Oh yes," she breathed. "I want him."

Mrs. Blythe patted her hand. "Then you shall have him. Let me tell you what I can do for you. . . ."

When the man across the street saw Lady Greenleigh leave the bordello and drive away in her carriage, he forced himself to wait another half an hour for verisimilitude. Then he strode importantly to the front door of Mrs. Blythe's famous establishment and rapped the knocker smartly.

Once inside and face-to-face with Mrs. Blythe, he bowed respectfully. "I'm sorry to intrude, but my Lady Greenleigh has asked me to return to you on her behalf." Then he waited. If luck was with him, the woman would let spill something useful now. He'd learned that people made their own conclusions and were compelled to fill any extended silence with them.

After a long moment, Mrs. Blythe sighed. "She had second thoughts, I suppose. I'm surprised she actually had the fortitude to approach me in the first place. I was sure once she considered it, she would regret asking me to help her stage her Hunt Ball."

Interesting. The man nodded somberly. "It is a very important event."

"I suppose it is too late to reassure her that I had only the most tasteful entertainments in mind. I know the most wonderful soprano . . ."

The man felt a spurt of excitement. This fell neatly into his plan. "No, madam," he interrupted smoothly. "My lady does not wish to relinquish your aid. In fact—" This was going to do the trick as nothing would. "In fact, my lady wishes for you to find something much more radical for her."

Mrs. Blythe's eyes narrowed. "Ah. I see. I had wondered why she came to me, specifically." She snorted impatiently. "She couldn't bring herself to say it herself, could she?"

The man nodded sympathetically. "She is new to her position, madam. I'm sure she was simply too timid."

"Ladies." Mrs. Blythe shook her head. "So she wishes that sort of party, does she?"

"Indeed. She wishes to be a most notorious hostess."

Mrs. Blythe folded her arms. "Inform her that I have the perfect entertainment. It is, after all, what I do."

The man nodded. "Indeed, madam."

Perfect, indeed.

Olivia couldn't think of anything but Mrs. Blythe's advice on the way home in the carriage and through tea and through the household's bustle and preparation for the journey day after tomorrow.

Mrs. Huff was rushing about in a flurry, directing this and that, even sending instructions to the other staff by fast courier!

Apparently, the house in Scotland had not been used for two years. Of course, there was a caretaking staff in residence at Kirkall Hall, but evidently Mrs. Huff didn't trust anyone but herself to manage the preparations for so many guests.

Leaving the woman to it, for she'd not welcomed a single suggestion from Lady Greenleigh, Olivia dawdled in what she had come to think of as her "morning room," a smaller parlor done in more cheerful colors than the supremely elegant pale tones of the rest of the house.

The butler tapped twice and opened the door. "There is a parcel come for you, my lady, from a 'Mrs. B.'"

Olivia started, then turned away from the butler to hide her blush. "Oh yes, thank you, Kinsworth." Goodness, was that her voice, so high and nervous? She cleared her throat and strived to sound normal. "Put that in my room if you please."

She forced herself to wait, even attempting to go over the menus with the cook, Mrs. Arnold. Rather, Olivia listened while Mrs. Arnold told her in no uncertain terms what she would be eating for the next several days. Finally, she nodded agreement—apparently that was her role in this household, to nod agreement to what the servants wanted to do—and escaped upstairs, ostensibly to dress for dinner. Duty done.

On the side table in her room sat a paper-wrapped parcel the size of a small luggage case. Olivia looked for Petty, but the girl was nowhere in sight and likely wouldn't be unless Olivia sent for her—in which case Olivia could count on it being several sullen minutes before the girl arrived. Assured of her privacy, Olivia ripped the paper from her gift.

It was a box of sorts, almost like a barrel on its side. It was stained dark and was heavily carved with sumptuous images of exotic fruits—at least, they looked like pomegranates and bananas.

On the front there were two golden clasps. After a moment of fiddling, Olivia learned the trick of them and flicked them both open.

The box fell apart, unwinding away from her like a rolled carpet. "Oh, how clever!" What had been a box was now a flat tray made of compartments hinged together. In each of the five silk-lined compartments, a single object lay, itself wrapped in matching golden silk. Biting her lip, she reached for the first one.

Mrs. Blythe had told her what was inside, but de-

scription did not satisfy one's curiosity. Olivia picked
up the first object and let the silk wrapping fall away.
Oh my. Perhaps those hadn't been bananas after all.

"What the hell?"

Dane's appalled bellow from the doorway startled
Olivia, making her drop the carved ivory vagina ex-
pander on the floor. It rolled away under the bed.

13

"Now look what you made me do!" Olivia glared at Dane. "It will be soiled under there!" She dived beneath the counterpane to retrieve it, only to find Dane lifting her bodily from the floor with a great arm about her waist. "Got it!" She waved it triumphantly at him.

He set her on her feet, glaring at her. "Do you mind telling me what the hell that thing is?"

He looked down at what she held in her hand and paled. "Never mind. I don't want to know." He released her and turned away. "I suppose I cannot deny you your own pleasure. Only . . . please don't let the servants find it."

Olivia planted both fists on her hips. "Oh, you don't know everything, Lord Greenleigh. These are for the both of us."

He turned to stare at her, distaste evident on his face. "No thank you. I'm afraid my inclinations don't run to—"

She pulled out the note from Mrs. Blythe. "Here. Read this."

He took the note and read it aloud. " 'As I related to
you earlier this afternoon, these relics are the Pleasure
Rods of the Rajah, created at the request of the second
Rajah of Najimbi for his bride in order for her to train
her body to accept a man of great size. Alas, they were
never used. It seems the young rajah had a rather in-
flated idea of his own proportions and felt that no pure,
virginal woman could receive him. The story goes that
neither the wife nor the rajah was quite as advertised.' "

Dane stopped reading and looked askance at the
opened box. He folded the note and flipped aside the
golden silk covering the next offering in the case.
"So these ivory . . . things are supposed to help us
somehow?"

Olivia knelt by the case and began unwrapping each
one. "Yes. You see, they come in graduating sizes. Once
a woman becomes comfortable with one size, she may
move on to the next—oh, dear heavens." She'd unwrapped the fifth and final rod. It was as thick as four
fingers and its length lay across her two palms and then
some. She blushed and rewrapped it quickly. "Well, at
least I'm sure we won't need to use *that* one!"

Dane rubbed the back of his neck sheepishly. "Actually . . . I think we will."

Olivia stopped with her hands still cradling the final
rod. "Truly? Does that mean you don't mind?"

To his surprise, considering he was not one to "aug-
ment" his satisfaction with objects, Dane felt his first
glimmer of true hope in years.

"I'm surprised you are willing," he said slowly. He
didn't want to sway her from it, but neither did he want
to make her go through such a thing if she wasn't—

She leaped to her feet and flung both arms about his neck. "Oh, thank you, darling! I know we can make it work, I just know it!"

An alarming thought struck him. "Who gave you these, and how did she know? You haven't been—"

She shook her head, causing a rather adorable downfall of fair hair. "You needn't worry. I trust her discretion completely. She helped me enormously with the arrangements for the Hunt Ball. She's a good friend of the Prince Regent's, you know. Her name is Mrs. B—"

Dane held up one hand sharply. "No, perhaps I'd better not know. I'd never be able to look her in the eye in a social situation."

Olivia only smiled fondly at him. "Dane, you know this means we'll be able to have children. You could be a father this time next year!"

What a startling thought. He pictured a sturdy, fair-haired boy with gray eyes, and a smile crept across his lips. Olivia sighed happily and snuggled closer to his chest. What an astonishing woman she was, to go through this for him, for their future and their family-to-be.

"I want lots of children," she said dreamily. "Lots and lots."

He chuckled and held her close, tucking her head into its perfect spot beneath his chin. If she did this for him, she could have all the children she could stand to raise. "And dogs."

She nodded against his chest. "And dogs."

Dane gazed over her shoulder where four of the five ivory rods lay beside the case. The thought of using them to drive her urgent responsiveness to new heights . . .

His body began to respond to his thoughts and the way her full breasts pressed to his chest. She must have been thinking along the same lines, for her body seemed to melt languidly into his. "Dane," she whispered. "We could start right now."

"Hmm." Dane let his hand slide off her hair and down her side to cup beneath one lovely breast. "Do you wear any sort of ladies' drawers, my dear?"

"Of course not," she replied with a small smile. " 'Tisn't healthy."

Lovely, country-bred woman. Dane bent his body, reaching for her hem and taking advantage of his position to lay his mouth over her sprigged muslin bodice. He breathed over her nipple as he stroked his hand beneath her hem and up her stocking. Her body responded, quivering in his grasp already, though he'd touched no higher than her knee.

He passed over her garter—he ought to have her leave her stockings on sometime—and ran his palm up her inner thigh.

She gasped slightly and parted her legs a bit, allowing him in. He straightened, his hand planted firmly over her mound, and used his other hand to pull her bodice down to just below her nipples. They thrust out like ripe cherries and he plucked at them as he lowered his mouth to her neck. "What do you want, my lady?" he whispered. "You must choose. My hand or my mouth?"

She hesitated, her breath quickening. Her nipples turned to stone beneath his teasing fingertips. "Ah . . . might I not have both?"

He chuckled at her greed and slid his longest finger inside her. It slipped in readily, for she'd gone moist in a matter of moments. He took her small gasp into his mouth as he drove slowly into her, in and out. After a moment, she began to ride his hand's motion, thrusting her pelvis toward him, then back, then forward again.

His vision glazed as he thought about how she might ride him someday, grinding hard against him as he drove himself deep. She moved her lower body faster, her urgency escaping her in small cries as she lathed his hand in dampness, until he felt her climax tighten her flesh about his probing finger. He didn't stop there.

Using her wetness, he slid another finger alongside the first and pressed within her slowly but not tentatively. She wriggled in surprise. "Take it," he ordered softly. "Take everything I give you."

She nodded, still breathless from her orgasm, and permissively held still while he drove into her again and again, first slowly, then faster. At last she could bear it no more and began to move on his hand. Dane wrapped his other arm around her waist to balance her against her own frenzy and lowered his mouth to one exposed nipple, then the other, sucking them rigid while she bucked in his grasp.

She climaxed again, great heaving shudders that sent her knees right out from under her. She sagged in his embrace. He pulled his hand from her, drying it on her petticoat as he let her skirts fall. Then he tugged her bodice up and stood her on her feet.

She was breathing hard and her hair had fallen from its pins and her face was flushed—and he thought she may have bitten her bottom lip at some point, for it was plumped and pink. It only made him want to make her climax again.

She must have caught the look in his eye, for she backed a step and held up a hand. "No, please. . . ."

He took one long step and caught her to him. "I can make you take back that 'no,'" he growled playfully.

She dropped her forehead to his chest. "I know you can," she said, still breathing hard. "But the clock is about to chime for dinner and I haven't changed yet—"

There was a rattle at the doorknob of the outer room. It separated them like a spark. Dane turned away to adjust his aching erection within his trousers and Olivia quickly rolled up the clever case with the rods inside it.

She had just latched it shut when Petty entered. "What gown do you wish, my lady—" She stopped short when she saw Dane. "Oh, so sorry, my lord!" She began to back from the room.

Dane smiled at the girl, although Olivia noticed he kept his hands folded before him. He was obviously striving for a casual air, for she'd never seen him be so friendly with one of his staff. He was usually most businesslike. "What is your name, girl?" he asked Petty.

Petty bobbed and shot a triumphant look at Olivia. "I'm Elspeth, my lord."

Dane nodded. "A lovely name." He turned to Olivia. "Don't you think so, my dear?"

Olivia wished she could tell him what he did to impressionable young girls with his smile and his looks and his form and his easy compliments. What he did to her as well, for that matter.

"Indeed," she replied. "So it must be Elspeth and Leticia? And Henrietta, of course." She turned to Dane. "Did you realize that you employ Elspeth's younger twin sisters as well?" She smiled fondly at the maid, whose eyes shot sparks back at her. "And what a hardworking trio they are."

Dane smiled at her proudly. "You already know my staff well, I see, right down to the housemaids. Well done."

Olivia cast Petty a triumphant glance of her own before she bobbed her own little curtsy. "Why, thank you, kind sir!" Then she gave him a little push. "Now, I must prepare for dinner. If I'm not mistaken, Proffit is gnashing his teeth in impatience even now."

Dane rolled his eyes. "Proffit's a genius, but he will fuss so." But he went, with a bow to her and a distant nod to Petty.

Olivia turned to look at the maid. "Elspeth? Really? I should think you'd prefer to be called that instead of Petty."

Petty scowled. "Don't think my preference matters much. My mum named us all such pretty names, and my da never uses them." She shrugged. "So no one does."

She reached into Olivia's wardrobe and selected a pale green silk. It was prettier than the deceased gray silk and had a much more flattering neckline. Olivia suspected the modiste, driven past her last nerve, had simply disregarded Lady Greenleigh's specifications.

Mother did tend to have that effect on people.

"That handsome Lord Dryden is dining with you again, my lady."

Olivia searched that sentence for some kind of snide subtext, but it was nothing but truth. "Yes, he's handsome indeed." She smiled to herself as she turned to let Petty unfasten her sprigged muslin. "Not as handsome as his lordship, however."

She heard Petty sigh. "No, indeed, my lady. Although Letty likes him better, but she's always gone daft over the dark ones."

Olivia turned her head to look at Petty over her shoulder. "Are we having a normal conversation, Miss Elspeth?"

Petty blushed and looked away. "Seems like." She shrugged. "Gossip was, you were going to fire us all and bring your own people in."

Olivia blinked. "My people are more than ready for their well-earned retirement. I don't think anyone here needs to worry, although Mrs. Huff is beginning to drive me mad."

Petty gasped. "Oh no, my lady! Mrs. Huff is right kindly, once you get to know her. She gave me and my sisters our positions as a favor to my mum. It's only her bones aching so that makes her cross. She's got the arthritimus real bad, she does."

Olivia bent to let Petty pull the fresh gown over her head. "I . . . ow . . . do . . . out . . . at."

Her head popped out the neckline. Petty was frowning at her. "What was that, my lady?"

Olivia smiled. "I know what to do about Mrs. Huff's . . . ailment." She couldn't bring herself to repeat Petty's mangling of the word, but she didn't want the girl to feel criticized, not when she was finally being almost friendly.

Olivia went to the writing desk and pulled out a sheet of paper. She inked her quill and quickly jotted down a list of herbs and ingredients. "Take this to Cook and have her make up a gallon of this tonight. Tell Mrs. Huff that she must wring cloths in it and lay them over her joints, and do it again as long as the mixture stays hot." She handed the list to Petty.

The girl took it hesitantly, seeming rather uncomfortable. "Yes, my lady, but . . ."

Olivia crossed her arms. "But Mrs. Huff won't have anything to do with it if it comes from me."

Petty nodded, her gaze on the floor. "Don't be angry with her, my lady. She's been keeping house for his lordship for ten years and she's afraid no other employer will want her with her joints so bad."

Olivia nodded. "What if you told her you got the recipe from someone else?"

Petty smiled slyly. "Like my mum."

Olivia grinned and dusted her hands briskly. "Now, what do you have in mind for my hair tonight? Something that won't fall out, I hope."

Petty slipped the list into her sleeve, then made a sour face. "Like it's my fault your hair won't stay pinned. Mayhap if you didn't spring about so. . . ."

Olivia seated herself in the vanity chair, serenely confident that Petty would make her look wonderful. Now she knew that sour demeanor was just . . . well, it was just Petty, that was all.

In no time Olivia was dressed for dinner. She only hoped dinner could be dispensed with as quickly. She and Dane had a rendezvous planned tonight that just might change everything.

14

Dane found it very difficult to sedately eat his dinner. He kept seeing Olivia with her head thrown back, fully dressed with only her nipples revealed, clutching his shoulders and giving her all to him without reservation.

The fact that an entire such night stretched before them only made the fork shake more so in his grip. He sat there, his cock still half-erect, his palms sweating, thinking of what more heights he could bring her to tonight.

That was not all. His own dark fantasies had begun seeping into his "education" of her. He wanted to command her to fall to her knees and take him into her mouth. The fact that his sensually obedient wife might just do it only further inflamed his imagination.

He let his gaze rest on Olivia's bosom across the table. The pale green gown showed off her soft pink skin to perfection, but the bodice was a mite too snug. Her abundant flesh pressed upward, as if she were going to overflow her neckline with a bounty of womanhood.

Dane's erection stiffened further. He'd once heard

of a prostitute who would press her large breasts together and—

". . . don't you think so, Dane?"

Dane jerked his head around to stare blankly at Marcus. "What?"

Marcus flicked a knowing glance at Olivia and her amazing bosom, then grinned. "Nothing. Never mind." He put down his fork. "Shall we skip the usual formalities and kick me out now? Or shall we play a few inattentive rounds of cards first?"

Olivia slammed napkin to tabletop with lightning speed. "Oh-so-sorry-you-must-go. Do come again soon!" She stood.

Dane leaped to his feet so abruptly his chair teetered behind him. "It was a pleasure to see you, Marcus." He never took his gaze off his wife's sparkling, eager eyes. "Go home now, if you please."

Presumably, Marcus left on cue. Dane neither remembered nor cared. All that counted was that in a matter of seconds he had Olivia alone in her bedchamber, the door shut and the green gown on the floor.

"Not the floor," she protested indistinctly—probably because his tongue was in her mouth. "It's my best."

Dane only growled and kicked it away. "S'too tight anyway," he muttered as he sucked on her neck. "I'll buy you ten more."

She shrugged and grabbed his shirttails. "You can buy a new one of these while you're at it—" She ripped the shirt up and off him, careless of the torn seams.

"I like your chest," she panted, stroking her spread hands over his pectorals. "You're like a stone wall, except where it ripples under your skin."

"I like your chest more," he said, panting as he divested her of everything but her stockings and garters. "No, leave those on," he said when she reached for her garters.

"Where's the box?"

"Did you lock the door?"

"I'll build up the fire."

"Why are you building up the fire? Come here!" Olivia blinked in surprise when Dane tossed the bed pillows to the carpet before the fire and stretched out there.

He looked like a decadent pagan god, lounging there with the orange firelight licking his golden skin and hair, wearing only black trousers. The room suddenly felt unbearably chilly where she stood clad in nothing but her stockings and garters.

She grabbed up the carved case and dropped to her knees on the carpet before him. "You must remove your clothing as well," she said primly. "'Tis only fair."

He drew back, his inviting smile beginning to fade. "Olivia, I don't think—"

"No, I don't think you do." She crossed her arms.

His eyes nearly crossed. She was beginning to get a glimmer of how her bosom affected him. Tit for tat, after all, since his entire body affected her that way. A body she would very much like to see all of.

"If we are going to surmount—" Her own choice of words halted her. "I mean, rise above—" Oh dear, the image *that* provoked! She pressed the back of her hand to her heated forehead. Blast her ridiculous tendency to redden! She took a breath and tried one more time. "If we are to breach this—"

Dane fell back on the pillows, laughing. "You can stop now," he said with a smile. "I think I understand."

She tilted her head, smiling as she watched him laugh at her. She didn't care as long as he was truly laughing in this easy way, without a shred of his lazy, genial facade in evidence.

She flipped the catches on the case and let it roll open away from her. "Very well then. Time's a-wasting," she said crisply. She unwrapped the first rod. "I take it that this is the usual size?"

He blinked. "How would I know?"

She paused, caught by something carved into the rod. "Heavens, I think these are little people! And they're—" She looked up him with her eyes wide. "Can we do this?"

He snatched the rod away from her and held it close to the fire, peering at it. "Ah. Well, ah . . ." He swallowed hugely. "Yes, if you like." His casual air was not convincing at all. "I suppose so. Someday."

He cleared his throat, his laughter flown before the dark hunger that now sparked in his eyes. "You know, my lady, I'm striving very hard to pay attention to what you're saying, but . . ."

"But the night flies by." She flopped down on the pillows beside him. "Have at, then."

"Have at?" Dane leaned over her, stroking a finger down her cheek. "No need to be so dispassionate about it," he said softly.

She arched her neck, excited by the fierce desire gleaming in his blue eyes. "You know," she said dreamily, "when I'm with you, I couldn't be dispassionate if I tried."

His slow, knowing smile sent shivers through her. He had her in the palm of his hand and he knew it. She let herself be there, willing and trusting, for he was Dane. Strong, gentle, masterful Dane, who she knew would never hurt her, nor desert her, nor deny her.

That warm, protected place in the palm of her husband's hand was her home.

Dane smiled down at his willing bride. Her face shone with just the right amount of wifely affection. He'd done well, keeping matters amiable and light, attaching her fancy using her body's responses and not her heartstrings.

He took the ivory rod, warmed from his hand, and stroked it down the center line of her body, between her breasts and down over her belly. "Open," he commanded softly.

Her eyes widened in surprise, but she did so, letting her thighs fall open compliantly. She obviously thought he meant to thrust the rod directly inside her. She would allow it, too, but that wasn't his intention at all. He suspected that the raised carvings of the rod had another use than merely instructional.

He slid an arm beneath her to raise her breasts high—his reward for his restraint. He took one softened tip deep into his mouth, the way she liked. Her answering gasp fueled his lust, but he had to hold back. It was up to him to bring her along patiently. If this wild plan was to work, he must keep his distance, within and without.

He held the tip of the rod poised just at the top of her slit, not quite touching her sensitive button. As he sucked and teased first one nipple, then the other, she began to writhe, unconsciously straining her pelvis upward against the blunt tip of the rod.

He let the rod slip down a bit, letting the length ride slowly over her little bump, following her crease down like a guide. He let the rod dip into her dampness, using her own desire to wet the ivory, making it slip most sensuously against her.

There was a way to use the carvings, and he had an inkling of how. As she began to feel the effects of the carvings sliding fluidly over her swelling clitoris, her breath began to quicken sharply, tiny cries reflecting the rise and fall of smooth ivory on her sensitivity.

He rotated the rod, watching her face. "Do you like this side?" He twisted it again. "Or this?"

Finally, he turned the rod the way a man's cock would press if he lay between those sweet thighs—soon, by God, someday soon!—and slid it smoothly up and down.

She went mad in his embrace.

Olivia reached out, grasping for balance against the wild sensations radiating from her center. In response to her reaction, the rod slid more quickly. Up and down, again and again, the bumps and lines in the ivory caressing and kneading her nub into violent ecstasy.

Ascend and descend, on and on, sweet, sharp pleasure, until the now-familiar bubble of bliss began to grow within her. It swelled, expanding sharply. The rod rose and fell. Fighting the dizziness, she opened her eyes a slit to see Dane watching her, power and satisfaction on his face.

I am yours. She was owned and cherished and his.

She could fly free within the protective circle of his hold. He wouldn't let her fall.

He bent to take her nipple in his mouth again. That was all she needed.

The bubble burst in a thousand shimmering threads, sending white-hot shivering ecstasy radiating through her. As she floated down from the heights, her body still throbbing, she felt Dane change the angle of the rod.

Her eyes flew open and locked with his. He gazed down at her, his expression somber. "This should be me," he whispered.

She raised her arms to wrap about his neck. "It is you," she whispered back. "It is ever you."

He bent to kiss her softly, possessively, as he slowly pressed the rod within her.

Olivia closed her eyes and waited for the pain. Mother had made it very clear that there would be pain.

The rod was warm and slick and hard. The bulbous head pressed her open, the length sliding in behind to fill her. She felt a pressure. Dane stopped at her tiny protest.

"I think that is your maidenhead, sweeting," he said softly. "Once broken, it will bother you no more."

She blinked up at him. "I'm ready," she said, tensing her body in expectation.

Dane smiled at her. "I think I'll kiss you more, first." He bent to kiss her, a long, sweet wet kiss that made Olivia sigh with delight. She relaxed, going soft and pliant in his hold.

He thrust the rod deep.

She cried out, clutching at him, ready for the agony

to overtake her. There was only a sharp sting, like the pricking of a finger.

She relaxed again, letting out a breath of relief. Dane slowly pressed the rod deeper, then smoothly withdrew it. "Yes?"

"Yes," she breathed. He continued the motion, once more twisting the rod until he found the best aspect. The carvings slid in and out, pressing here, drawing there, exciting small tugs of pleasure deep within her. "Oh!"

Dane paused the motion. "More?" he teased.

She clung to him. "Oh yes, *please.*"

He took his time, first slowly, until she writhed against him. Then carefully faster, letting her wetness ease his speed. She bucked, gasping, helpless in her pleasure.

He found he enjoyed watching her take her pleasure. Sometime he might have her do it herself as he looked on. Let her perform for him . . . quivering at her own hand . . . in the bath. . . .

Lecher. He was most base, he decided. She was already giving him such a gift, bearing this outrageous invasion for him. The fact that he could probably convince her to do it notwithstanding, there was a line he could not pass, a level of sexual debauchery he could not ask of her—

"Oh *yes!*" she cried. "Oh, please, *more.*"

Or perhaps he could.

He watched in wonder as she arched her back and tossed her fair hair on the pillows, her lips open as she gasped her pleasure, her breasts quivering with the tension in her body. He threw his thigh across her nearest leg to hold her still and drove the rod in deeply a final time, sure it would drive her over the edge.

It did.

She bucked wildly in his hold. Her soft body writhed and tortured his imprisoned erection, making him shake as well. She called his name out loud, her broken cries husky and abandoned.

He nearly lost his own control, nearly spilled himself right there like a randy lad. If she kept that up—

She went limp, her breath leaving her in a wordless sigh. He withdrew the rod and set it aside. Thankfully, he'd held his seed—or perhaps he wasn't all that thankful. His tormented body ached for release, any release. He wanted to undo his trousers and have her put her hands on him, to stroke him as she had the night before, with her soft hands directly on his sensitized flesh.

He could not do it. He could not reveal himself to her in all his abnormality. He still did not trust her nerve, it seemed.

Memory assaulted him. *Good God! Get that 'orrid thing away from me!* He didn't know what was worse, honest revulsion or horrified fascination. His aching cock subsided at the memory. He'd experienced both and he wasn't willing to go through it again. There was time.

They had the rest of their lives, he and Olivia.

He found that thought very comforting. As he pulled her soft body close and drowsily tucked her head beneath his chin, it never occurred to him to worry about how comforting the thought was.

15

Dane rolled over, sleepily reaching for his bride.

She wasn't there.

He started and sat up, blinking about him. He was disoriented at finding himself on the floor until he remembered it was his idea.

Olivia sat tailor-fashion nearby, the reddish glow of the coals on her skin, still clad in nothing but her stockings and garters. She held another of the rods in her hands, peering closely at the pictorial carvings. She turned her head and smiled as he sat up.

"Did you rest well, darling?" She went on all fours and crawled to him. What a sight! His cock shifted at the way her heavy breasts hung and the way her pert rear beckoned. She came close and collapsed into his lap, nuzzling his neck with her forehead. "I feel rather astonishing," she purred.

"You look rather astonishing," he gasped. "I thought you would be in pain."

"So did I." She shrugged. "Well, that was a great

deal of fanfare for nothing. Not that I'm complaining, mind you."

He drew his brows together. "It didn't hurt?"

She shook her head. "Only a bit. Wasn't it supposed to be much worse?"

He blinked. "Ah . . . to be truthful, my lady, we are both operating on secondhand information here. I have never taken anyone's virginity before."

She tilted her head back and smiled at him. "I shouldn't think well of you if you had." She held up the second rod. "As a matter of fact, I felt quite 'comfortable' with the first one." She gave him a demurely naughty smile. "And you know what that means."

He blinked. "Again? Are you sure?"

She nodded with certainty. "I realized something, you see. I am not a small woman. My mother has often pointed this out to me. It seems at last that I have found a benefit to being oversized and awkward—"

"You are nothing of the sort!" Dane was surprised that she could even think such a thing. "You are tall and stately, with the figure of a goddess. I should not wish you to be a small woman." He frowned. "I always feel as though I'm going to crush them."

Olivia's lips quirked. "I have sometimes felt the same way."

Dane tilted her chin up with one finger. "You are perfect for me, just as you are."

She swallowed and blinked at that, and then her eyes took on that grateful gaze again. This time Dane didn't mind so much at all.

She cleared her throat. "As I was saying," she continued huskily. "I am not a small woman. Therefore, it only makes sense that I would . . . ah, *graduate* sooner than someone more petite."

He narrowed his eyes. "Or can it be that you want another such climax?"

She lazily slid her hand into his hair and pulled him down for a hot, wet kiss. "Why, my Lord Greenleigh," she murmured against his mouth. "What a naughty thing to say."

He pulled her back down onto the cushions, chuckling deeply. "I fear I've created a monster."

She rolled her naked body sensually on top of his. "Absolutely." She growled playfully. "It's all your fault. Now you must pay. I want more."

He flipped her over and, taking the second rod from her, pinned her roving hands above her head. "As my lady commands," he said, and proceeded to give her just that.

The next morning, Olivia did not have time to seek out Dane. In fact, she learned that he'd breakfasted early and left to take care of a few things before they all departed for Scotland tomorrow.

It was packing day. The house was in a flurry, servants rushing this way and that, with a much more cheerful Mrs. Huff directing the traffic.

Olivia glanced a question at Petty, who nodded back with a sly smile. Olivia's cure for joint ache had worked its magic, it seemed.

She and Petty spent most of the morning in Olivia's bedchamber, packing up the gowns and possessions that had only been unpacked five days ago.

Had it truly only been five days? Five days since

she'd waited in this room, not knowing what to expect from the stranger she'd married?

She held the green gown up to inspect it for damage but then only dreamily clutched it to her bosom as she recalled how Dane had stripped it from her last night.

Goodness, what a night!

The second rod had been an entirely different matter. She'd been fortunate to have a man like Dane, who had labored over her for what seemed hours of pleasure, purely to ensure her readiness. She sighed deeply, remembering the way he'd held her tightly when she'd climaxed again. She closed her eyes, recalling how he'd whispered that she was beautiful and amazing and strong as she'd ridden the falling pleasure to come back to herself in his arms.

It had been a bit disappointing to wake in her wide bed without him this morning, but she supposed that was how marriage was conducted. After all, her parents didn't share a bed. Lord and Lady Cheltenham rarely shared the breakfast table if they could help it.

Of course, tomorrow Olivia and Dane would be traveling together. Surely they would share a room when they stopped at an inn tomorrow night. Olivia smiled dreamily at the thought. She must be sure to order a bath first thing when they arrived. It would be like a little honeymoon for them, for they'd had to pass on the traditional month together.

Someone cleared her throat. Olivia opened her eyes to see Petty standing there with an I-know-what-you're-thinking-about glint in her eye. The maid held out her hands.

Olivia looked down to see that she was crushing the

green gown to her bosom, creasing the already-abused silk. She shrugged sheepishly and handed it to Petty. "His lordship thought it was a bit tight in the bosom," she told the maid.

Petty sniffed. "I thought it looked right fine, but what do I know about ladies' gowns and such? Nothing at all, that's what."

Olivia ignored Petty's irony and forced herself to focus on her tasks. Abruptly she realized there was a very serious problem with her wardrobe.

"Petty! What am I to wear to the Hunt Ball? Mother ordered a ball gown for my trousseau, but it hasn't come yet—"

Petty pulled a heavy card dress box from beneath the bed. "It came yesterday evening, my lady, but I didn't have the chance to tell you." She bent her sour gaze on Olivia. "What with you two lockin' the door and all."

"Petty, you are insubordinate!" Olivia hugged the astonished maid. "But I forgive you! Let's try it on, shall we?"

When Petty bent to undo the string ties on the box, Olivia's enthusiasm began to fade. Mother had chosen this gown as well. If Olivia recalled correctly, it was a flounced blue satin with a bell skirt, which Mother was convinced was on its way back in. The style made buxom Olivia look like a flour sack tied in the middle.

"Oh dear." She had to wear it. She had nothing else. At the very least, it would be grand. If awful.

"Oh, my lady!" Petty's breathy, unqualified approval made Olivia open her eyes. "You'll look a sight in this!"

From the maid's hands hung a sleek column of sky

blue silk, falling from a low-cut Empire bodice that went to perfect tiny cap sleeves at the shoulders.

Olivia gasped, her hand at her mouth. It was perfection. It was divine. It was nothing her mother ever would have ordered for her.

"I am going to find that modiste and kiss her silly," Olivia vowed.

Petty, who knew the difference between Lady Cheltenham's taste and good taste, nodded emphatically. "That one knew what side her bread was buttered on. Better to make a wealthy viscountess look fine than please a poor countess."

Moments later, Olivia turned toward the mirror. Oh my. "Petty, I don't look fine."

Petty shook her head. "No, my lady, you don't."

Olivia grinned down at Petty. "I'm going to boggle his mind!"

Petty grinned back. "Himself isn't going to know what hit him."

Then Petty's smile retreated and she looked away, busying herself with checking the gown's hem. Olivia sighed, but what could she say to the girl? Dane was never going to be hers, it was a ridiculous fantasy, but hearing that from Olivia would only cut deeper.

To say anything else would be a lie. So Olivia said nothing. Still, she mourned that brief camaraderie as Petty silently removed the gown and packed it away for the journey.

Olivia took pity on her discomfort. "Petty, why don't you go check on Mrs. Huff? Remind her to bring a packet of the treatment on the journey. I'll make sure the kitchen at the inn makes it up for her."

Petty nodded and escaped without ever looking up.

The quiet was lovely after the bustle of the day. Olivia dropped into the chair by the fire, letting out a great yawn. She'd hardly slept last night, she realized with a smile.

A catnap in the chair was just the thing. Petty would return shortly, so she ought to take advantage of these few moments alone.

She turned, cuddling into the corner of the great chair. The first night here, Dane had held her in his lap on this chair after that silly dizzy spell. It was too bad one didn't take great overstuffed chairs along on journeys to Scotland. . . .

The door burst open and Petty flew into the room, her eyes wide.

"My lady, there's a gent come to see you and he's a right stunner!"

Olivia snuggled deeper into the cushions. "Tell him I'm already married."

Petty shook her shoulder with deferent urgency. "My lady, I think he's an upper servant looking for work. Oh, my lady, please hire him, do!"

Olivia cracked her eyes open. "A servant, seeking work from *me*?" Surprising, since she'd not advertised for one. Furthermore, what was Petty's urgency?

Curiosity alone was enough to shake Olivia from her nap. Besides, meeting this paragon of male beauty definitely sounded like more fun than packing.

Moments later, when she received the fellow in the third parlor—because apparently Mrs. Huff didn't think he rated the first or second parlor—Olivia had to admit that he was a fine-looking fellow indeed.

Fair-haired and blue-eyed and with very nice manners as well.

Of course, he was a bit young and too slender for her taste and he was no taller than her and he tended toward a mournful expression—

Yet Petty couldn't take her eyes from the young man. Olivia watched the way the maid sent furtive adoring glances at him.

"So tell me, Mr. Sumner, what leads you to believe I'm in need of a manservant?"

He shrugged, blinking dolefully at her. "I'd only hoped, my lady. I'd heard you were marrying and I thought you might be taking on a few new people since his lordship's household was growing." He sighed. "I know it's presumptuous, me coming here like this, but Lord Walter was always willing to listen when someone needed work and I thought—"

Olivia held up a hand. "Lord Walter? You were employed by my brother?"

He nodded vigorously, turning his hat around in nervous hands. "Yes, my lady. I was valet to his lordship for two years, until his death a month back." He blinked rapidly, as though near tears. "I miss working for his lordship, I do."

The valet who had witnessed Walt's death. The sole witness, in fact. Olivia stood abruptly. "Wait here."

She left the room, not caring that Petty stayed behind. Let Petty have a new fancy. In a few steps, Olivia was outside Dane's study. She hesitated, for he'd made it clear he didn't like being disturbed.

Then again, she had no idea if she was allowed to hire servants on her own. Mostly the housekeeper hired staff, and Olivia would much rather ask Dane than face down the imperious Mrs. Huff.

She tapped at the door.

"Come."

She entered to see Dane alone, working on something he casually slid beneath the blotter as she approached. Honestly, did these men think she was a prying sort?

Of course, their caution made her itch with curiosity, but she was a lady. She could control herself.

Besides, she was here on a mission. She wanted to know what really happened to Walter and why he was hanging about with such sordid sorts and why he would drown when he was a keen swimmer.

"Dane, may I hire a manservant?"

He sat back and smiled at her. "Good afternoon to you, too, my lady."

She blushed. "My apologies. How are you today, my lord?"

He tilted his head, cocking a saucy brow at her. "I'm a little tired actually. Something kept me from my rest last night."

She reddened further. "Dane," she hissed in embarrassment. "Don't *talk* about it! It's daytime!"

He threw back his head and laughed. "Very well. Strictly business, then. Why do you need a manservant? I've a household full."

Olivia nodded. "True, but they all work for you and Greenleigh. Especially with all this traveling, I think it might come in handy to have a manservant of my own. He needs the work, and he can help Petty take care of my things, and with lifting and carrying and such."

"And you feel sorry for him."

"Well, yes. He was with my brother for two years and now he's without employment. I never met him because he stayed in London when Walter visited, but I've only heard good things about him."

Dane took a breath. "You know, sympathy is not really the correct way to hire servants."

"I know. But it was my parents' responsibility to give him references when my brother died, and they did nothing."

She was rather naive if she thought a good servant would go unemployed for months just because of that, but it would do no harm for her to hire the fellow. Dane made a note to have the fellow's background investigated immediately. The Chimera had made him more suspicious of England's servant class.

"You may take him on a trial basis. If he isn't a great help on the journey, I shall leave him on the side of the road."

She dimpled. "You would not."

To his surprise, she circled the desk in a run. "You are a dear, Dane." She bent to press a quick peck on his cheek. Dane found himself enveloped in a perfumed cloud of faint rose scent and girl. He also managed a very rewarding glance down her bodice. Damn, she had a superior figure!

She scampered from the study, leaving Dane fighting back a brand-new wave of lust. Just when he'd finally managed to get his mind off last night and onto the business of convincing the Prince Regent to participate in his little plot!

16

"But I loathe Scotland," the Prince Regent announced peevishly to Dane and the Falcon in his private chambers that afternoon. "The cold makes my arse hurt. I shall spend the autumn in Brighton."

"Of course. *After* you attend Greenleigh's Hunt Ball in Scotland."

"Why on earth would he want me there?"

The Falcon crossed his arms. "*We* want you there."

The Prince glared back and forth between the Falcon and the Lion. Dane kept his own gaze steady. George was his monarch, it was true . . . but he was George's sworn protector. As such, it was his job to protect His Highness, even from himself.

George wasn't going to go willingly. "I'll need a wing to myself."

Dane nodded. "Of course."

"I'm bringing my entire household."

Dane nodded again, suppressing a sigh. Greenleigh could absorb the cost. "Of course."

"And my dogs. And their servants."

Dogs. At least Olivia would be happy. Dane nodded again. "My carpets are yours."

George glared at them both. "But *why*?"

Dane smiled. "I wish to impress my bride."

George openly sneered. "Oh, please. All you have to do is walk into the room to impress your bride." He tossed back his wine. "Congratulations, by the way," he muttered grudgingly.

Dane bowed. "You honor me, Your Highness."

"Oh, sod off, you buggers. I'll be there."

Dane bowed again, more deeply. "Thank you, Your Highness. I shall expect you by early afternoon in two days time."

George waved them away. "I'll be there when I get there. Now, go away. You're giving me a crick in my neck."

"How would you like me to dispose of your summer frocks, my lady?"

Olivia frowned slightly. "I thought I would simply leave them here."

Now it was Petty's turn to frown. "For who?"

Olivia had that feeling one gets when two people aren't speaking of the same thing but think they are. "Petty, what do you think I should do with my gowns?"

Petty became very busy with wrapping Olivia's shoes. "I'm sure I wouldn't know, my lady."

Olivia folded her arms. "Which is what people say when they do know."

Petty wrapped another pair. "I can't . . . it wouldn't be proper, my lady."

Olivia sighed. "Since when has that stopped you?"

Petty shrugged, unwrapping and rewrapping the first pair of shoes.

Olivia shrugged right back. "Petty, you know very well that I haven't the slightest idea what you expect me to do with my gowns. I've never 'disposed' of anything that had another wearing in it. My mother trimmed and retrimmed hers for three years before giving them to her lady's maid—"

But Olivia didn't need to retrim a thing. As Dane's viscountess, she was allowed—nay, expected—to begin each season with an entirely new modish wardrobe.

She was supposed to give her old gowns to Petty. It was one of the perquisites of the job. Of course, most maids didn't wear the gowns. They sold them and kept the money as a sort of bonus for keeping their mistresses looking well.

Olivia decided to start over. "By the way, Petty," she said airily, "I want you to have my summer gowns."

"Yes, my lady. Thank you." Petty smiled in obvious relief. Apparently there were some lines even Petty would not cross.

Still, what a bother. That meant Olivia would have to go through an entire new series of fittings next spring.

Olivia stroked a hand down the bed curtains. "It's odd. I only just now acquainted myself with all the rooms in this house, and now I'm leaving again. By the time I learn Kirkall Hall, I shall be leaving again to Christmas at Greenleigh. And at Greenleigh—"

"At Greenleigh, it's like to take you years to learn every room, my lady. There's more than a hundred of them."

"Cheltenham has sixty-four rooms," Olivia said

proudly. Then she shrugged. "Most of them are closed off and full of cobwebs and leaks."

For the first time, it struck her that she would not be spending Christmas at Cheltenham. She'd been so busy and so wrapped up in Dane that she'd not thought the coming year through.

There would be no excited preparations for her family's return. She wouldn't be receiving her traditional inedible fruitcake from poor Mrs. Abersham, who couldn't see well and often mistook the ingredients (it was best not to mention the time it was cow suppositories instead of dates).

Walter had so looked forward to that fruitcake every year. He would dissect it on the great scratched dining table, crowing with delight at each outrageous ingredient. For years, Olivia had been able to make him laugh at will simply by saying, "Moo!"

Walter . . . oh God, poor Walter. And poor Olivia, for she would never spend another Christmas waiting to find out what her beloved brother had found for her that year—would it be a Chinese puzzle box or a stuffed and mounted Brazilian lizard or a diary clad in deep blue leather? He'd always known just what to bring her to make her laugh and to make her feel understood.

Abruptly Olivia wanted to be alone. "Petty, go and find yourself some dinner. If we've forgotten anything, we can send for it later."

When there was silence at last, Olivia reached under the bed for her lockbox and pulled the bed curtains around. She cried a bit while writing, but as always, she felt much the better for putting words to her feelings.

Nothing would bring Walter back, but she would never be too busy to remember him again.

Which reminded her of Sumner. She wouldn't be able to pin Sumner down about the details of Walter's death until they arrived at the lodge—and even then, not until after the Hunt Ball.

Nervous knots formed in Olivia's stomach at the thought of the Hunt Ball. She'd put so much faith in others. Mrs. Huff, Mrs. Arnold, Mrs. Blythe. How could she be sure that no one would let her down?

She closed her eyes in anticipated horror. What if the food was wrong or the lodge wasn't ready for guests or the entertainment was banal?

She thought of Mrs. Blythe and her outrageous penchant for purple. Such a woman could never be banal. A comforting thought. Yes, even if the food was poor or the lodge uncomfortable, her guests would always remember Lady Greenleigh's Hunt Ball.

"Ready for bed already?" A deep, teasing voice came from just outside the bed curtains.

Dane!

Olivia stuffed everything—the diary, the open inkwell, and the inky quill—beneath a pillow just as Dane swept open the bed curtains next to her.

Mrs. Huff's steely indignation was nothing next to the embarrassment Olivia would feel if Dane ever read her childish scribbling about him!

Dane took one look at his bride's guilt-ridden expression and all his pleasure at finding her alone was gone. He'd virtually sneaked upstairs in his own house, determined to find her and sweep her away somewhere private. He'd been hoping for a repeat of yesterday's predinner escapade. It had been nearly a day since he'd caressed her breasts, and he was nearly fading away from deprivation.

Now she sat, shoulders hunched defensively, gray eyes wide and shining with badly done "innocence."

"Hello, Dane," she said brightly, falsely.

Every suspicious fiber of Dane's being—which meant most of his being—leaped to attention. This afternoon she'd been as warm and open as ever. Now he was quite sure that this was a woman with something to hide.

Dane slammed the lid on that sick suspicion before it could infect him. Olivia wasn't that sort. She was embarrassingly frank, wildly sensual, and entirely without guile.

He gazed down at her, his face expressionless. "What are you doing, Olivia?"

She licked her lips and flicked her gaze away, every so slightly. "Resting."

He nodded, betraying no suspicion. "Hence the bed."

She nodded agreeably, looking relieved. "Yes. Right. The bed."

Dane's gaze swept the area. There was a small lockbox he'd never seen before. It was about the size of a cigar case and it was standing open. "What do you have there?"

Olivia shot a panicked glance at the box, then relaxed. Whatever it was she was hiding wasn't there . . . but from the way she'd reacted, it typically was.

"Oh, these are some keepsakes from ho—from Cheltenham." She pulled the box toward her. "See, here is the token I won for my flower arrangement at the Cheltenham fair." She dangled the medal from her fingers. "I'm not very good, I'm afraid, but the fair was my doing, so I think they let me win."

Dane was frankly confused by her behavior. This was a girl who would host a fair for her cottagers but not expect to win. He was wrong. She might be hiding something, but it was likely as benign as a hole in her stocking.

Relaxing, he held out his hand to help her to her feet. "It's nearly time to dress for dinner."

As she rose, her shoulders slumped slightly. "What is it?" he asked.

She shook her head. "It is nothing. I sometimes weary of changing my gown six times a day, that is all."

Dane laughed, the last wisps of suspicion blowing away on the refreshing breeze of her frankness. "I could tell Mrs. Huff that you have the headache. She'll send a tray up here."

Instantly happier, Olivia blinked coyly at him. "And how would you like to be rewarded for that rescue, O kindly knight?"

Dane reached out to hook a fingertip in her bodice and pulled her closer. "You may feed me clotted cream and candied cherries," he whispered, relaying his meaning by plucking softly at the points of her nipples through her gown.

Her breath caught and she swayed. "Oh yes," she breathed. She reached out a hand to slip it beneath his waistcoat, her fingers stroking his chest.

Dane tugged the neckline of her gown low, revealing the tops of her breasts to the rosy aureoles. Turning them both, he sat on the bed and pulled her to stand between his knees. He bent his head to kiss her breasts, then stroked the side of his face against the silky softness of them. He heard her gasp at the way his stubble abraded and awakened her skin.

Her fingers twined through his hair, pulling it from the neat queue he wore. His long hair fell down around her breasts, softly insinuating itself over and between like warm strands of silk.

She pulled the rest of his hair free and tossed the black ribbon away. "I like your hair," she said dreamily. "It's prettier than mine."

Dane shut his eyes for a moment, then gave in with a chuckle. "I shall let you say it, although if anyone else called me pretty, I believe I should call him out."

"Hmm." She laced her hands together behind his neck. "Is that like a woman being called 'stately'?" She sighed. "It simply means that one is tall and none too slender."

Dane took a gentle, playful bite of succulent flesh and growled. "You're not stately. Dowagers are stately. You are—"

"What? What am I?" Her voice told him she'd never heard complimentary words. With her mother, that seemed quite likely.

He kissed the top of each breast—*I'll be back soon, my darlings*—and raised his gaze to hers. "You are . . . lush. Succulent. Desirable. Delectable. You are like a ripe fruit, or a sip of cream, or a bowl of custard—"

She leaned back to gaze at him, frowning. "Ought I be inferring anything from this listing of foods?"

He laughed. "Only that I hunger for you."

She smiled slightly. "And I for you."

"Then shall I ring for two dinners in your room?"

She blushed. "They'll know what we're up to."

The fact that she believed the servants *didn't* know was charmingly naive. There was probably some sort of pool going on right now about how many times a day the master and the lady came together.

Dane stood. "Two dinners it is." He went to the door and caught an under-underfootman scurrying down the hall. Quick instructions settled the matter quickly, and the fellow was too impressed by speaking personally to his lordship to dare risk a knowing glance.

When Dane returned to Olivia's bedchamber, he found her standing demurely in the middle of the room with her hands behind her back. "Dane, I have a surprise for you."

He smiled and walked toward her. "I hope you're the surprise, especially if that means I am permitted to do the unwrapping."

She took one hand from behind her back to halt him. "My surprise is that I want you to use *this*."

From behind her back she pulled the third Pleasure Rod of the Rajah. Dane blinked. "No. It is too soon. You aren't ready—"

She lifted her chin. "It is for me to say if I'm ready, and I am." She blushed deeply and ducked her head. "I want *you*," she said softly. "I want you so that I cannot sleep, or think, or—" She shook her head as if shaking off a spell. "I want to be your wife in truth."

Dane felt a hot twinge somewhere in his chest. She was pushing the schedule of "training" because of him. He wrapped his arms about her, rod and blush and all, and tucked her head beneath his chin. She laid her cheek on his chest.

"You do not have to do this," he told her softly. "I don't want you to push yourself too far."

She shook her head. "I don't think I am. I—I don't know what it is, but no matter how large they seem at first, all I have to do is think about *you* and everything seems to fit."

How fortunate he was in her. Generous, selfless woman. He'd chosen so well it almost seemed as if someone all-knowing had chosen for him.

A tap on the door separated them. Olivia thrust her hand behind her once more as three servants bustled in with trays. In seconds, there was a fine cloth covering a side table, silver candlesticks lit, covered plates steaming on the cloth, and two comfortable chairs—hers and the one from his room—all put in place before the fire.

Olivia was plainly astonished. Dane grinned and peeked beneath the silver dish covers. "Beef and boil," he announced cheerfully. He picked up a full wineglass. "Care to get me drunk and have your way with me?"

Olivia laughed, then joined him, plunking the Rod of the Rajah upright on the table like a centerpiece. "If anyone asks, that's yours," she said playfully.

Dane pushed it closer to her plate. "You'll ruin my reputation for manliness in all of London."

She pushed it back. "What do you think will happen to my reputation?" she said, grinning.

He scowled teasingly. "If you don't put that away, I'll be forced to exact retribution."

Olivia pursed her lips. "Oh, very well." She leaned across the table and dropped it into his coat pocket. It thrust obscenely through the fabric, looking for all the world like an off-center erection.

Olivia tilted her head and smiled. "It does take after you, does it not? Always so . . . solid."

Dane gazed at her, openmouthed with shock. "You vixen!" he said accusingly. "You're going to pay for that!"

He pulled the rod from his pocket and waved it with mock threat. Olivia squeaked and made as if to run from him. He jumped up, laughing—then stepped on her hem, tripping both of them to the floor.

An hour later, a perspiring Olivia emerged from under the tablecloth, adjusting her bodice and panting slightly. She lifted the lids on the plates.

"Now you've done it, Dane," she called down to the pair of legs sticking out from beneath the tablecloth.

"Our dinner is stone-cold."

17

The next morning the journey to Kirkall Hall began. Olivia had another chance to witness the efficiency of Dane's staff as they loaded the trunks and barrels and cases on three carriages and one wagon.

One carriage was for her and Dane—a fact that pleased Olivia no end. The upper staff rode in the second large carriage and the understaff in the third.

Sumner and Petty rode with Mrs. Huff, Kinsworth, and Proffit—a fact that pleased Petty no end. She was nigh unto driving Olivia mad with her chattering on about Sumner this and Sumner that.

Not that Olivia blamed the girl. She knew just what it was like to have a man completely occupy one's mind.

Lord Dryden proposed to ride his horse most of the way but allowed that he might ride in the carriage at times. Olivia rather tersely inquired if he intended them to adopt him as well.

He'd bowed and smiled. "I could do worse, my lady."

Still, it was all Olivia could do to keep from dancing with impatience. The only traveling she had ever done was to journey from Yorkshire to London a month ago, and that had been under the pall of losing Walter. She scarcely remembered anything but her mother's constant complaints and the way the springs of their ancient carriage seemed to drive spikes up her spine by the end of the first hour.

Not so with Dane's—and hers!—luxurious vehicle. It was large enough to seat six, or three people and Dane. The motion was so smooth that she could even nap on one wide seat if she liked.

Mrs. Huff loaded in an impressive hamper for them. Then a footman—bother, would she ever learn all their names?—helped Olivia in before Dane. She hand-carried her reticule, which contained her diary, and had Sumner bring the carved case of the rods.

"My cosmetics," she'd blithely explained to Sumner, who only nodded indifferently.

In moments, everyone was loaded in and the procession began to roll. Olivia hopped from one side of the carriage to the other, eagerly watching the city roll by.

Dane laughed. "You've been in London for weeks. Why so interested now?"

She tilted her head at him. "Because now I'm *leaving* London, and I won't be back until next spring. When you leave someplace, you want to take your last memories of it with you, don't you?"

Dane only laughed and opened his news sheet. "For me, London is rather like an old shoe, I'm afraid. Comfortable, but accustomed."

"Laugh if you like," she replied primly. "*I* will never become blasé about new adventures."

Dane gazed at her fondly for a long moment. "I know."

So milord was keeping milady close on the journey. And that dinner in the room last evening . . . the one that had been taken away cold and uneaten.

Yes, things were looking most promising. By the end of this intimacy, milord would be neatly strung about milady's pretty pale finger.

The second carriage rolled past. Familiar faces inside . . . the watcher had become well-acquainted with all the staff now. The housekeeper, the butler, the lady's maid, the valet—

A new face in the bunch, with fair hair and a high, pale brow. Pale blue eyes seemed to meet the watcher's for the merest instant. Then the new man looked away.

Well, well, well. And here he'd been afraid the fellow had disappeared forever.

Young Lord Walter's valet had come in useful before. Now the fellow had managed to put himself in a most useful position again.

The symmetry pleased the watcher. Lord Walter Cheltenham had been his original target, after all, for much the same reason Lord Greenleigh was now.

Lord Walter would have been Cheltenham soon and unlike his retiring, monosyllabic father, he'd been a fellow of energy and intelligence. He could have been a real power in the House of Lords, that is, with the proper leverage.

Yet Lord Walter hadn't taken the financial bait. His

engagement would save Cheltenham. So the watcher had used Wallingford and the others to lure Walter into some sort of decadence so he could apply a bit of careful blackmail to stir him from his righteous stance.

It hadn't worked.

No, Lord Walter hadn't ended well at all.

No matter. Lord Greenleigh was next on the list.

By the time the caravan had reached the other side of Bedfordshire, Olivia was heartily bored. By Nottinghamshire, she thought she might go mad. Dane was slouched on the opposite seat—it had been very dear of him to ride backward—sound asleep. Being by nature an immovable object, he scarcely even swayed with the motion of the vehicle.

It was gray and chill outside, the road went on and on, and aside from brief moments of interest when they encountered towns and villages on the way, the landscape had been a rather monotonous series of fields, hedgerows, and stone walls.

The one bright spot had been when the road passed through a small wood, brightly strewn with orange and gold leaves. Olivia had caught one vibrant specimen through the window. She toyed with it now as she watched Dane sleep.

He was so tired, poor dear. She ought to be as well, for she was the reason for his weariness. He'd spent hours caressing and stimulating her, driving her higher every time.

The result being, unfortunately, that she—the satisfied one—slept like the dead while he, being the unsatisfied one, tossed and turned the night long. She'd heard

Proffit talking to Mrs. Huff about it, concerned at how mangled Dane's bedclothes were and how weary his lordship seemed.

Olivia slipped carefully off her seat and onto his, into the tiny triangle left by his stretched-out limbs. Resting her hip against his, she stroked his golden hair from his brow and bent to kiss his forehead. "Poor man," she whispered soundlessly to him. "Soon we shall be together, my darling," she promised. "Husband and wife, as we should be."

The very thought sent fire singing through her. The carriage was large. The seats were as wide as cots. There was no end to the mischief they could get up to if they pulled the isinglass shades. . . .

Inspired, Olivia dug the fourth rod from the case beneath the seat. Twisting toward Dane, Olivia planted her bosom directly in front of his face, certain that if he awoke confronted with his deepest desire, he'd not be able to resist.

"Wake up, my darling," she cooed. "I want you to touch m—"

Just then, the carriage halted. She hadn't even been aware that it had slowed, so gently had the driver eased the horses. Therefore, when the inevitable bounce-back occurred, even one so minor, she wasn't braced at all.

She went flying to the floor, landing hard on her bottom. "Ouch!" Most of her nether regions were already a bit sore from last night's athletics, plus the fall jarred her spine and made her bite her bottom lip.

Dane—who of course hadn't been jostled an inch—leaned over to peer down at her. "Are you all right, Olivia?"

Hurriedly, she hid the ivory plaything beneath a fold of her skirts. Unfortunately that left her no time to correct her disarray.

The footman, who had already opened the door, gazed at Olivia with horror. He leaned away to shout something sharply to the driver, who then leaped down to gaze into the carriage as well. In less than an instant, the entire staff stood there, staring at their downed viscountess.

Dane helped her up carefully, then he turned his furious gaze upon the driver. "What do you mean by this, man? Her ladyship could have been injured by your ineptitude!"

The driver could only shrink before Dane's anger. Olivia saw the gazes of the other servants, who of course knew the driver had done nothing wrong, turn toward her with chilling assessment.

She felt like an idiot, a clumsy, lack-witted rustic who didn't know how to ride in a carriage. "Er, my lord, it wasn't Errol's fault." At least she had one name down. "I wasn't in my seat."

Dane turned to gaze at her oddly. "Where were you?"

All the eyes were on her. She didn't want Errol to be sacked, but she certainly couldn't very well say, "I was on your lap."

And, yet, somehow she did, quite without realizing it. Muffled snickers rippled through her audience, reinforced by careful derisive glances. Even Dane put his hand over his mouth, his blue eyes laughing at her above it.

The driver, however, gazed at her with sympathy

and near worship. She'd humiliated herself to save him and he knew it.

Dane turned and dismissed the lot of them with a wave. "We're stopping for an hour. Make yourselves scarce, but don't be late or you'll be left."

Dane turned back to her, one corner of his mouth quirked up. "I appreciate your candor, my dear. However, in the future, if you wish to explain something to me in private, you only must need say so. There was no emergency. Errol was in for a tongue-lashing, nothing more."

Of course. She'd been stupid, thinking Dane would impulsively fire a long-held employee over a bumped bottom. Dane stepped outside, but Olivia stayed where she was until she was sure all the servants were out of sight.

She was never going to be elegant or refined or even the tiniest bit poised. She had simply never learned. Covering her face with her hands, she knew she couldn't entirely blame Mother, for Olivia had spent much of her time avoiding those very lessons when her parents were home. She'd preferred to ride to the village or the river or very nearly anywhere just to evade them.

Mother had scolded halfheartedly and always soon left Cheltenham, leaving Olivia to her hoydenish ways, much to her delight. Walter had been the family's bright hope, not her.

Olivia kept her thoughts on Errol's sympathetic gaze as she righted herself and dusted off her skirts. One less servant who despised her. She would win them over one by one, if it took her years.

She was served a meal in a private dining room in the coaching inn, but she merely picked at it. Dane was somewhere with Marcus, doing whatever it was they did for hours on end and—

Olivia stabbed a bit of cold pork with her fork and gazed at it pensively. What did Dane and Marcus do all day long, anyway? Estate matters. Investment matters.

Thinking of the way Dane and Marcus had sought out the company of the other two gentlemen at Mother's dinner party . . . those matters certainly seemed to include that nice Lord Reardon and that sharply handsome Lord Wyndham.

A bit of memory drifted back to her, memory that had been fogged by the following bout of heated passion in the downstairs hallway.

What we need is the right woman.

A frown creased her brow as she stared unseeing at the bite of pork. The right woman for what?

The watcher kept an eye on the comings and goings in the inn from a dark corner of the taproom where he nursed an ale mug that never emptied. His rough woolen disguise of a rumpled farmer irritated him, and the pads plumping his cheeks dried his mouth, but his focus never wavered.

Something was wrong. Greenleigh should have been completely besotted by now. The girl was perfect for him, according to the watcher's information—which was excellent. His source was impeccable, albeit dead. He knew precisely what Greenleigh wanted, and in a perfect circle, he'd been given it by Lord Walter's own loving description of his sister.

So what could have possibly gone awry? He knew the girl was doing her part, for the incident in her carriage had spread with the first round of ale bought by Greenleigh staff. She was artless and clumsy in her efforts, to be sure, but he'd expected that of her, counting on it to amuse his lordship.

The valet appeared in the doorway, his gaze searching the taproom. The watcher waited until the young man's eye was on him, then lifted his ale in a tiny salute. The valet flinched, then nodded hesitantly.

Excellent. One of his more useful pawns was back in the game. Having a man in the household should speed up those tedious matters of the heart. The valet knew the plan well for he'd helped devise it some weeks ago. Of course, it had been intended to be used on dear, departed Lord Walter, but now Walter's sister could help him capture a king, instead of a mere knight.

How enjoyable it was, to watch the patterns flow and merge. Espionage was an art and a science combined.

And he was a master of both.

"My lord, if I may presume?"

Dane stopped in the inn hallway. As he was intent on the conversation he'd just had with Marcus—in which Marcus informed him that he had the nagging sensation they were being followed—it took Dane several moments to place the fair-haired man with the mournful expression. "Yes?"

The man bowed again. "Sumner, my lord. I only wish to thank you for giving me the opportunity to serve my lady. My prior connection to her family—"

Dane had almost forgotten about Sumner. He'd

assigned the Liar's Club to scrutinize the man's history, then he'd put the fellow from his mind. "Yes, well, the choice was her ladyship's." He turned toward Olivia's private dining room.

"I must extend my sincerest felicitations as well, my lord. You and Lady Greenleigh make a most handsome couple. It does my heart good to see her happy. Her brother spoke of her so fondly." The valet smiled sadly. For the first time, Dane noticed that the man could be called handsome. He was tall, but not overly so, and lean like a whippet. Blue eyes, fair hair . . .

"Lady Cheltenham was a very busy woman, and I believe Lady Olivia was just the slightest bit . . . abandoned."

Dane went very still. This he knew from personal experience. He certainly didn't appreciate hearing it from a servant.

"Oh, there you are, Dane." Olivia appeared before him in the hall, slightly mussed, with a long lock of fair hair having come down from her pins. Her bottom lip was swollen from being bumped in her fall.

She looked like a woman who had just been taken up against a wall. Dane wondered if she would like it that way, pressed high with her thighs wrapped about him—

The roar increased, drowning out every thought but one.

She belonged to him.

Olivia was greeting Sumner, asking him how he was bearing the trip. Sumner gazed at her moonily and said he wished it could go on forever.

"It is time to leave," Dane blurted. They both turned to look at him, obviously surprised by his forcefulness.

He swept Olivia before him, moving quickly to the first carriage. He installed her with no more than a word or two, leaving her gazing after him curiously when he turned and walked away.

Marcus was readying his second horse, having tied his first to the back of the following wagon.

"You may ride inside now," Dane told him, taking the horse's reins.

Marcus blinked at him, then stared. "Are you unwell, Dane?"

"I need air," Dane said shortly, and mounted Marcus's horse. Thankfully, Marcus rode powerful animals much like Dane's. He'd never have the patience to await the saddling of one of his own right now.

He rode ahead, leaving the servants scrambling for their seats as the carriages rolled out after him.

18

The inn at Huddersfield, midway between London and the Scottish border, was full. Dane moved the lot of them in anyway. Olivia could not get over what a Viking god with a pocketful of gold could accomplish in less than three minutes.

She felt terrible as she watched the farmers and merchants—and hastily dressed wives—rushed from their rooms to make way for Greenleigh and his staff. Dane seemed to expect nothing less.

He'd not spoken to her once since installing her in the carriage and riding away. Marcus had done his best to tease her out of her worrying mood, but Olivia just knew it was her fault.

She'd been a complete Bedlamite, climbing into his lap in the carriage. And then to blurt it out in front of everyone! She could never hold her tongue, especially not when it mattered.

Mother had been right all along. She was an embarrassment, a millstone, a country clod. She'd finally turned away from Marcus's gentle teasing to gaze silently out onto the darkening fields.

Once in her room at the inn, she'd asked for the bath after all, for she felt chilled inside and out. Dane wouldn't be coming to her tonight, she was sure. She left the case of rods in the carriage, tucked deep under her seat. She didn't even think she could bear to look at the evocative carvings on it at this time.

At last, the bath was poured, her nightdress laid out, and Petty gone from the room. Olivia turned the key and slipped off her wrapper. At least if she cried in the bath, she could always tell herself she had soap in her eyes. She stepped one foot, then the other into the steaming water, then slid entirely into the comforting heat. The scent of jasmine rising with the steam almost made her smile. It seemed Petty had found the other bath scents after all. A thank-you for hiring Sumner, Olivia thought.

She only hoped Sumner returned the girl's sentiment.

Dane spent far longer nursing his ale in the private dining room he'd hired than the mediocre libation deserved.

It was his plan to stay down here until Olivia was asleep. He'd not been able to bribe another room from the innkeeper. Apparently the rest of the guests were of sufficient rank to give the man pause.

If Olivia was asleep, then perhaps he could keep his senses long enough to get some rest. If she was awake, eager and agreeable and so convincingly adorable, he wasn't sure he was strong enough to resist her.

Dane had always held his own position in the world with ease and power, untroubled by doubts. To find such possessiveness within himself was disturbing, to say the least. He ought to have found a servant's infatuation with his wife scarcely worth noticing, or amusing at the most.

Instead, he had felt very much like sacking the smitten fellow. His playful threat to leave Sumner by the side of the road was beginning to sound like a very good option.

He'd obviously been spending too much time in Olivia's company. His constant state of arousal was fair to making him obsessive. There was only one thing in his life Dane was willing to give that sort of devotion to—his duty.

So he'd exchanged places with Marcus on the journey. It ought to have been a relief to be alone with his thoughts, able to focus at last on his plans for Prince George.

Instead, his thoughts had been filled with Olivia. Olivia with her hair falling down. Olivia in his thrall, her eyes closed and her head thrown back. Olivia laughing at him, her gaze bright and fond. Olivia wanting him despite his problem.

She'd just been so damned . . . *unexpected*.

He gave up pretending to drink the ale and pushed it away. And in Dane's line of work, *unexpected* could be a very bad thing.

He'd never expected his father to turn traitor, had he? He'd never had a moment of suspicion of Henry Calwell. Dane's father had been his favorite person, and they had spent many hours happily debating the state of the union. Dane had relaxed his natural reserve, waxed political, even joked about Liverpool's tightfisted rein on intelligence! He felt sick thinking what he had spilled unknowing to a traitor wearing his father's face.

Dane's one comfort was that he'd never breathed a word to his father about his appointment to the Royal Four. He'd told his father that the previous Lion was mentoring him in investments—the same pretext he now gave for Marcus. Since the Lion had been a visibly prosperous man, Dane's father had approved heartily.

A clock chimed somewhere. Dane let his eyes close briefly. He was so bloody tired. Surely Olivia was asleep by now.

As he left the dining room and crossed the nearly deserted tavern, he felt that ever familiar twinge.

Marcus had said he felt watched. Dane felt it, too, a creeping sensation up the back of his neck. Unlike Marcus, however, Dane was fairly sure he knew who had his eye on him.

Blood will tell.

Certain members of the Four didn't trust him. Not Nate. Reardon was besotted with his own lady and bound to see the best in everyone right now.

Wyndham, on the other hand . . .

Wyndham had been highly critical of the way Dane's father had died before he could be questioned. It had been Stanton's point that much useful information had died with Henry Calwell and had he been truly repentant, he would have given that information to England instead of taking it to his grave.

His grave on the grounds of Kirkall Hall. There'd been no well-attended funeral, no grand procession to their chapel in Greenleigh. Dane had buried his father quietly in his favorite place in the world. As the miles melted away, so seemed the distance that Dane had built between himself and his father's memory.

Dane hadn't been back since the day he'd found his father in the library, dead by his own hand and the bullet in his brain. A note, with a single line at the top of the page.

I never meant to hurt anyone.

And his signature, sans title. *Henry Calwell.* As if he were just an ordinary man, with feet of clay, not a peer of the realm. Not a privy adviser to the Prince Regent and the Prime Minister. Not an admired and trusted father.

Not that it mattered. He was dead and the whore who had sold herself for the French cause had disappeared like a puff of smoke. A good man, a learned and important man, lured with sex, bound by shame, then crushed like a bug under the bitch's shoe.

He turned his key and opened the chamber door.

Oh, dear God. He was being punished.

Olivia was in the bath, her head tilted back on a rolled piece of toweling, her face damp and rosy in the rising steam. Dane crossed the room without willing a single step, his eyes glued to the tub.

The soap had subsided, leaving only a misty film that lay across her astounding breasts like a very low, very translucent bodice. With each deep sleeping breath, her nipples peeked from the water like curious mermaids, then submerged again when she exhaled.

Soapy, wet, glistening Olivia. His fantasy come to life.

Deep in his mind, barely heard above the pounding

in his blood, was the thought that she'd arranged herself thus in order to captivate and distract him. Yet how
could she have known it was the one thing he dreamed
of above all others save the dream of losing himself in
her sweet body?

Then again, he'd wager most men would be rather
captivated right now.

He would test himself, he decided abruptly. He
would command her to fulfill his darkest fantasy . . .
and then he would walk away. He would prove to himself that she had no acute hold on his will.

He would try to make her bring about her orgasm by
her own hand. While he watched.

He reached into the water and dampened his fingers. Then he let a single drop fall onto her upturned
cheek. She twitched, then opened her eyes and blinked
up at him.

"Will you do as you're commanded?" he asked without preamble.

Her eyes widened and her cheeks flushed. After a
long moment, she nodded silently. Dane observed that
her softened nipples were now rigid and crinkled, despite the heat of the water.

"Touch your breasts," he ordered. "Soap them, then
wash them clean."

Without taking her pale moon eyes from his, she
reached over her shoulder to dig her fingers into the
porcelain container of soft soap. Slowly, she rubbed it
between her two hands to make a lather.

He waited, betraying no expression. His interest
here was purely experimental, nothing else.

She shivered the tiniest bit, then sat up slightly to

raise her upper torso from the water. With both hands covered in bubbles, she began to run them over and around her two lush breasts, leaving gleaming trails of white to drip off her rigid nipples. Her flesh rose and fell, plumped and pressed, as her hands rotated around but not touching the points.

"Wash your nipples," he said tonelessly. "Wash them very well."

Her tongue came out to lick her lips. She was still gazing at him solemnly, even as she kneaded her rigid nipples.

"Pinch them."

She did so, finally closing her eyes at the pleasure/pain. It was relief, for now he could not be distracted by her yearning gaze.

He watched for a long while, curious how long she would continue.

As long as he wanted, apparently.

"Rinse the soap off now."

She did so, cupping her hands and bringing the water to her throat, letting it wash away the film of white.

Her nipples were hard points, made deep red by her efforts to please him.

"Sweep the soap away so that I may see all of you."

She opened her eyes and waved her arm, pushing the soap film to one side. The water was still cloudy, but he could see her belly, her navel, and her pudendum.

"Close your eyes." She did so, instantly. "Slide your hands down your body."

She spread her fingers wide and let her palms glide from beneath her breasts and over her belly, her fingers touching over the center line of her.

"Open your thighs."

He saw her smile slightly, a tiny wave of relief crossing her features. She thought he was going to stroke her now. He turned away from her gladness to cast his gaze about the room. "Are the rods still with the baggage?"

She nodded, her smile becoming sensual. She thought he would trot right out into the cold to fetch them.

"Well then." Dane crossed his arms and took a stance at the end of the tub. "You'll just have to use your fingers, then."

Her eyes flew open. "Wh—what?"

"You heard me," he said cruelly. "Fuck yourself with your fingers."

She flinched at the foul word and drew her hands away from her thighs. "I—"

Dane leaned over the tub, gripping the sides with both hands. His face was little more than a foot above hers. "Do as I say."

She cringed away, against the slanting back of the tub. Her big gray eyes filled as she stared up at him. Her bottom lip quivered. Dane refused to relent. He *needed* to know she had no hold over him.

Then she blinked the moisture away and narrowed her gaze. "If you like soap so much—" She used both hands to lift a great wash of bathwater. It hit his open eyes and he spun away, cursing.

When he rubbed his stinging vision clear, she was out of the water and clad in her wrapper.

She glared at him, her arms crossed beneath her breasts—which, by the way, were completely revealed by the now-soaking wrapper. Her dripping hair only made matters worse.

"That wasn't nice," she said, her tone flat.

He wasn't going to pass this test. From the furious, betrayed look in her eyes, he'd already failed. Her hurt tore at him.

Weariness struck him. He was so bloody tired of keeping his guard high. He let his shoulders drop and sank to sit on the edge of the bed. "I'm sorry, Livvie."

He dropped his face into his hands and rubbed it, but the fatigue was bone deep. "I'm an ass. You're quite correct. That wasn't nice."

"Well, as long as we're in agreement—"

He held up his hand against her anger. "Please. I know. I'm so very sorry."

He heard movement—and a good bit of dripping—across the floor. Her bare crinkled toes stopped just inches from his booted ones. "Well, it isn't as if you're not allowed to make a mistake or two," she said slowly. "Who would I be to declare that?"

He shook his head. "I—"

"I mean, it isn't as if you truly know what you're about."

He jerked his head up. She was gazing at him with . . . understanding? He frowned at her, then glanced away when she raised a brow. "I don't know what you mean," he said stiffly, although he was very much afraid he did.

She was wrong, of course. Well, about it being the reason he'd mangled this evening, anyway.

She knelt before him, her wrapper falling into her own puddle. She raised her hands to cradle his face, gently forcing him to look at her. "You made a mistake because beginners make mistakes. You've never . . . have you?"

His jaw hardened. "No." He pulled away from her, rolling aside on the bed. "There's never been a woman who—" He stared into the fire, then laughed darkly. "I don't know why I thought I could keep that secret. It is rather the point, isn't it?"

She clambered up on the bed behind him and wrapped her arms about him, pressing her wet wrapper-clad breasts to his wet shirt-clad back. "I think it's lovely. It is a gift we give only to each other."

And just like that, he was forgiven. Understood and forgiven. Deep down, in a place he wasn't ready to look, he knew that her assumption was quite correct. He'd tested himself, true—but he'd tried to fulfill his fantasy of her in the bath even while he told himself he was uninterested.

It isn't as if you truly know what you're about.

"Oh!" Olivia sat up from the circle of his arms. "I just remembered—" She scrambled off the bed and ran to the hook where she'd hung her traveling dress.

Dane found himself with a view of curvaceous woman through damp muslin, lit from behind by the fire. The vision struck him dry-mouthed with a sudden bolt of fresh lust. He scarcely noticed that Olivia was trying to work something out of the pocket of her dress.

Then she whirled, showing him a flash of pale thigh where her wrapper parted, and waved a familiar, blunt shape at him.

"I had Rod number four in my pocket!"

He blinked. "Why?"

She shrugged and looked away. "Ah, for emergencies?"

Dane fell back on the bed, chuckling helplessly. "Were you going to cosh a highwayman on the head with it if we were accosted?"

She moved to bed and crawled up his body until she sat astride his lap. Then she stroked the rod down her throat and smoldered at him. "We wouldn't want to lose any of our lovely progress, would we?"

Dane closed his eyes against her playful, erotic pose and pulled her to him, holding her hard against his heart. "Where did you come from, sweet Olivia? You should mock me, a man of my age with so little experience."

She wrapped her arms around his neck and laid her head on his chest. "I like you just as you are."

Her simple acceptance slid beneath Dane's guard like a whisper, but it felt like a balm to his heart. He took her head gently in his hands and raised her face to look into her eyes. "You defeat me, my lady."

She smiled softly. "You defeated me when you got stuck in the mud. I believe I may have a bit of a rescue compulsion."

"Save me, then," he whispered.

He kissed her tenderly, a mere sweet pressure on her lips.

She smiled, then kissed him back.

Hard.

The bathwater went chill and the coals faded to a dusty gleam. Her wrapper was kicked unceremoniously to the floor at some point—perhaps when Dane's practiced application of the pleasure rod made her cries fill the room.

Finally, she lay quiescent in his arms, her face

flushed, her eyes closed in exhausted sleep. Dane carefully pushed back a wayward strand of hair caught on her dampened cheek. She'd given him all of herself once more, holding nothing back as currency, playing no hands for her own advantage.

He'd never met anyone like her in his life.

She was so giving, so honest—it made him feel like a liar for treating her as he had. He'd bought her like a brood mare, acquired to improve his stock. He'd installed her in his home, in his bed, like a mistress—ignoring her all day, attending to her solely in lust and ambition. Then he'd abused her, insulted her, and frightened her.

He owed her so much more than that. He owed her respect and admiration and affection and—

Love.

Was this love or merely obsession?

Long suppressed emotions swelled within him, fair to breaking his chest with their power. It seemed that he was remembering how to feel.

He didn't like it.

How could he be who he needed to be if he could be swung by his emotions—if he could be strung through the heart?

His sudden tension woke Olivia, who blinked at him curiously.

He went very still. "I think I'm going to check on the carriages and horses," he said tightly. He unwrapped her arms and slid off the opposite side of the bed. "Go on to sleep. I'll see you in the morning."

Olivia found herself left, chilled, and confused, as her absolute Gordian knot of a husband fled the room as if she'd splashed fire on him instead of water. "Hot. Cold. Hot. Cold." She fell backward onto the pillows with her empty arms flung wide. "God, a sword if you please."

Alexander the Great had used a sword to slice through the knotted puzzle that had mystified thousands in ancient Phrygia. Olivia was going to have to use something slightly more subtle.

At least, she would if she could figure out what.

19

The next morning, Olivia waited in the carriage as the servants ran to and fro, securing the things that had been used overnight to the wagon and carriages. Everyone seemed to know precisely what to do. Dane must have made this journey often in the past. Olivia had gathered from Mrs. Huff that the previous Viscount Greenleigh had favored Kirkall to Greenleigh and that Dane had visited him there as often as possible.

Finally, Dane and Marcus separated themselves from the madness and strode toward the carriage. Olivia sat back quickly and smoothed her skirts, preparing to welcome her husband with a smile. She wasn't sure she was the source of Dane's turmoil last night, but she was determined to do nothing to add to it today. She would be the perfectly poised, gracious, *graceful* Viscountess Greenleigh.

Walter used to tell her that every day was a fresh start. Today she would give Dane no cause to regret his choice. Today she was a new and improved Olivia.

As Dane approached, a footman hurried to open the

carriage door, but Dane only leaned his head into the carriage. "I believe I shall ride again today, my dear. Marcus will keep you company."

Olivia felt her smile begin to slip and pulled it back with a will. "Of course. I do envy you the fresh air, my lord. I'm sure you will enjoy your ride immensely." She turned her gracious-if-it-killed-her smile onto Lord Dryden. "I shall be delighted to share the carriage with you, Marcus. Won't we be a merry pair?"

Marcus quirked his lips and nodded as he mounted the steps and sat opposite her. Of course he had ridden with her last evening when she'd been a bit damp and depressed. Olivia doubled the brightness of her smile. "I'm feeling very much better today," she said. "The sun is shining and we shall arrive tonight. I am very eager to see Kirkall."

Dane grunted. "There will be foul weather later. We'll push hard to beat it to the lodge." He spared a nod to Olivia. "I shall see you later today." Then he shut the door and strode to his mount, his well-built body full of coiled-spring tension. He looked like a great cat with an itch to kill something.

Olivia turned from her view of Dane's back to see Marcus watching him with concern as well. Then Marcus smiled and sat back on the velvet cushions. "And how shall we pass the time, my lady? Are you fond of anagrams?"

Word games. Olivia refrained from making a face. A viscountess would never make a face. She nodded sedately. "If you like, my lord. Shall I begin?" He nodded graciously. "Hmm." A smile flickered across her lips. "Render sundry red."

Marcus closed his eyes for a long moment. "Render . . . surrender—" His eyes popped open and he laughed aloud. "Surrender, Dryden!"

He shook his head, still laughing. "I think I may have met my match, my lady. Very well, you choose the game."

"Well." She pursed her lips. "There is a game called 'Tell Me Amusing Stories about My Husband.'"

Marcus smiled conspiratorially. "I do know a few. Let's see, there was the time he leaped off a bridge to save a young lady—"

Olivia tilted her head at Marcus. "I saved him, you know. His feet sank into the mud like a draft horse."

Marcus frowned. "Oh, I suppose you know that one, then. I hadn't realized that time was you."

She blinked. "That time? Were there others?"

Marcus grinned. "Oh, lend me your ear, my lady."

Olivia settled down into her favorite position for listening to Walter's storytelling, curled up with her feet beside her on the cushions. "Go on," she said eagerly.

Outside the carriage, Dane rode a few yards ahead. It was not far enough to drown out the merry laughter coming from inside.

Marcus was only keeping her amused, just as Dane had asked. But how could he think with all that chiming laughter that made him think of her smile and her lips and her kiss—

He had to keep his mind on his mission, the immediate one and the grander one that consumed his life. He was the Lion. He could not let his attention and his judgment be pulled aside by a woman, no matter how magnetic.

Another trill of laughter rose on the air to tickle his attention awry. Marcus was certainly being charming. Dane didn't like it.

Moreover, he definitely didn't like the fact that he didn't like it.

The entire party was weary and more than ready for the journey to end by the time they pulled up to the gates of Kirkall.

The gatekeeper was ready for them and had torch-bearers run before the carriages through the closing gloom of the day. Olivia had eventually fallen into trivial conversation with Marcus, then silence. Then she had curled up on her side of the carriage to sleep. Not a very viscountess-like thing to do, but it was only Marcus after all. He might as well have been Walter, she felt so comfortable with him.

Olivia took a footman's hand to step out of the carriage and looked about for Dane. He was difficult to miss, for he was standing in the center of the activity, directing the chaos into order.

Marcus took her elbow. "I'll go in with you. I've been here a few times, so I know my way about."

Olivia smiled at him, then stopped as she caught sight of Kirkall Hall. "Why don't they call it Kirkall Castle?" It certainly looked like a castle to her. The dark stone walls rose up to lose themselves in round towers vaguely outlined in the gray mist that hung low over them. Tall, narrow windows looked as though they might have archers ready within even now.

In the daytime, it would be either lovely or looming. At this time of the evening, it looked rather magical.

She smiled at Marcus. "How wonderful. I shall be the lady of the castle. You shall be a knight."

"If I am the knight, then what is Dane?"

Olivia turned to gaze at her husband, who had not exchanged six words with her all day. "The dragon? The ogre?" She turned back to Marcus with a smile. "The giant?"

He threw back his head and laughed. Olivia saw Dane turn his head toward them for the first time. His expression was unreadable at this distance, but he was definitely not smiling.

Olivia smiled anyway and waved gaily at him. Just because he was in a mood was no reason not to enjoy being at Kirkall at last.

Then she saw a footman stepping into her carriage to retrieve the small items within. With a start she remembered the case of rods. Dashing through the lines of servants carrying in bundles and baggage, Olivia caught the fellow as he left the carriage with his arms full.

"I shall take my . . . my cosmetics case."

The fellow looked down at his burden. "I'm sorry, my lady. I don't think I have it."

He didn't, so Olivia waved him on and clambered into the carriage to feel beneath the seat. She'd put it all the way back on that side. . . .

There was nothing. Perhaps it had slid over during the journey. She went down on her knees to search thoroughly beneath the seat.

Oh no. Her stomach flipped over. She wriggled around until she could search beneath the other seat. Nothing.

She jumped from the carriage and sought out Sumner.

"Sumner! Did you carry in my cosmetics case already?"

He blinked at her vaguely. "The carved box? No, my lady. I haven't seen it since I loaded your carriage in London."

Olivia felt sick. What if someone opened it? She'd made such a point of carrying it herself—everyone on the staff knew it was hers.

Wait. No need to fret. She forced herself to breathe deeply. They knew it belonged to her. Therefore, it would surely end up in her chamber, untouched. She was Lady Greenleigh after all. No one would paw through her things.

Still, she'd best find her room before Petty began to unpack her baggage!

She found Marcus again, who showed her to the bedchamber traditionally used by the mistress of the house. Petty was already there, brushing out gowns and directing her sisters to prepare the room to Petty's high expectations.

Olivia cast her eye about the room and even re-arranged a stack of hatboxes, but the case was nowhere to be found. There was no help for it.

"Petty, have you seen a carved case?" She held out her hands to measure. "About this size?"

Petty scarcely looked up from her fluffing. "Oh, that gift from Mrs. B.?"

"G—gift? Did you, ah, did you look inside?"

Petty lifted her head and frowned at Olivia. "Of course not, my lady. It were latched."

Olivia took a breath. "Right. Latched. So no chance anyone will peek?"

Petty, Letty, and Betty all turned to look at her

oddly. Oops. She spread her hands apologetically. "It's only that it's . . . intended to be a surprise for his lordship. So I need to find it."

Sumner entered, carrying an unsteady pile of items that threatened to fall. Petty jumped up to help him, elbowing her sisters out of the way while smiling sweetly at the fellow.

"Did you find your cosmetics, my lady?"

Luckily, Petty was too busy simpering to notice the sudden cavernous hole in Olivia's story. "Er, no. Do please check the other rooms, Sumner."

He blinked at her. "All of them?"

She bit the inside of her mouth to keep from losing her composure. "Well, you may stop looking when you've found it. Will that do?"

He scurried away and Olivia went back to quietly panicking. The box was latched. No one would look inside. Sumner was searching.

Everything would work out and she wouldn't have to tell Dane that the box full of ancient ivory penises was roaming freely about Kirkall Hall.

Dane finally retreated from what was really Kinsworth's and Mrs. Huff's turf and let his staff do their jobs. Taking charge had served to keep him from having to speak to Olivia or Marcus for several hours. Now it was late and he likely wouldn't have to speak to anyone until tomorrow.

Then the guests would arrive and everyone would promptly retire to prepare for the Hunt Ball tomorrow night.

It flashed across Dane's mind that he still didn't know what sort of entertainment Olivia had arranged. Then he decided it really didn't matter. Whatever party the Prince Regent attended became George's party anyway. He did tend to sweep everyone up into his enthusiasm, whether it be for drinking, eating, or flirting.

Dane entered a bedchamber, then halted. The chamber was cold and unlit, the furniture still hung with dust cloths. This was his old room, the one he'd used since he'd been moved out of the nursery.

He was lord of Kirkall Hall now.

He turned and left the silent room. The master's chamber was down another hall. As Dane found the doorway to the room that had been his father's, he glanced at the next door. Olivia would be ensconced in there, undoubtedly too exhausted from her tiring day of having far too much merriment with Marcus.

He was being childish, of course. He'd been the one to ask Marcus to ride with her. Of course, Marcus hadn't seemed at all reluctant to help out. . . .

Dane shook off those infectious thoughts. He'd been the Lion too long. He was seeing conspiracy everywhere.

He entered the master's chamber to find it lit and warmed by a cheerful blaze in the hearth. All trace of his father's things had been removed. It was just another room.

The study, on the other hand, was going to be a problem. He didn't think he could go into it without seeing his father lying there, looking broken and empty, with the pistol still smoking in his hand.

So he wouldn't use it. He'd lock it up and use another room. A study was simply a room with a desk, after all.

He strode to his dressing table and tore his cravat off with quick, hard jerks. Where the hell was Proffit?

He undressed himself to trousers and pulled on a dressing gown. He wanted some bread and cheese and tea. There was no one in the hall. In fact, there wasn't a single servant in sight.

Dane had the sudden eerie feeling that he was in the wrong house. Ridiculous. He shook it off. *"Proffit,"* he bellowed down the silent hallway.

A door opened behind him. "They're busy."

He turned to see Olivia standing in her doorway, huddled in her wrapper. "Busy doing what, might I ask?"

Her gaze dropped. "Busy searching for the Rods of the Rajah," she murmured.

Searching? Dane felt a pounding in his head. "You lost the Rods of the Rajah? *Here?* They're rattling about somewhere in *this* house?" His father's house. Ivory penises, left out where anyone could find them.

He rarely raised his voice. It was certainly raised now. "Do you have any idea the caliber of guests we have arriving tomorrow?"

"How could I?" she asked resentfully. " 'Forty guests' could be almost anyone!"

"Trust me when I say that they are forty powerful, influential guests!" At least no one was bringing along innocent maiden daughters. He rubbed both hands over his face. He hadn't slept at all last night, instead pacing Marcus's room until his friend had thrown a pillow at him and told him to pace in the tavern.

"Aren't you even a little upset about the other part?"

Dane dropped his hands, prepared for the worst. "There's more?"

She folded her arms, staring at him as if *he'd* upset *her*!

"Yes, there's more. Without the last rod, we cannot finish the training."

He let out a weary breath. "Oh, that." He shrugged. "I cannot worry about that now."

She gazed at him for a long moment, her eyes hurt and confused. Then she slipped back into her room and quietly shut the door.

20

The sky had scarcely lightened the next morning when Petty flew into Olivia's bedchamber. "My lady! My lady, wake up! The Duke and Duchess of Halswick have arrived early!"

Olivia woke instantly and completely, ice suddenly forming in her stomach. Duke and duchess?

Do you have any idea the caliber of guests we have arriving tomorrow?

As if her thought had summoned him, Dane strode through the connecting door in trousers and shirt, Proffit trailing after him with his arms full of clothing and Dane's cravat flying from his hand.

"Petty, go make sure the blue room is ready," Dane barked. "Her Grace favors blue." Petty took off at a run. Olivia scrambled behind her dressing screen, pulling off her nightdress while Dane continued.

"Olivia, have Mrs. Huff prepare a hearty breakfast for us all. His Grace must have traveled through the night. I think it is safe to say they will be hungry."

He snatched his weskit from Proffit and shrugged it

on. "Her Grace is known for her finicky tastes. Tell the kitchen staff that she will only drink tepid water laced with lemon and she will require a plate containing precisely nine dates before she goes to bed every night."

Dane strode back and forth with Proffit trailing him, handing him items to put on.

"The tepid water is because her teeth hurt her and the dates are for her digestion. She requires buttermilk with every meal. Then there are the kippers—"

Petty rushed back in. "Her Grace is already in her room. Her maid said she's well satisfied with it." She began to help Olivia dress behind the screen.

Sumner followed Betty in carrying her coal bucket for her. The morning gown went over Olivia's head, muffling Dane's instructions. She stuck her head out from behind the screen. "What was that about kippers?"

Dane stopped to gaze at her coolly. "Weren't you listening? I said you must never serve kippers at any table containing Her Grace. The very smell of them makes her violently ill."

Ew. "Right. No kippers."

"Her Grace will have her own staff giving her requests to the kitchen, but it is up to you as the lady of the house to personally make sure her specific needs are met."

Petty was doing up the buttons on her gown, so Olivia stuck her hand up from behind the screen like a schoolchild. "Will there be any more such particular guests arriving today?"

"We'll discuss that later. Right now, Her Grace will be preparing to meet us in the breakfast room."

Proffit tied the last perfect loop into the knot in

Dane's cravat. Dressed to perfection, Dane strode to the door. "We must get there first, Olivia."

Olivia, with one stocking on and her hair still in a braid, glared around the screen at her husband. "That is easy for you to say. I wear twice the garments you do."

Dane remained unsympathetic. "I'll expect you within moments," he said, and left.

Olivia closed her eyes. "Betty, Sumner, go down and make sure the kitchen staff knows about the water and the dates and the buttermilk and . . . what was the other thing?"

"Kippers, my lady."

"Yes, the kippers. Go. Hurry."

With the male intruders finally gone, Olivia threw herself into the chair before her dressing table. "Hair, Petty, quickly!"

Moments later, just as Dane had commanded, dressed and hair temporarily tamed with an embarrassment of pins, Olivia was ready to greet her first guests in the breakfast room. She did think it was a bit rude of them to arrive at cock's crow with a list of demands, but apparently a duke and duchess made their own manners.

She and Dane waited. And waited. She wished she could sit, but there was no doubt in her mind that the moment her rear touched the cushion, the persnickety Duchess of Halswick would make her entrance.

The door opened and Olivia straightened and pasted a welcoming smile on her face. Kinsworth entered. "My lord, my lady, Lord and Lady Reardon have just arrived."

Olivia's smile turned real. "Have more places set immediately, Kinsworth."

The butler eyed her without expression. "Yes, my lady."

At that moment, the servants' door opened in the wall paneling and a flurry of activity left the table beautifully set for six. Olivia took a breath. Right. The Greenleigh staff certainly didn't need her to tell them what to do.

By the time Kinsworth returned to announce Lord and Lady Reardon, Olivia was dying to see a friendly face. Willa's fit the bill entirely, and Olivia even received a brief, cheerful hug. "I hear the Duchess of Halswick is here," Willa whispered to her. "Did anyone remember to tell you about the kippers?"

Oh no. The kippers. She ought to have checked on that before coming to await the duchess. Should she remind Kinsworth?

The thought of the butler's dry contempt made her hesitate. Then again, Dane had instructed her to see to it *personally*—

At that moment, Kinsworth entered once more, faint bemusement etched on his face. "Lord and Lady Cheltenham have arrived, accompanied by Miss Absentia Hackerman."

Oh no. Mother wouldn't!

Apparently, she would. Lady Cheltenham must have heard about the house party and the ball through her gossip web and decided that Olivia couldn't very well throw her out on the drive, Hackerman girl and all.

Although, by the furious look on Dane's face as he turned to glare at Olivia, that might actually be a possibility.

To make matters worse, Lord and Lady Reardon

obviously knew something was amiss. Nate sent Dane a mystified glance and Willa blinked and frowned slightly. "I, ah, didn't realize I would have the pleasure of seeing your parents again so soon."

Olivia swallowed. "My . . . what a . . . happy surprise for us all."

The staff did their magical plate performance again, making the arrangement for nine look as though it had been planned for weeks. Just then, Kinsworth announced the Duke and Duchess of Halswick and Lord and Lady Cheltenham and—*dear God, why did they have to bring her?*—Miss Absentia Hackerman.

She was going to kill Mother for this.

If she could find her behind the roundly voluptuous Duchess of Halswick. Somehow Olivia had imagined a spare, er, more abstemious sort of lady, not this brightly gowned dish of tightly corseted female flesh and jiggling décolletage.

The duchess threw herself down in her chair and waved them all down as well. "Sit. Sit. You can put me through the introductions later. I'm completely fagged, you know. Can't bear the carriage. Makes me queasy."

As they sat, plates appeared before them containing perfect coddled eggs and artfully arranged slivers of ham. Tea for the ladies, coffee for the gentlemen, buttermilk for the duchess, all done so smoothly that it was as though their minds were being read. Olivia began to relax.

The duchess crammed a large forkful of eggs into her mouth and kept speaking. "I made him ride all night, just to get it over with, didn't I, Ducky?"

The Duke of Halswick was elderly and nearly blind, if one correctly deduced the reason his nose was nearly in his plate. Ducky didn't answer.

The duchess waved her fork in the air. Lord Reardon neatly ducked a splat of eggs. "Anyway, I said to Ducky—"

She stopped, mouth open. Olivia had never seen a human being go from pink to green in less than a second. "Your Grace, are you—?"

"Kippers!" The duchess clapped her hand over her mouth and shot up from the table, causing her glass of buttermilk to flood the table. Everyone except the elderly duke rose abruptly as well, but there was no helping the woman. She dashed from one side of the room to the other, her vast bosom bouncing high, obviously looking for some vessel to—

The Duchess of Halswick fled through the door, there to heave violently onto the carpet down the hall.

The Greenleigh staff rushed to help her, quickly followed by the Halswick servants.

The breakfast party remained standing at the table, shocked motionless by the sounds still echoing through Kirkall Hall.

Lady Reardon placed a plump hand over her own mouth, swallowing hard. Miss Hackerman quietly snickered, then wiped the amusement from her face when Dane turned his furious gaze on her.

He threw down the napkin still clutched in his hand and strode around the table to the duchess's plate. With a fork he flipped her now-congealing eggs over to reveal—

"Kippers." Dane's voice was flat and ominous. Three fishy little herring eyes gazed accusingly at Olivia. Dane dropped the fork to clink loudly on the plate.

Olivia flinched at the sound. "I thought—"

Dane cut through her stammer with one word. *"Personally,"* he said flatly. "I told you to see to this *personally."* His hard blue gaze stabbed her right through the heart. "I cannot understand how a hostess of your experience could allow this to happen." He turned and stalked from the room.

Crushed, Olivia slid her horrified gaze about the rest of the table. Her mother looked indignant and properly horrified, as if Olivia had ruined *her* breakfast party. Father looked vaguely disappointed and concerned.

Abbie Hackerman stood with her hands folded demurely before her, but her face shone with spiteful satisfaction. If Olivia hadn't been so sure that Abbie had only just arrived—

Yet worse than any of that was the pity glittering from Lady Reardon's eyes.

Olivia felt her hands begin to shake. She was a pathetic excuse for a viscountess and now the world would know it. Miss Hackerman would make sure of that.

A last resounding retch echoed loudly down the hall. The Duke of Halswick raised his head from his plate and blinked blearily at them. "Is that my Pippy?" He turned back to his plate, pushing his eggs about with a shaky fork. "She must have got hold of some herring."

"I'm s—sorry. I'm so sorry—" Olivia turned and ran away from the breakfast room and past the crowd gathering down the hall. She took the stairs at a run, her eyes beginning to blur. She'd never seen Dane like that before, so hard and cruel, not even that night in the inn. The look in his eyes!

She ran down the upstairs hall, gasping from her swift climb. Her room was close—

She rounded the corner and ran full-speed into a solid wall of dark green superfine. "Whoa there!" She felt herself grabbed and steadied. "Olivia? Olivia, what is it?"

She blinked and swallowed, shaking her head sharply. "Oh, Marcus—" She looked up into his face.

His worried jade gaze cost her the last of her control. He was so much like Walter. "Oh, *Marcus*!" She threw herself upon his chest so forcefully that he staggered back. His arms came about her, his hands awkwardly patting her back.

The story poured out of her, out of sequence and incoherent, yet Marcus seemed to understand every word. "Shh. Shh." He smoothed her hair. "It can't be as bad as all that."

She shook her head, smearing tears across his weskit front. "It is! It is just that bad, and worse! It is as though someone is conspiring against me! And Dane said—Dane said—"

She fell apart again, the sobs coming from deep within her, from the place that had known all along that she was going to fail, that she would never be able to fool anyone, that she was never going to be good enough—

Marcus held her more tightly, chuckling softly. "Livvie, Livvie, it's only a house party. The Season is over. By the time March rolls around again, no one will remember anything about this. For that matter, after tonight's Hunt Ball and your marvelous mystery entertainment, no one will remember it tomorrow!"

Marcus's words filtered through her misery. Perhaps . . . perhaps he was correct. Mrs. Blythe's hired performers should arrive at any time. There was every chance that the ball would be a resounding success, eclipsing this morning's fiasco into obscurity.

She sniffed back her tears and tried to catch her breath.

"That's the ticket," Marcus said soothingly, his arms still around her. "Breathe deep now."

She did as he said, releasing that breath with a shaky smile. She swiped at her face with one hand. "Oh heavens. I've ruined your weskit."

"I never liked it anyway," he said with a grin. "Now, run and wash your face and change your gown." He dropped a quick kiss on her brow.

Olivia tilted her head back to look up at him in surprise. "Walter used to do that," she murmured.

Something flashed in Marcus's eyes as he gazed down at her. "So it's brother I'm to be," he said softly. He ran his knuckles gently down her cheek, erasing away a last tear. "I suppose that's just as it should be—"

"Olivia!" Dane's deep exclamation separated them with a jolt.

Olivia's gaze flew to the top of the stairs where her husband stood, his face like granite. He strode toward them, filling the hall with his size. Marcus pushed Olivia behind him, then held up both hands before him.

"Dane, calm down. She is upset, that is all. I only—"

Dane could only see the way they'd stood so close together, Marcus's arms about her, his hand on her cheek, her face upturned to his, ready for Marcus's kiss—

The pain was lethal, like a sword to his heart.

He didn't even remember hitting Marcus, but there his closest friend was, downed on the carpet. Olivia knelt beside him, patting his face and checking his pupils.

She looked up at Dane, her gaze confused. "What are you doing? He's your friend!"

Dane fled the pain and the sharp awareness that had sprung to life within him.

He loved her. It was astonishing and uncanny—and absolutely the worst thing that could ever happen to him.

Down the stairs and out the door, around the house to the stables. His stride grew and his pace quickened. He wasn't running—quite. The grooms must have seen him coming, for his favorite horse, a white stallion called Galahad, was already nearly saddled by the time Dane strode into the stables.

He mounted Galahad straightaway and rode through the stable door, ducking low. The big hooves hit the gravel drive hard, sending pebbles flying behind them.

21

Olivia made it to the front door of Kirkall Hall just in time to see Dane race by her, his gaze hard on the horizon, his jaw set. *"Dane!"* She picked up her skirts and ran after him. "Dane!"

He was already out of earshot. She saw the horse leave the long drive and race off toward the large wood to the east.

He was gone. Olivia staggered to a halt, breathing hard, and stood there dumbfounded at how her wonderful new life had turned to rubbish in just inside an hour.

The rattle of carriage wheels on the gravel drive penetrated Olivia's hurt and confusion. Another delivery. At least the remaining guests were not expected for several hours yet. She didn't think she could bear to deal with more strangers now—especially highborn strangers who would expect her to be what she was very evidently not.

She stepped to one side and turned, prepared to wave the delivery around to the back of the house.

Oh no. A grand, ornate coach and four rounded the drive, heading right for her. The horses stepped high despite their journey, as only the finest of stock could do. Under the dust and grime of the road, the buckles on the horses' tack gleamed with the unmistakable sheen of gold.

The polished ebony coach itself was large, luxurious, and positively draped in footmen, footmen wearing the unmistakable gold on white livery of—

Oh-dear-God-in-heaven. Olivia's knees went weak. It couldn't be. This was a dream—a nightmare containing all her worst fears and imaginings. Only in a nightmare would she be standing in the drive looking like a madwoman, her hair wild, her face undoubtedly ruddy, her slippers left somewhere back down the drive. . . .

She closed her eyes. She wished she could wake up now. She wished she would open her eyes and see the ceiling of her bedchamber, having never sat down to that unspeakable breakfast, having never stepped into Marcus's arms, having never seen that look in Dane's eyes, and most deeply, fervently, especially she wished that she was not about to greet the Prince Regent of all Britain in her bare feet.

The crunch of wheels stopped directly before her. Olivia opened her eyes just as the rather astounding number of footmen burst into action. Two ran forward to take the reins of the horses so they shouldn't take the merest step that might unbalance His Highness. Two more ran to the back of the coach to unstrap a finely carved stepping stool—very nearly a set of stairs all on its own—and juggled it into position by the carriage door. Another young man stepped forward smartly to dust the stool with a silken cloth—for apparently such a task was too much for the two who had put it in place.

For a giddy moment Olivia wondered how that young man's pay was entered into the palace housekeeping ledger. His Highness's First Orderly of the Stool? Royal Stepping-stoolie?

Then a foot clad in a surprisingly dainty slipper stepped from the interior of the carriage onto the highest step of the stool. That's when it occurred to Olivia for the first time that His Highness had not rolled up her drive by accident. She and Dane were hosting a house party and a Hunt Ball.

The Prince Regent was one of her guests.

For an eternal moment she couldn't draw a breath. Having the prince stay was an honor, a privilege—an event that most ladies would have spent months preparing for. Mother had spoken many times of one lady who had ordered a set of china designed just for the occasion and then demanded the molds be broken so that no one else might claim that *their* plates had been touched by the Royal Fork.

Yet Dane had never said a word. Betrayal stole Olivia's breath. He demanded that she be Society's premier hostess—and then he cut her feet from under her with his own sword.

Nothing she had prepared could possibly live up to a Royal Visit. Not her menus, not her decorations, not her wardrobe—

Oh God. She was His Highness's hostess!

She looked down at herself, but nothing had changed. She was still rumpled and barefoot, and there was a whitish stain running down the front of her skirt.

A beringed hand reached out to grasp the open door for balance. Olivia remembered her manners and dropped in the lowest curtsy she could manage without getting her face any dirtier than it already was. Oh God, was that sour buttermilk on her skirt?

It was, and worse.

"Oh, get up, girl!" The much-imitated Royal Voice was terse and strained.

Olivia rose quickly—too quickly. Her head bumped something on the way up—hard. In horror, she looked up to see the Prince Regent of all Britain rubbing his chin in pain.

"Clumsy wench!" The First Knight of the Stool pushed Olivia away, making her stumble in the gravel.

The prince flicked the man away with an impatient gesture. "Good God," he muttered, testing his jaw. "Spare me bumbling housemaids! If this is the best Greenleigh can do, I'd best get back in that thrice-bedamned arse-shattering carriage!"

Olivia's head hurt, but worse was the ache in her chest. Dane had been afraid she would fail and she was, miserably. The prince was about to leave in a well-deserved huff. And why not, when she had butted the Royal Jaw with all her might?

With horror, she felt the tears coming. She pressed both hands over her eyes, but it was all just too bloody much! The final humiliation seemed almost fitting, after all.

She burst into tears in front of Prince George.

Dane was halfway across the wood before he remembered that the Prince Regent was due any moment and he'd forgotten to explain that to Olivia. George was apt to get up to some sort of mischief if not carefully watched and Dane wanted to be ready to steer his highness toward some of the ladies he had invited to the ball.

Dane pulled Galahad to a halt. The stallion reared, protesting having his run cut short. Dane leaned down to pat the thick white neck before him.

Olivia had laughed when he'd introduced her to Galahad two days ago. "Galahad? The Virgin Stallion? Am I the only one who thinks that is odd?"

A reluctant chuckle escaped Dane. Olivia never could keep the first thing in her mind from flying from her lips.

He sat up, drawing in a deep breath. He knew Marcus would never covet another man's wife. He believed that Olivia was about as devious as a clear, blue sky. Even the ridiculous kippers incident must have been a simple mistake, not some sort of carelessness.

It wasn't them he was riding away from, he realized. It was himself.

He could not allow himself to love Olivia. There was no place for love in the Lion's life—no room for anything but duty.

His first mistake was in believing that he could attach her passions without incurring any such response within himself. Any man without worldly experience would be susceptible, especially to a woman such as Olivia.

So he simply wouldn't permit it. If he stayed away from her—if he kept from her bed for a while, avoided the warm, generous clasp of her arms—surely the feeling would fade. People fell in and out of love all the time, after all. Passions flared and then went to ash. That was the natural process of the human heart.

He would withdraw to a position of cool unconcern until the passion wore itself out. When he was sure that he could refrain from involving himself too deeply in her, he would go to her again. He wasn't sure how long it would take, but they had the rest of their lives together to iron it out.

With relief, Dane reined Galahad into a turn and urged the stallion to a gallop back across the wood to Kirkall Hall.

When Dane returned to the house, Kinsworth informed him that His Royal Highness had already arrived.

More carriages were rolling up the drive. "Where is her ladyship?"

Kinsworth blinked owlishly. "I'm sure I don't know, my lord."

"What of Lord Dryden?"

"His lordship has had a fall and is in his room recovering."

That was best not thought on.

Despite the missing mistress, it was clear that the household had the preparations in hand. Dane turned to greet the arriving guests on his own, growing more concerned about his missing wife by the moment. Where had she disappeared to?

The last guests arrived and installed in their rooms, the last servant directed belowstairs, the last carriage gone from the drive, Dane was finally able to turn his attention to finding his truant bride. His misconduct this morning should not have kept her from her duty as Viscountess Greenleigh.

Dane found Olivia in the last place he expected.

When George's manservant announced Dane, he strode into the vast boudoir that had already been set up in the east wing and saw none other than the missing Olivia comfortably ensconced on a sofa next to George, her hand in his.

The pain struck again. Fortunately, Dane was prepared for it this time. He did not send his ruler to the carpet with a blow.

"Your Highness." Dane bowed stiffly. "I see no introductions are necessary."

Olivia smiled tentatively at him, but Dane turned away from her. Cool unconcern.

George was obviously quite smitten, however. It had been Dane's goal from the outset, though he'd not foreseen this precise turn of events.

Olivia, for her part, seemed at ease with George. But then, she had a knack for being pleasing. The degree of which Dane himself had only today begun to grasp. "I see that my lady wife has everything . . . well in hand." At his emphasis, he saw Olivia's eyes widen with startled understanding.

Dane bowed again. "If you will excuse me, Your Highness, I must see to the other guests." He turned to Olivia. "Please continue to see to His Highness's needs," he instructed her coolly.

After all, he had been hoping to find a likely woman to throw in George's path. He might currently be distracted by his passion for Olivia, but his duty came first. If she was what George wanted, then she was what George would get, no matter the cost.

Leaving the room, Dane was stunned to realize that

it all fitted quite beautifully together, now that he saw it clearly. He could control George through Olivia, for hadn't she proved herself nigh irresistible to himself?

It was a perfect plan. Dane simply hadn't realized it would hurt so much.

When her husband turned and left her in George's room to "service" him, Olivia was beyond being hurt. She was furious and quite willing to let Dane stew in his own juice. George smiled at her, kindly and interested as he had been since she'd burst into tears, but Olivia put a stop to that as well.

"I'm sorry, Your Highness, but I fear my heart belongs to that insufferable horse's arse who just left."

George was disappointed but cheerful. "That young man needs to be hoisted on his own petard," the prince said thoughtfully. "Manipulative lot they are."

Olivia turned to gaze at the Prince Regent. "And yet you trust him, and his friends, do you not?" She had many questions about what Dane and his group of gentlemen were up to, but she had no doubts. She knew Dane was honorable. The question was—did Prince George?

For the merest moment, the Prince Regent wiped the lazy, foolish facade from his expression and gazed back at her somberly. "I would trust him with my life. More, with my kingdom."

Then he grinned devilishly. "That doesn't mean I have to make things easy for him. He and his cohorts believe me to be thoughtless and hedonistic, interested in only pleasures of the flesh."

He said it casually enough, but Olivia didn't think

he felt easy at all about that estimation of himself. "That's ridiculous," Olivia said staunchly. "Mother took me to see Carlton House and I saw the drawings of the Brighton palace in the news sheet. You're nothing short of brilliant."

He tilted his head, giving her a pleased, rather shy smile. "Do you really think so? Are you conversant with architecture?"

She shook her head with a smile. "Only as it applies to rebuilding flour mills and such, I fear. But beauty is beauty, is it not?"

He chucked her under the chin softly, naughty invitation in his eyes. "Indeed. Are you sure you don't want to come away with me and leave that horse's arse to his own devices?"

Her eyes began to burn again and she looked away. "Thank you, but no. I happen to be very attached to that horse's arse, although currently I can't for the life of me remember why."

The prince laughed, tapping her lightly on the nose with one finger. "Mayhap because he is a handsome blond giant of a man?"

"Well, yes." She blinked. "Then again, there are many handsome men in the world. I feel nothing for any other."

George shook his head. "Lucky bastard," he said as if to himself. "If you were mine, I'd call me out, prince or no."

Olivia sniffed back her tears and smiled at him. "You're sweet."

He clapped a hand to his chest and fell back on the cushions. "A direct hit, my lady!" He grinned regretfully at her. "When a bloke hears that, he knows he hasn't a chance in hell."

Not knowing quite what to say to that, Olivia could only shrug helplessly.

George laughed at her and sat up once more. "I say we give the Dane a taste of his own medicine." He bowed playfully over her hand. "Will you be my escort to the Hunt Ball tonight? Play along with me, dear lady. I promise that His Arseness will suffer for it."

Olivia took one last look at the door, her eyes narrowed. Under her anger roiled blank desolation, for what sort of husband would turn and leave his wife in another man's hands, prince or not?

Dane had left her here to satisfy His Highness, like an unwanted lady-bird. She raised her chin and smiled at George. "It would be my pleasure, Your Highness."

22

Kirkall Hall was alight with a thousand beeswax candles, their sweetness filling the air as they lit the way for two-and-twenty couples, one prince, one slightly bruised earl, and one rather petulant shipping heiress to waltz the evening away at Lord and Lady Greenleigh's Hunt Ball. There was otherwise an astonishing lack of young ladies present. Olivia was beginning to have her suspicions about Dane's reasons for this event.

The musicians Mrs. Blythe had recommended were performing beautifully, Mrs. Arnold's late supper had been exquisite, the house itself gleamed with polish, and the staff stepped lively to keep every guest perfectly happy.

The Duchess of Halswick had speedily recovered when she learned that the Prince Regent was in attendance. She had even forgone her evening cup of buttermilk, confiding to Lady Reardon that it made her breath stink. Willa had professed extreme doubt at any such thing—from a discreet distance—and then quickly moved away.

Olivia gazed at the scene from her place at the side of Prince George. She'd done rather well, she decided indifferently. Even her mother seemed impressed. Unfortunately, the only person whose opinion she cared about was brooding by the refreshments, his looming black-clad figure frightening everyone away from the cool drinks and confections offered there.

George glanced her way and saw where her gaze tended to stray. He patted her hand where it rested on his arm. "Time for us to dance, my dear."

Olivia nodded and allowed him to lead her to the floor, their hands held high. The musicians immediately swung into a waltz tune, for it was well known to be the Prince Regent's favorite dance.

Thankfully, Olivia was an accomplished dancer. Dancing with her parents and Walter had whiled away many a snowy evening at Cheltenham, when nothing else seemed to keep them warm.

She moved lightly in George's arms and he raised a brow, impressed. "What a lovely partner you make, Lady Greenleigh. Now, throw your head back and laugh as if I've said something entirely amusing. It will keep up my reputation as a shameless rake and it'll make that great idiot over there jealous." He wiggled his brows suggestively.

Olivia managed a smile. "You're—"

"Sweet. Yes, so I've heard. Don't bandy it about, will you? I've a certain standing in Society as an overindulgent lecher."

Now she truly did laugh, making George swing her faster about the floor. The other couples gave way before His Highness and soon they had the center of the ballroom to themselves.

Olivia caught sight of Dane's black expression as she turned. He looked miserable. She immediately felt better. "I think he's spotted us."

"I think he's gutted and skinned us," George said after he'd checked Dane's location. "Or me, at least, in his imagination."

Olivia decided to change the subject. "Have you noticed that aside from Miss Hackerman there are no young ladies present?"

George looked at her oddly. "Yes, that had come to my attention."

" 'Tis odd, is it not?" Olivia said absently. Dane's discomfort made her realize something wonderful. He did care that she was with George, just as he had cared that she stood too close to Marcus.

Dane, her casually composed husband with the genial facade, cared very, very deeply.

A warm glow began deep within her. She smiled cheerfully at George, who grinned back, surprised. If she was correct, then tonight she would go to Dane, ready for him at last.

So the fifth rod had been lost. It made little difference. None of them had been terribly difficult to bear. She was sure she could accept Dane if they were careful and took their time.

The thought of being in his arms again made white-hot shivers go through her. As the waltz came to a close, Olivia turned to George to thank him for his great courtesy and comfort but to tell him that she needed to seek out her husband.

At that moment, the ballroom doors burst open and a barbarian army of scantily clad women danced in, bearing a litter with what looked to be a naked flower-covered virgin sacrifice aboard it.

Mrs. Blythe's entertainment had arrived.

When Dane saw his wife shiver with pleasure in the Prince Regent's arms, he couldn't bear it anymore. Tossing the drink he'd not been drinking into a potted palm, he turned to stride from the ballroom.

Marcus caught up with him in the back hall. "Dane, you're an ass."

Dane didn't stop. "How flattering. I'm so moved."

Marcus grabbed Dane's arm to halt him. "I wasn't poaching. I wasn't even flirting! I was . . . I was only thinking. Just for a moment. A single thought, of what if she'd rescued *me* instead."

Dane whirled. "She *told* you about that?"

Marcus rolled his eyes. "Dane, she talks about nothing *but* you." He threw out his hands. "I had to sit through an entire day in the carriage with her, listening to a litany of the manly virtues of Dane the Mighty Viking Viscount!"

Dane blinked. "She called me a mighty Viking?"

Marcus nodded wearily. "So I spared a moment to wonder what it would be like to have a woman be mad for me that way. That is all. Completely. Olivia thinks of me—" He rubbed the back of his neck. "I remind her of her brother," he muttered.

Dane narrowed his eyes at his friend. "Well, you do have that . . . that *brotherly* quality."

Marcus glared. "I do not. I am a very dangerous individual."

"You're too slow to block on your left. I shouldn't have been able to lay you out like that."

"I *let* you hit me," Marcus protested. "I deserved it." He rubbed his jaw. "I simply didn't think you were going to hit that hard."

Dane shrugged, feeling a little bit better. Olivia might be in the arms of the Prince Regent, but at least he'd not driven away his closest friend as well.

"So are you simply going to hand her over to be His Highness's plaything? You've only been wed a week!"

"Eight days," Dane corrected gruffly.

"I've never really liked this plan anyway, for if one woman could influence the prince for good, then couldn't another one just as easily influence the prince for bad?"

Dane stubbornly looked away. It was a good plan. He'd seen it in action.

"How can we really be sure we can trust any woman who would break her marriage vows like that?" Marcus had very firm ideas about adultery.

At the time, Dane had argued that most Society marriages tend to be rather open, at least once a woman had borne her husband an heir. His perception of marriage had always been that it was a business arrangement, not a matter of the heart.

All the ladies he had chosen to present to George had already had their sons and were known to be open to a bit of discreet dalliance. Most Society husbands would see the value of such a connection, especially if their wife brought a royal bastard home.

Dane truly didn't appreciate having his words thrown back in his face now.

Suddenly an uproar broke out in the ballroom. Wild cries and shocked screams echoed down to where they stood. Dane and Marcus turned as one and ran back down the hall.

The highborn guests of Lord and Lady Greenleigh's Hunt Ball shrank away from the outrageous display before them.

Several tall, broad-shouldered guards leaped out from where Olivia had stopped noticing them, to stand before the prince, who craned his neck vigorously. "Move, you great buggers! I want to see!"

They had cut Olivia off from him and the aghast crowd further forced her away. Olivia gazed about her at her horrified, scandalized, avid guests and saw her visions of social redemption come to a crashing end.

A new gasp erupted from the crowd, causing Olivia to yank her gaze back to the sight before her. There were nearly naked women, apparently clad in flowers, and now they had been joined by a nearly naked man, painted like a primitive, with a—oh dear, look at the size of that codpiece!

On closer inspection—well, suffice it to say that it wasn't a codpiece at all. Olivia felt faint. The "high priest" was dancing suggestively around the platform where the bound "virgin"—at least one assumed, since she wore primarily white flowers. Oh heavens, it didn't appear that she was wearing anything *else*!—writhed in cadence with the suspiciously appropriate music now coming from the players' balcony.

Apparently Mrs. Blythe was *that* kind of hostess.

Olivia stood, frozen, petrified, praying for a hole to open up in the lowlands of Scotland to swallow her down.

When Marcus and Dane first burst back through the ballroom doors, the cringing crowd momentarily pinned them on the far side of the room. They couldn't very well fight their way through, although from what they could see and hear, there was something seriously amiss in the center of the ballroom.

"Are those dancers naked?" Marcus hissed as they pushed their way gingerly through agog gentlemen and fainting ladies.

"No," Dane answered grimly. "They have flowers. And some feathers."

Marcus and Dane reached the edge of the clearing in time to see a muscular fellow raise a strange scepter high, apparently prepared to plunge it into his, er, enthusiastically moaning victim.

Dane recognized the scepter just as a cry cut through the music and mutters of the crowd.

"Give me that! That's *mine!*"

Oh God. She couldn't have just done what he thought she'd done.

Olivia burst from the crowd and snatched the fifth carved ivory penis from the "high priest" and clutched it to her bosom possessively.

Olivia hadn't been thinking of anything but disappearing until she'd spotted the fifth rod. Then the only thought in her mind was that she and Dane needed it to fulfill their dream of a family. It was when the case of rods went missing that all seemed to go wrong. Suddenly it seemed that their entire future hinged on that rod.

It wasn't until the first shrill laughter broke out that she realized what she had done.

23

Moments later, after Mrs. Blythe's dancers had been hustled out of the ballroom by red-faced and snickering footmen, Dane turned to Olivia.

"My lady, would you care to explain yourself?" His voice was tight and his gaze was furious.

Olivia knew there had been nothing in Mrs. Blythe's descriptions about such a performance and she couldn't bring herself to believe that the woman would purposely destroy her.

The rumors turning the staff against her. The missing rods. The *kippers.*

She opened her mouth to explain it all to Dane, but the chill in his gaze made her hesitate. She swallowed. "It seems . . . I believe . . . I'm being sabotaged."

His face hardened. "I should have respected you more for taking responsibility for your failure. You've made us into laughingstocks and you've compromised my . . . plans."

Olivia flinched, but raised her head high. "Your plans to manipulate the Prince Regent, you mean?"

Dane went very still, his gaze intent on hers. "What do you know of that?"

Olivia raised a brow calmly while bright hard spikes of humiliation and hurt spun inside her. "You said that all you needed was the right woman, did you not? You and Marcus, and Reardon and Wyndham—you wish to keep an eye on the Prince Regent, even in the bedchamber?"

Dane jerked slightly at that, then only nodded.

Olivia took a breath and shrugged slightly. "Then isn't that what this ball was for from the beginning? To find the Prince Regent's new mistress for him?"

He nodded again. His gaze was that of a stranger.

Olivia looked down at her hands clasped before her. She untangled her worried fingers and smoothed the front of her dress. Then she looked back up at Dane.

"Then your plan has worked beautifully. The Prince Regent has invited me to take that position."

Then she waited, breath stopped, heart stilled. *Please. Tell me no. Tell me you'll never let me go.*

Dane gazed at her for a long, long moment, his face frozen. She could see a glimpse of something wild behind his eyes. For an instant she had hope, for he seemed about to break the bonds of his own will.

Then his gaze cleared and his expression became blank. "If you would be so kind, my lady, it would be a service."

A service. As if she'd agreed to post a letter for him, or stitch a button on his coat.

Dane was completely calm as he gazed at Olivia. His chest was filled with ice. The pain was gone, as was the conflict and uncertainty within him. He was the Lion . . . and she was useful to the cause.

Then the Prince Regent fought free of his persistent Royal Guard and came to stand with Olivia. He gazed at Dane with cutting disdain. "I've always respected your judgment, Lord Greenleigh. Until now." He shook his head. "You must be the stupidest man alive."

Dane was dimly aware of the crowd hanging on every word. He heard them murmur at the Prince Regent's words, then gasp as George held out his hand to Olivia.

"My Lady Greenleigh, would you care to join my party in the east wing? We are a merry bunch, my friends and I." He cast a dismissive gaze toward Dane. "I daresay you could use a bit of fun."

For the past moments Olivia had been focusing her attention on moving air in and out of her lungs. If she had not, she thought she might have stopped altogether.

It would be a service.

She felt nothing. Her heart beat dully in her chest, as if it scarcely cared to keep her alive. Dimly she heard the Prince Regent speaking. He was a sweet man but old enough to be her father. She must be respectful and listen. She tried, but everything seemed to come from far away, muffled and indistinct.

Dane still stood before her, almost in arm's reach. Even as he crushed her heart, she realized that what he crushed was love.

She loved him. Not adored, not wanted, not desired. Loved. Loved until the pain she'd mistakenly caused him made her own soul ache in sympathy. She loved him. She willed herself to reach for him, to touch him. It might make him real again—

With a jolt, reality snapped back into focus. Dane wouldn't want her touch. He'd made it more than clear that he didn't care at all.

She loved, but she was the only one. No surprise there, for he was Dane . . . and she was nothing.

So she would give him what he most desired, her first and last act of love. She brought her chin up and faced him for the first time. "I suppose I won't be needing this anymore." She handed him the fifth rod and then turned to George, who still extended his hand. She curtsied low. "Your Highness, I would love to join your party."

Rising, she placed her hand in his. They turned without one more glance toward Dane and walked away.

Dane looked down at the thing in his hand. He'd taken it automatically, having been struck by something in Olivia's eyes.

She wasn't angry. She wasn't resentful or guilty or embarrassed. She'd looked at him with . . . understanding?

It shook him, causing a tiny voice within him to doubt. *Perhaps you are wrong.*

Perhaps she is precisely what the Lion needs.

Dane threw the ivory rod from him. It skittered across the floor and rolled into the watching crowd. Ladies leaped aside and gentlemen scrambled to get out of the way of the outrageous thing.

Dimly Dane recognized that he was going to suffer from their assumptions about why his lady needed such a device in the first place.

She belongs to me.

It seemed quite clear at that moment that before

Olivia went away with the Prince Regent or Marcus or whomever she chose next—

He had to have her, just once. Then, and only then, could he wash his obsession from his mind and body.

With that instant of clarity, he moved. Swiftly overtaking the new royal couple before the Guard could stop him, he wrapped his arm about his lost lady's waist and tossed her over his shoulder. "So sorry, Your Highness, but I believe I owe my lady a wedding night."

"What—," Olivia gasped, then struggled in his hold. His shoulder was too broad to dig into her stomach, but his grip was like stone. She could only push herself up by her hands against his back and watch the astonished Prince Regent and other guests disappear from sight.

Dane's long strides were faster than most men ran. The halls of Kirkall were a blur. By the time Olivia had caught her breath, they were outside.

The Greenleigh grooms, eerily efficient as ever, had Galahad bridled by the time Dane arrived.

He took the unsaddled horse from their protesting hands without a word. Olivia felt him give an easy heave and found herself sitting sideways on the broad white back. Dane was going to carry her off on a white horse?

Girlish fantasies aside, Olivia would really rather be sure of his intentions first.

From a distance.

He let go of her for only an instant, but it was enough to slide off, land lightly on her feet, and take a single running step. Then she found a great arm wrapped about her waist again and her feet left the ground.

And then it was too late. She was perched precariously upon the racing stallion with only two options. Cling to Dane or fall to certain injury at this great speed.

The hard ground would not give her a second chance.

Then again, she wasn't entirely sure that's what Dane intended, either.

24

Finally the trees gave way to a clearing. The moonlight fell into it, filling it like a bowl of bright milk. There was a cottage in the center. The thatched roof hung nearly to the ground except where the eaves rose above the low door. Roses climbed the sides of the door, twining together above. It was likely a charming effect in summer, but now the bare, thorny branches seemed threatening.

Olivia had the uncanny feeling that the moment they were inside, the growth would cover the door, locking them in forever.

Dane swept her from the horse and kicked the door open, carrying her away into the darkness within. Forever might be just what she needed to win Dane's heart.

Once inside, she was deposited on something soft—a bed dressed in sheets that smelled of lavender. He fell upon her, his mouth hot on her neck. She felt the scrape of his beard on the tops of her breasts, the sting of his teeth as he sucked on her skin. She writhed, pushing at him, but he only took her by the wrists and pressed her hands high above her head. If he had been any other man above her, she would have fought to the death to escape . . . but he wasn't any other man.

He was her man, her passionate, desperately alone Viking lord, and no matter what his intentions were, she knew what hers were. She was fighting for her love.

Having her pinned at his mercy only seemed to excite him further. He wrapped one big hand about both her wrists and used the other to tug the bodice of the blue gown low. He reached in urgently, pulling her breasts free to be pushed high by the neckline. He took one nipple into his mouth and wrapped his hand around the other breast, squeezing hard.

She gasped, protesting, so he simply covered her mouth with his own while he continued to tease and torment her breasts with his free hand, his hot, hard hand that took vengeance on her soft flesh. Hard fingers took her nipples between them, pinching sharply, causing jolts of pleasure/pain to run through her. She gasped into his mouth and he kissed her deeply, his tongue penetrating her lips over and over.

Then his hand traveled down her body, over her gown, until he cupped her mound in his big hand. He rubbed her there, roughly but with a knowing touch. The layers of cloth eased his roughness into a heated caress until she felt her body begin to respond. Her hands were still pinned, his tongue still violated her mouth, her breasts were still exposed, her nipples sore and tight in the cold air, and he continued to massage her through her gown.

Dark erotic pleasure radiated from beneath his hand.

Her body turned to hot wax in his hands. Her core began to throb and swell with arousal, much to her dismay. She ought not to want this roughness. She ought not to let it have this effect on her. His punishing kiss and his intentionally rough handling of her were meant to scandalize and dominate.

It seemed she was partial to being conquered by her Viking lord.

Oh, she was wicked, just as he said. Wicked and shameless all the way through, for she was going to orgasm with his fingers digging into her, pushing her petticoat inside her, rubbing and pressing and—

She lost control, crying out into his mouth, shuddering in his grasp as her climax swept hard through her, stealing her will and her voice until she was only a shivering creation, formed by his touch.

He was as surprised as she, she realized dimly on her way back down from the heights. His massive erection pressed hotly against her hip and his breath came hard. She seemed to be sweeping him away just a bit as well.

His kiss turned softer, almost wondering, and his hand soothed her now, helping her slip down once more into the moment. He took his mouth from hers and kissed the tops of her breasts more gently, then laid his head upon them. She could feel him fighting for breath, fighting for control, fighting to keep his retaliation foremost in his mind.

She couldn't allow it. "I want you, Dane," she whispered to him, to his reluctant heart. "You cannot force the willing. I want you so that I burn for your merest touch."

He shook his head, burying his face in her breasts. She persisted, for she was fighting with everything she had. "Test me. Press me. Try me in any way you like. You cannot steal what is freely given. You cannot make me beg for mercy." She rotated her hips, pressing up against where his hand still rested in her lap. "All I will ever beg for is *more.*"

He threw his head back then, pulling away from her. She reached for him, but he'd moved away. She heard the swift rustle of cloth. Then he was back, his bare skin beneath her hands.

He was wild on her now, sucking her nipples deep into his mouth, pulling her hair from its pins, yanking her gown and petticoats high to press her thighs wide. She surrendered completely, answering his urgency with her own, digging her fingers into his hair as she pressed his mouth down on her breasts. She raised her hips to welcome his touch on her wetness as he slipped two long fingers deep into her.

Then his hand moved away for a moment and came back covered in something cold and creamy that quickly turned warm and slick with her heat. He used it to coat her inside and out, thrusting his fingers in again and again, long after she was well covered. She rode his hand, rocking in a rhythm he set her to, allowing him to do his will on her as long, please God, as long as he did not stop touching her.

He brought her close, then backed off the rhythm. She cried out in protest, but he was merciless. He forced her high once more, only to stop before she hit the peak. She was nearly crying now, desperate for satisfaction, shamelessly begging him for more.

"You've never seen what it is you think you want," he growled. "Touch me now and tell me you want 'more.'"

He took her hands and wrapped them around himself.

Oh, dear heaven. He was huge and thick and so very hard. He throbbed at her touch, growing more so. Then he pulled himself from her hold.

"I—," she began.

"I care not what you think of me," he said. He pressed her back down upon the bed and laid his body between her thighs. The big, blunt tip of him pushed hard against her slick opening "I am demanding my marital rights, my lady," he said coldly.

He thought she'd been about to protest, to recoil, to pull away in revulsion. He thought he would be forcing himself on her. Her poor darling, so ready to be fended off.

In answer to his threat, she twined her long legs about his hips and pulled his mouth down to hers for a deep, wet, loving kiss. He went very still, profound astonishment positively radiating from him.

"I love you, you phenomenal ass," she whispered against his mouth. "All I ever wanted was to be your lady."

His breath caught. She wished they had a candle— and not only so she could feast her eyes on his amazing physique but also so she could see his eyes, to see if there was anything else there behind the desire and the anger and the surprise . . . any answer at all to her declaration of love.

He said nothing but only slowly, carefully, began to press inside her. The slick, cold hardness of the rods had done nothing to prepare her for feeling her man within her. He was warm and smooth and *Dane*.

The air left her lungs in a long sigh as he drove slowly, inexorably, within. She felt the sting of flesh stretched too far and hissed slightly. He stopped instantly, holding himself there until she felt her body relax further. She rotated against him, taking another half inch by herself. He followed her signal, pressing into her once more.

She stopped him twice more, each time hoping she would not have to stop entirely. Her body seemed to know what to do, and all she had to do was think about that day, someday, when he would sweep her up into his arms and look at her with love in his eyes. It never failed to turn her protesting flesh to supple submission again. Gradually, cautiously, he filled her absolutely. It was difficult and daunting . . . and *heaven*. At last, he was hers.

Dane could not believe it when he felt himself buried entirely within her. It was a dream, a gift, an impossible undertaking that no woman could do, yet she had done it. She still had her limbs wrapped tenderly about him, holding him right where he was.

She'd said she loved him. He willfully dismissed that. Words only, after all.

But this—this came close to breaking his heart with the thrice-damned *generosity* of it. He felt her tightness ease into comforting snugness yet more as he lay within her, his face buried in her sweet-smelling hair as it cascaded over the pillow. He dared not thrust, though his body trembled with the need to. He dared not think about what it might do to her—

"Move inside me," she whispered. "I want to feel you come in again."

She was incredible. Turning his head away with the ecstasy of withdrawing from her, he closed his eyes against the feel of her heated sheath caressing every inch of him, the way her tightness tugged at him with exquisite suction, the way she sighed with loss when he left her—

"Come back," she called softly.

He cupped her shoulders carefully in his hands and drove inside her once more. He gritted his teeth for control as he forced himself to penetrate her unhurriedly, allowing her body to accept him in its own time.

"Yesss," she breathed in his ear. "I love how you fill me."

He arched over her, his body shuddering with tightly reined desire as he deliberately moved within her. He'd imagined himself thrusting wildly into her, vengefully, without care or concern, yet he found himself highly attuned to her body's quiet signals. The way she clenched her thighs when something hurt, the way she relaxed beneath him when it pleasured her. The soft break in her breathing, the hint of smile he heard in her words.

He kissed her, unable to resist feeling her mouth open beneath his willingly, welcomingly. The taste and feel and soft, womanly acceptance of her . . . he could lie in her arms forever.

"Dane," she whispered to him, "I want more."

He blinked, startled from his careful rhythm, from the place he'd retreated to in order to control the pounding in his blood. "What more?"

She traced her fingertips down his bare back, her

touch like cool fire on his skin. "I want your climax now."

He shook his head. "I—I cannot. I don't dare—"

"Well, I do," she said firmly. She wrapped her calves over his lower back and brought him down into herself, deep and hard. Bright ecstasy exploded behind his eyes even as she cried out sharply.

Dane pulled almost entirely from her, concerned. "You should not have—"

She did it again. The pleasure stole his breath even as she cried out again.

He pushed himself up and away, though her legs still encircled him. "Stop!" he gasped. "You cannot—"

She let out a fierce hoarse sound as she forced him within her once more. "It . . . doesn't . . . hurt," she gasped. "I want . . . you."

Black erotic need nearly stole away the last of his awareness at her words. She wanted him, all of him, fast and hard. It was his deepest fantasy come true. "Wait—" He managed to speak, although it cost him. "The . . . the cream."

"Yes." She released him and he reached for the small pot of sweet tallow he'd used on her before. His desperate hands fumbled it and nearly dropped it in the dark. He caught it in midair by some outrageous good luck and brought it back to where she waited for him. He knelt before her again and pressed it into her hands. "Cover me with it to ease the way," he told her, his voice husky with the ferocity of his restraint.

She took the pot. Then he felt her hands, chilled and slippery, wrap around his cock. He gasped and threw his head back as she slid her slicked grip up and down his length, the fingers of her two hands wrapped tightly around him. It was very nearly as good as being in her body—but not quite.

"Enough!" he gasped. He pulled her greasy hands from him and wrapped her arms around his neck. "Kiss me," he demanded roughly. "Kiss me hard."

She rose to kneel bosom to chest with him, his cock pressed between them, her nipples hard points against his chest. She wrapped her arms tightly around his neck and then she kissed him as if her life depended on it. No gentle press, no tender touch of tongues. Her kiss was as hard and needful as his had been punishing and angry before.

It did him in.

25

Surrendering completely to his need, Dane toppled Olivia backward, rolling with her until he was lying between her thighs once more. This time when he entered her, he was not slow or gentle or careful. He thrust in deep and hard, nearly sliding her up the bed with his ferocity. She screamed his name out loud and wrapped her thighs tightly around him. He pulled back slowly, savoring the feel of her sheath pulsing around him, then thrust hard again.

She took every thrust with a cry; she answered every withdrawal with a lost whimper. The sweet, lustful animal sounds she made only drove him higher. The black cloud of abandon threatened him again, daring him to turn his lust loose on her at last. Control . . . control . . .

She raised herself on her elbows and kissed him hard. Then she bit him on the chin.

Control fled and he unleashed himself upon her at last. He took her hard and fast, wrapping her hair around his fists to turn her mouth up to his hungry kiss as he drove them both wild. She clung to him, her cries incoherent as she climaxed, her body shuddering beneath him.

Her tight sheath throbbed around him, sending red jolts of aching rapture into what was left of his brain. He exploded into her with a roar, thrusting hard even as he emptied his seed into her.

For a moment, dark, perfect pleasure ruled. Then his mind began to move again, his thoughts sluggish.

He'd done it. He knew now what the everlasting fuss was about. Although, he suspected as he collapsed next to his softly panting woman, he was fairly sure it wasn't that good for most men. If it was, they'd stay indoors and never do anything else. He lay limply next to her, one muscular thigh thrown over hers. The smell of her, of him, of what they'd made together, rose to envelop them both in the close, musky air of the cottage. Dane closed his eyes.

Olivia relaxed beneath the press of his heavy, sleepy body and breathed him in. She didn't dare speak for fear of reminding him that he wasn't very fond of her right now.

Dane might have been wreaking vengeance or fulfilling a physical need, but she loved him and she'd been given another—or last—opportunity to show him.

He might have been using her . . . but she had been loving him. It had been a risk, surrendering to him that way. She might find herself ever deeper in love, and alone. Fear of that very thing lived inside her heart even as she lay in his arms.

Yet if she failed, it would not be because she'd chosen

not to fight. She closed her eyes. Failing wasn't the same as giving up.

And she was never one to give up.

Just after dawn broke the night, Dane watched Olivia sleep limply on the bed, her blue silk gown twisted around her, ruined forever. She lay with her arms open, as if she'd welcome him back into them any time he liked.

He resisted the temptation. He had some thinking to do and he wanted to figure out his problem without the interference of his desire for her.

Then stop looking at her. Or listening to her breathe. Or thumping the wood about in the wood box hoping it will wake her up so you can have her once more before you have to be rational again.

He closed his eyes against the sight of her, leaning his elbows on the old, polished mantel and resting his head on his palms. The truth was, she'd affected him more deeply than he'd thought possible.

Never in his life had he felt so *accepted.* Not only by her body but by her heart and soul as well. His body, his problem, his anger, his fear, his every doubt—she had accepted all of him, swallowing him into her well of warmth and comfort and desire. She had accepted all his darkness and asked for more, until they were both spent and exhausted. This exhilarated and terrified him. He found himself in great danger of forgetting everything else . . . and that he could not allow himself to do.

She was so open, so giving, so generous—so dangerous. She threatened every fiber of the Lion's control.

His duty was beginning to pale beside thoughts of her.

It wasn't supposed to have been like this. He was a peer, wedding the daughter of a peer. Their union should have been pleasant, solicitous, and comfortably distant.

Dane had the feeling that Olivia didn't know the meaning of the word *distant.* With her, every moment was immediate and real, bursting with vitality and intimacy.

Perhaps it was that she cared so deeply about things. Unlike the usual Society woman with her practiced ennui, Olivia shimmered with interest and diligence.

Even the tightly knit Greenleigh staff was susceptible. Petty was her willing slave. The driver, Errol, could speak nothing but praise of her. Yesterday, in an obvious attempt to defend Olivia after the kippers fiasco, even the severe Mrs. Huff had reported to him that she was much mended by her ladyship's bone-ache cure.

He smiled at the thought. Then he shook off the spell. Damn, she was doing it to him again! He could not go three minutes without slipping sideways into her!

He heard motion behind him and turned to see her stretching languidly, a smile forming on her lips before she even opened her eyes.

Something ached within him at her smile. He forced himself to turn away and knelt to add wood to the fire.

"The wood box is full and the cottage is spotless," Olivia said behind him. "What is this place?"

Dane fixed his gaze on the rising flames. "No one lives here, if that's what you're wondering. It is for my use alone." It was the cottage he'd ordered prepared for her—five days ago, after she'd entrusted herself to him with the first rod. Even the small pot of unguent had been on his order. He'd planned on bringing her here after they'd completed the "training," so they could be all alone and take their time.

The honeymoon she'd never been given.

She came over to him, her bare feet padding on the carpet, her toes peeking out from the blue silk pooling at her feet. Dane closed his eyes, thinking of the way she'd looked in the gown, an elegant goddess with eyes full of pain.

Now she laughed and knelt beside him, holding her hands out to the fire. "This isn't a place for guns and dead birds. You don't actually shoot grouse up here, do you?"

Just as he was about to speak, someone pounded on the door.

Olivia started, but Dane was already halfway across the cottage. "Marcus."

"How do you know?"

Dane flicked a glance at her as he opened the door. "Because he's the only one who knows where I would go."

Marcus strode in. "His Majesty was fired on early this morning."

26

Dane went very still. "Tell me."

Marcus paced and rubbed his face, obviously having had a very long night. "He was with the Duchess of Halswick in the east wing. Apparently there was a shout of 'Fire,' so of course he was rushed outside. While he stood there in his dressing gown, surrounded by Royal Guard who were dutifully lighting his way with torches—"

"Oh, bugger," Dane breathed. "Might as well have painted a target on his ass."

Marcus closed his eyes. "I know. He wasn't harmed, unless one counts having nine guardsmen flung over one's prone body."

Dane's jaw clenched. "I should have been there."

Marcus stiffened. "I was there. I moved him outside, then directed the staff to search for smoke or flames. I was only seconds behind, on my way across the garden to him. That's when I heard the pistol shots."

"*Shots?* How many?"

Marcus nodded. "Three. So, three men, do you think?"

Dane rubbed his jaw. "Perhaps. Or one man with three pistols."

Olivia raised her hand. "Ah, if you'll pardon the interruption—how do you know they were pistols and not hunting rifles? It is grouse season."

Dane shook his head quickly. "The sound is entirely different." He turned back to Marcus as if she weren't there. "How were the shots spaced? Three nearly together? Far apart?"

Marcus shook his head. "Two nearly together. One after."

Dane nodded. "One man." He mimed shooting a pistol in each hand, then grabbing up one more to shoot it as well.

Marcus nodded. "Exactly. Then we have him. You'll never guess who."

Dane became dangerously still. He slowly turned his head to look at her. "The only person here who wasn't properly investigated. Sumner."

Marcus turned to gaze at her as well, his brow creased in a shocked frown.

"It is Sumner," Marcus said slowly. "One of the housemaids recognized his voice as that of the one crying, 'Fire.' "

That would have been Petty. Poor Petty, to have her newest fancy turn wrong before her eyes. Olivia quite knew how she felt.

"He already as much as admitted it," Marcus went on. "We have him in custody even now."

Olivia could only gaze at Dane, a chill growing in

her belly. "I—Sumner was employed by my brother. I had no reason to—"

Dane shook his head. "No, of course you didn't." Still, the man who had made love to her for hours was gone, replaced by the cool stranger once more.

Dane turned to Marcus. "Bring her back with you. I'll ride ahead." With that, he turned and strode from the cottage. Moments later, they heard the pounding of Galahad's heavy hooves fading away.

Olivia took a shaky breath. "Marcus, I don't know what is happening, but you must believe I had nothing to do—"

He turned from her. "I'm afraid it won't be comfortable riding before me. I'll put you up behind. We'll go slowly. It might give Dane time to—" He didn't finish but only bowed her through the door ahead of him.

Olivia again had the feeling that there was some scheme going on. All her mishaps—things she had dismissed as clumsiness or bad luck or some fault of her own! Someone had been conspiring against her all along.

And now she had a fairly good idea who it was.

George had been tucked into the vast bed he'd selected, surrounded by what had to be most of the pillows from the east wing, with the Duchess of Halswick fluttering over him, getting in the way of the superbly competent Royal Staff.

Dane bowed deeply. "Your Highness, my deepest apologies—"

George waved away Dane's regret. "Ballocks. I'll be all right once my physician tends my back. The important thing is, lad—did you get the girl?"

Dane straightened. "If you are referring to my wife, Lady Greenleigh is being safely returned to her room."

George blinked. "Oh." Then he frowned. "I don't believe she gave up on you. If she wasn't mad for you, she could have simply taken my offer."

Dane rubbed the back of his neck. "If Your Highness will recall, Lady Greenleigh did accept your company, until I . . . stopped her."

"That was simply desperation to leave the ballroom." George rolled his eyes. "You're a bigger fool than I thought if you don't realize she was dying for you to sweep her off her feet. That girl *is* mad for you, Greenleigh. Fully, can't-see-straight, no-other-man-exists mad for you." He looked disgruntled. "She turned me down flat, told me I was 'sweet.' You know what that does to a bloke's pride? Made me feel like her favorite uncle, whether I liked it or not."

Dane didn't respond. The real problem wasn't that she didn't love him or that she had the Prince Regent wrapped about her soft, pale finger.

The real problem was that it was the Lion's duty to protect the Crown . . . and he'd been off playing bed games, his duty forsaken for a roll in the sheets.

Never again.

When Dane entered the secure chamber where Sumner had been deposited, he saw the younger man standing at the window. Dane ordered the guard to remain outside, for even loyal ears could hear too much.

"Who are you in truth? Who do you work for?" The man was involved with the Chimera. Dane would wager his life on it.

Sumner turned, his mournful face a study in sorrow. "A simple servant, pledged to serve the wrong people."

Dane narrowed his eyes. "My most recent information states that you were Lord Walter Cheltenham's valet for two years and that you were the sole witness to his death last month."

Sumner shrugged. "More or less correct."

"Where have you been since then?"

The man sighed. "Trying to put it all behind me."

Dane was losing his temper. "Sumner, you shot at the Prince Regent of England! Speak before I hang you myself!"

Sumner sat abruptly, less in disrespect than in sudden weakness of the knees. "Hanged?" His voice was a faint murmur. "Yes, I suppose I will be hanged, won't I?" He rubbed both hands over his face, then looked up at Dane. "Then I ought to tell you everything . . . just to be sure she doesn't try again."

There was a woman involved. Somehow that didn't surprise Dane. The Chimera was known for using female operatives. Dane sat opposite the man and leaned forward. "To be sure who doesn't try again?"

Sumner tilted his head at Dane. "Lady Greenleigh, of course." His tone implied it was obvious. "Your wife."

Dane left the prisoner's chamber with a nod at the guard and strode purposefully down the hall. Sumner had tried to feed him some ridiculous codswallop about Olivia being part of plot against him. The man was obviously trying to gain some sort of bargaining chip against being hanged like a poached deer.

Nevertheless, the man had given some interesting information about Olivia's parents and their involvement. It would be easy enough to disprove, since Lord and Lady Cheltenham were still in residence.

As he walked to the west wing where the guests were staying, he let out a small laugh. Olivia might be many things, but the one thing she was not was a spy.

He slowed slightly then, thinking. She might be in the middle of something, all unaware. If even a fraction of Sumner's story was true, Olivia might actually be in some danger.

Olivia stared at Petty. "What do you mean, there's a guard outside my bedchamber?"

Petty nodded, her brow crumpled in worry. "I swear, my lady! He has orders that no one is to come in or out except for me or Mrs. Huff!" Petty's face furrowed again. "What's more, there's talk belowstairs that Mr. Sumner told his lordship that you were a traitor!"

Olivia put a hand to her midriff. "Oh, no." Sumner must be mad—or worse. Why else would he have done all those things to make Dane angry with her? Why else would he concoct such a ridiculous tale? Still Dane had no reason to believe the valet. The man had even shot at the Prince Regent!

An act which Dane had taken most seriously . . .

"I must get out of this room," Olivia said fretfully. "I must speak to his lordship!"

Petty wrung her hands. "His lordship is questioning your parents, my lady."

Olivia went very still. Why would Dane do such a thing?

Unless he believed Sumner's rantings. In which case he wasn't likely to believe her denial.

I should have respected you more for taking responsibility for your failure.

Hiring Sumner had been her wish—her responsibility. Olivia narrowed her eyes. "Then I want to speak to Sumner myself. I must convince him to stop this charade and tell Dane the truth!"

She turned to the worried maid. "Petty, will you distract the guard for me?"

Dane stared at Lord and Lady Cheltenham in complete disbelief. The graying conspirators gazed defiantly back. In their hands they held the drawing of the Chimera. Neither one had denied knowing him.

"We did it for Cheltenham," Lady Cheltenham insisted. "He holds a majority of the notes against the estate. He promised to tear them up if we assisted him."

Dane blinked. "You baited a trap for me with your own daughter at a French spy's request?"

"We knew nothing of any treason," Lord Cheltenham huffed. "We were told that you were looking for a wife, that you might like a girl like Olivia, and we were told where you'd be that day. The rest is your own doing."

That was true. He'd made his decision within hours of meeting Olivia and he'd not regretted it. "You exploited your own daughter," he said wonderingly.

Lady Cheltenham snorted. "Of course, we did. As did you. You wed her to be your broodmare, do not deny it."

It was an unpleasant truth, but truth nonetheless—at the time.

"Precisely how did this man intend to use Olivia against me?"

Lord Cheltenham looked at his wife. Lady Cheltenham looked at her hands. "She was to influence you with her charms," she said. "To give her information."

Dane laughed out loud. "What could he possibly accomplish with a woman who knew nothing of his plans?"

This time, Lady Cheltenham looked at her husband, who looked out the window.

Ah. This time Dane was prepared. "You're telling me that Olivia is knowingly working for this man."

Lord Cheltenham huffed. "She's a good daughter. She knows her duty to her family."

Dane shook his head. Olivia was no more working for the Chimera than he himself was colored blue. He stood. "You don't know her at all, do you?"

He turned to go, then he turned back. "My drawing, if you please."

Lady Cheltenham handed it to him silently. Dane looked down at the mild-faced young man in the sketch. "He wouldn't have exposed your bankruptcy, you know," he said conversationally. "He could hardly do that without bringing himself to unwanted attention." He waved the drawing at them. "This man would simply have killed you outright."

They looked startled, but Lady Cheltenham raised her chin. "I should have preferred death to scandal."

Dane turned and left them there, uncompromising and unapologetic. How in the world could warm, open Olivia have sprung from that chill union?

Olivia.

It was time to talk to Olivia.

"I'm here to speak to the prisoner."

The Royal Guard standing at attention only gazed at her uncertainly. He obviously knew who she was, which meant that he assumed she was an "intimate" friend of the Prince Regent's, and wife of the lord whose hall he stood in.

Olivia balanced the tea tray in her hands. "My Lord Greenleigh doesn't dare send a servant in there. We have no idea who might be in league with the traitor. You will stay with me at all times." She'd learned in the past week that it was best to inform, not request.

She'd contemplated donning one of Petty's uniforms, but after last night every person in the house knew her by sight, even the other guests' servants. She'd noticed them all eyeing her surreptitiously as she'd entered Kirkall Hall with Marcus, still ridiculously clad in her blue silk ball gown.

Now she was more respectably, if hurriedly, clad in the orange gown. The guard didn't precisely eye her bosom in the low bodice, but she rather thought it didn't hurt her case any.

Finally, he nodded and unlocked the door for her. She entered to see Sumner standing at the window, gazing out mournfully. They'd taken his coat and his shoes as an added precaution. The chill of winter was already here in the north. Only a fool would run out badly dressed.

Olivia set down the tray and stepped back. "You should eat and drink quickly. I must take the tray away again so you can use nothing for a weapon." The last she said for the guard's benefit. The fellow remained in the doorway, blocking the way but just out of earshot of a whisper.

"Why did you attack the Prince Regent?" Olivia tried not to scream at the fellow. "Why have you done all of this to me?"

"I couldn't let you go through with it," Sumner whispered back around a sip of tea, holding it cupped in his bound hands. "I had to get you away from him."

Olivia stared at him. "Go through with what? Bedding my husband?" she hissed.

Sumner's face took on a stubborn cast. "You think I don't know, but I do. I know about the bridge and the offer and the reason you had to use those . . . things."

Olivia swallowed, appalled. "I fell into the water," she protested faintly.

He shook his head. "You jumped, just when he was riding by, just as we'd planned."

Mother. "W—we?" It couldn't be that Mother had taken part in some elaborate plan—to what? Wed her off?

She leaned forward slightly. "You'd best eat all that now," she said loudly. "Who knows when you'll eat next." Then she pinned Sumner with her gaze. "What are you talking about? What does my mother's matchmaking have to do with trying to kill the Prince Regent?"

He picked up a tiny sandwich and popped it in his mouth hungrily. "I wasn't trying to kill him. I only wanted to draw Lord Greenleigh back here before you worked your wiles on him and make him keep you away from His Highness."

She blinked slowly. "All along it has been you who was trying to drive us apart."

He shrugged, popping another sandwich into his mouth. "Having your husband repudiate you is better than ending up like your brother."

Her breath stopped. "My brother?"

Sumner nodded sadly. "He actually found his own way out, away from the Debt Collector. Marrying that Hackerman girl would have paid everything off. He refused to participate and ended up in the Thames."

"Debt Collector?" Cheltenham's debt was severe, she knew that. Something clicked inside her mind. All the things that had been wrong about Walter's accident—murder. The way her parents had swept her up and turned her loose on Society in such a rush, using her to save Cheltenham—although Cheltenham had been poor for years. Another year or two likely wouldn't have meant the loss of anything but a few more roof slates. Unless this "Debt Collector" called in the notes.

"What does this man want?"

Sumner blinked sadly. "To win the war for France, of course."

Oh God. She'd been aimed at Dane like an arrow.

Someone must know about him and his . . . friends. She suspected and she'd only been with him for little more than a week.

And what of their plans? *What we need is the right woman.*

Time seemed to slow as Olivia worked it all out in her mind. Dane had aimed a netfull of women at George. Someone who owned Sumner and her parents had aimed her at Dane in much the same way. *Cheltenham needs you! You must do this!*

"I'm the lure," she said, her stomach roiling. How could she make Dane believe that she'd known nothing of this plan?

Sumner blinked at her. "As if you didn't know. You ought not to have raised your sights to the Prince Regent. I couldn't allow it. I had to stop you."

Olivia turned blindly and headed for the hall. She had to find Dane. She had to try somehow to explain—

The guard gazed at her curiously as she stumbled past him. "Would you like me to carry out the tray, my lady?"

She halted, then nodded. "Of course. Thank you."

She stayed where she was while the guard went back into the room and bent to pick up the tray. While she watched in horror, Sumner brought his bound hands down on the back of the man's neck.

"No!" It was too late. The guard crumpled to the floor.

Sumner nodded glumly at her. "Thank you, my lady. I would never have thought of it without you."

"Me? But I—"

Sumner ran past her, out of the room, and down the empty hall.

Olivia hesitated only a second. If she cried out for another guard, one might come in time or not. And if Sumner escaped completely, Dane would never, ever believe that she hadn't helped him.

Picking up her skirts in both hands, she ran flat out after the escaping valet.

27

Dane left the Prince Regent to his cooing new lady-love, striding from the east wing with Marcus on his heels. "Use Greenleigh footmen for outer guards and keep the Royal Guard close to the prince. I want someone at every mouse hole. No one is to see His Highness except the two of us. Even meals are to be carried in by the Guard."

"Right." Marcus peeled away from Dane at the next corridor to carry out his orders. "See you back at the prisoner's room."

But there was no one in the prisoner's room except a very groggy guard.

"I don't know what happened, my lord. I was fetching the prisoner's tea tray for your lady—"

"My lady brought him *tea*?"

"Yes, my lord. Then she forgot the tray and sent me back in for it. . . ." He blinked. "That was stupid of me, wasn't it, my lord?"

Dane shook his head. "My wife is safely in her room."

Marcus appeared in the doorway. "Bloody hell," he

said faintly. "Dane, Kinsworth just told me that Lady Greenleigh tricked the guard and escaped her room."

"So it gets better." Dane swept past him, running. "There's nothing else for miles. He'll need a horse."

At the stables, it seemed he'd taken a horse, or two.

Two horses gone, a traitor escaped, and Olivia was nowhere to be found. It was never a good thing when Dane couldn't find Olivia.

Sumner had ridden to a road where an unmarked carriage awaited him. Olivia watched from concealment as he boarded the carriage.

Who was that with him?

Olivia stepped closer, leaving behind the better cover of the evergreens for the nearly bare trees closer to the road embankment. However, her orange gown blended beautifully with the autumn foliage. She could stand to get a bit closer. . . .

The other face in the carriage turned toward her and her gaze was caught by the shadowed gaze of that pale face. In an instant, there was a glint of black metal raised to point at her.

Her gut chilling, Olivia scrambled backward into the trees—but it was too late. A single shot rang out.

Pain ripped through her thigh, knocking her backward onto the stony, leaf-covered slope. Everything went dark.

Once the carriage rumbled away and the sound of the hooves and wheels faded, there was nothing but the blustering autumn wind in the foliage as it blew the orange and gold leaves to drift over the still figure on the slope.

. . .

Leaving Marcus behind on Prince Regent watch, Dane took the largest of his footmen and pursued Sumner and the missing Olivia.

The tracks were fresh and easy to follow on the old path. Dane rode quickly, but it was too late. There were only the two abandoned horses at the end of the path by the road and the fresh wheel marks of a carriage in the mud. They rode hard to catch up with the carriage, only to lose the trail at a nearby well-traveled road.

She was gone.

Dane left Lord and Lady Cheltenham's chamber, for the second time nodding to the guard he'd placed at the door. They had no idea where Olivia and Sumner might have fled to. They seemed more appalled that Olivia had taken up with a servant than that she had deserted them to their fates.

It was all a plot to get influence over him—a plot he recognized all too well.

He'd been played masterfully. He'd thought her sweet and open, innocent in her enjoyment of what they had shared, responsive only to *him.* Yet, she did bring him the trunk of sexual devices—an odd act for a demure virgin. And she was in Marcus's arms only days after the wedding—and then in the Prince's room only hours after that!

And then in mine—for the most amazing, profound worthless night of my life.

He shook his head. He must stay focused on his duty. If he couldn't, then he must step down as the Lion.

And being the Lion was the only thing he had left.

Marcus caught up with him in the hall. "Well, what did you learn? Do they think Olivia was kidnapped? You must send more men out after her, Dane!"

Shaking his head, Dane turned away, moving slowly down the hall. He hurt inside, as if someone had torn out pieces of him with dull knives.

"You *want* to believe the worst of her! Why?"

Dane kept moving. Marcus followed, unwilling to let it go. "You know, I believe I've just deciphered you. You're a coward. You think that if you let yourself care, it will make you as weak as your father. She left without even her *cloak*. Honestly, Dane, do you think Olivia is a *spy*?" Marcus's tone said it was a ridiculous notion.

Dane turned to gaze at his friend without expression. "Her parents have admitted they are in the employ of the Chimera. They have been acting on his orders all along. She was planted in my path in order to ensnare my heart, or at least my passion, all to influence me in favor of the French."

Marcus paled. "You cannot be serious."

Dane kept his gaze level. "It does cause me to wonder how someone knew precisely what I would want in a woman. The information must have come from someone who knew me well."

Marcus drew back. "Are you accusing me?"

Dane tilted his head. "If the accusation fits . . ."

"How very flattering." Marcus narrowed his eyes. "But you're forgetting someone, someone who knew you better than I ever could."

With a start, Dane realized Marcus was quite correct. There was one person who knew him inside and out once upon a time. His father.

He rubbed his face. "Dear god, do you think the Chimera's plans extend that far back?"

"Why not? He'd been in the Liars' employ in one capacity or another for three years. I hardly think he's been sitting on his hands all that time."

The web of the Chimera's intrigue spun around them all, tying them together and pulling them apart.

She was cold. That was the first thing Olivia became aware of. Then she realized that her head was broken and her thigh was on fire.

Or perhaps it was her head on fire and her thigh broken.

Either way, it was all wrong. If she was hurt, shouldn't she be in her bed in . . . Cheltenham . . . no, London . . . no, Kirkall. She ought to be in her bed at Kirkall Hall, with Petty bringing her soup and obsessing over Sumner. . . .

Sumner . . .

Sumner was a spy.

She sat up quickly, then just as quickly rolled over and vomited. The dizzying whirl of the world didn't ease, but she managed to pull herself away from the noisome mess.

Until she tried to crawl. Hot agony raced up her thigh, blinding her. With a harsh cry, she collapsed again, black spots whirling in her vision. She lay there, breathing hard until the spots began to clear.

With one hand, she reached down to inspect her leg. There was a bloody hole in her skirt. It was safe to assume there was also one in her thigh. She swallowed. Perhaps she could inspect it in a moment. She dropped her hand and let her head fall carefully down again.

She was in the wood. Above her the nearly bare branches made a dark lacy circle against the gray sky. The wind made them sway . . . or at least she thought it was the wind. She closed her eyes before the movement disoriented her again.

"I'll wager that *my* pupils don't match," she murmured out loud. Her voice sounded odd against the whoosh of the wind and the crackle of the leaves beneath her.

How long had she lain here? She opened her eyes again, but the sky told her nothing except that she wanted to vomit again.

"I'll beat the duchess yet," she muttered. "Bother that Sumner. I'll never be able to eat kippers again—and I *like* kippers."

She felt the back of her head. The knot was frighteningly large and coated in dried blood. Turning her head carefully, she looked beside her to see blood on a half-buried stone the size of a cheese. She was fortunate to be alive.

So, she'd been here long enough to become thoroughly chilled and for the blood on her head and leg to clot.

They must be looking for her by now.

"Help! Help me, please!"

Calling out made her head pound, but she clenched her eyes shut and clutched the rocks on either side of her to keep her bearings as the effort of her screams made the world spin again.

No one came.

. . .

Dane was brooding. No one could stand him, and he didn't blame them.

Lady Reardon was the first.

"You scarcely knew her," Dane protested when Willa buttonholed him in the library. She was a pretty woman, curvaceous and lively, with snapping blue eyes, but he found himself thinking that she was too short and that her hair was much too dark.

She may have been small, but she made up for it in ferocity. "I may not know her well, but I know one thing, Lord Greenleigh, and that is that she loves you. Women know these things. There's something very wrong about all this. I can feel it!"

"So you want me to chase off after my runaway wife, is that it?" He folded his arms and squared his shoulders. She didn't back down.

He must be losing his touch. "I have duties and re-sponsibilities you don't understand, Lady Reardon—"

She rolled her eyes. "Yes, yes, you're the Lion, who protects the Crown, blah, blah, blah." She poked him in the arm, hard. "Your lady is in danger and—"

Dane caught her hand—a grievous offense to be sure, to grab another lord's lady, but he didn't care.

"What do you know of the Lion?"

She tugged her hand back and folded her arms. "I'm the granddaughter of a previous Cobra, you big lout. I'll wager I know more about the Royal Four than you do!" She narrowed her snapping eyes and poked him again, harder. "And if you grab me again, I'll tell Nathaniel—and see if he won't dust the floor with your arse, Viking throwback or no!"

She turned and flounced furiously from the library.

In the doorway, Marcus moved adroitly from her path; then he entered the library with his head turned as he gazed after her. "What did you do to Reardon's lady?"

Viking throwback? Did all ladies see him as some sort of marauder? Dane flexed his bicep to ease the primary poking spot. "I disagreed with her," he said tightly.

Marcus nodded sagely. "Oh. She thought you should be combing the countryside for Olivia?"

Dane shot his friend a dark look. "Do not begin."

Marcus threw out his hands. "I have no issue with your decision . . . although when you think about it, she likely has some excellent intelligence information on the Chimera. It might be worth tracking her down for that alone."

"And it might be a ploy to drag me away from the Prince Regent again!"

Marcus blinked. "Again? Wasn't it you who dragged her away last night?"

"A night for which I will undoubtedly pay for the rest of my life," Dane said quietly. His anger wasn't dependable. That was the worst part. He kept slipping into pain and loss and missing her lopsided smile and her husky laugh and—

If he could only hold on to a solid foundation of anger, he could manage to think all this through.

But George was the worst.

"You're a fool. An idiot. A great fair-haired waste of meat! That rat of a valet has *kidnapped* your lady and you immediately decide that she has run off with the bugger!"

Dane took a breath. He must not kill the Prince Regent. He must not kill the Prince Regent. It would be very bad. "One of your own Guard said Olivia helped Sumner—"

"Oh, goat shite! What are you listening to him for? The bloody Guard are hired for brawn and bravery, not for brains! *I'm* telling you that she wouldn't leave you, not for money or love or a room of her own in the palace!"

"I don't *want* to find her!" Dane's bellow echoed in the vast room. "If I find her, I might be forced to hang her!"

George stared at him for a long moment. "Good God, you are even madder than you are stupid. All Four of you are as mad as hatters on Sunday." He scowled and waved his hand. "Get out, you great giant fool. I hope she did leave you. You don't deserve her."

So Dane got out. Marcus could keep watch over His Highness for a while. As Dane left the east wing, he spotted the little lady's maid, Petty. She bobbed the scarcest bow and shot him a scathing glance as she scurried by.

Finally, driven out of his own house by the joint disapproval of all, Dane rode out through Kirkall Wood, as was his habit when upset. The wood was quiet and dim this gray afternoon and entirely unoccupied, thank God.

28

Olivia awoke again, this time facedown in the dry brown needles beneath the pines. She blinked back the constant pounding long enough to look over her shoulder.

The place where she'd originally fallen was out of sight. That meant she must be nearly halfway to the old path—mere moments of walking quickly but hours when moving at a dragging crawl. Uphill.

She took a breath and reached forward with her filthy hands to dig into the needles and chill earth. One leg wasn't working well—or at all—so she slid the other knee high. With a hoarse, nearly soundless cry, she hauled herself up eighteen more inches of hillside. Her damaged thigh sent a red haze of agony over her vision, but she clung to her position, waiting out the dizziness as she had fifty times before.

She lay there, panting, waiting for the pain to ease. If she'd had any voice left at all, she would have indulged in some therapeutic vulgarity, but she'd screamed it entirely away, calling for a man who wasn't going to come for her.

She'd screamed for him, cried for him, begged for him—yet never had she heard a single indication that anyone was searching the wood for her, not even to follow the tracks her horse must have left in the softened soil of the path. Some mighty hunter Dane was. No wonder he felt it necessary to shoot helpless birds.

She'd left the horse at the top of the path, tied to a branch. If it hadn't pulled free, she could—she hoped rather than believed—pull herself astride and ride back to Lord Gargoyle's perfect hall.

With any luck at all, she would bleed all over the creamy marble floor of the entrance hall before she died and the Gargoyle staff would never be able to get the stain out.

She took another deep breath. Reach. Dig. *Pull.*

Finally, she'd nearly crawled up the entire hill to the path. One more great heave and she should be able to see her horse.

She closed her eyes and hauled herself up the last foot and a half to drop her torso over onto the level ground. She nearly passed out again. . . .

No. She would fall back down the ravine. *Hold on.* She fought it back. She was nearly safe now.

The haze passed and she blinked thankfully up the path where her horse was tied.

Nothing. A clear view down the path and the small patch of road visible there. She turned her head to search the other direction. Maybe she'd moved too far back—

There was nothing there. The horse was gone.

The soft earth under her belly crumbled. Olivia flung her arms wide to catch herself, to no avail. She slid off the level ground and several yards back down the slope.

After the first mad gallop had worn off the worst of his fury—or whatever that feeling was—Dane allowed Galahad to choose his own path. Dane sat back in the saddle and closed his eyes, letting the sway of the stallion's long-legged walk rock him into some kind of peace.

The wood was so quiet. Most of the birds had already left for warmer climes and the small furred creatures were on their way to their long winter sleep. There was only the bluster of the wind through the orange carpet of fallen leaves and the muted thud of Galahad's hooves on the damp earth of the path.

Galahad whickered gently. Dane opened his eyes to see that they were on the old path to the road.

Olivia's escape route.

Even as he had that thought, something bright caught his eye. Reining Galahad to a halt, Dane dismounted and plucked a trampled hair ribbon from the mud. She never could keep her hair ornaments in. Orange. The guard had said Olivia had been wearing the orange gown.

God, Dane hated that gown, despite the rewarding neckline. The color made her look sallow and sad—

He clenched his eyes shut and crumpled the ribbon in his fist. Her wardrobe was no longer his concern, unless one counted the rope necklace he dreaded to give her.

Keeping his bitterness high, right where he could find it when he needed it, Dane forced himself to twist the knife by following her route as she left him.

Walking his horse slowly down the path toward the road, Dane assured himself that he was not wallowing in grief. He was merely making sure he never forgot the lesson he had learned. He must never allow himself to forget who he was.

Perhaps he would have his siren mural repainted with treacherous moonlight eyes and honey golden hair. . . .

Olivia had fought her way back within two yards of the path before she'd run dry of strength and will. Now it was all she could do to cling to what ground she'd won.

She looked up at the unreachable path with eyes fogged by what she was very much afraid was blood loss and fever.

Dane was there.

He'd come at last! In a moment, he would cast his gaze about—for surely he was searching for her—and he would see her, right here waiting for him!

He walked right on by, his gaze locked on the ground at his feet.

"Dane!" Her voice was a whisper, lost in the rustling of the breeze in the leaves. She pounded the earth, but it was lost under the thud of his white stallion's hooves on the ground.

She tried to crawl closer—surely Dane would hear her struggling; surely he would turn and look about himself, the great oblivious lout!

Her efforts cost her. The world spun and darkened. She reached—*please, help me*—

Her hand found a stone the size of her fist. She

pulled it from the soft earth and flung it wildly at her stupid, idiot, self-absorbed husband.

"Ow!" Then, "Olivia!"

She lifted her head to pin his shocked eyes with a furious gaze. *"Bastard,"* she hissed, then fainted dead away.

Dane burst through the front doors of Kirkall Hall with his filthy, bloody wife in his arms.

"Kinsworth, fetch that physician back immediately!"

A burly footman stepped forward to take Olivia from Dane, as if she were an oversize parcel. Dane held her close and strode past him. "Mrs. Huff, bring hot water and clean cloths! Petty! Damn it all, where is Petty!"

Petty appeared at the top of the stairs, then paled as she saw what he carried. "Is she dead? Is my lady dead?"

"Silly girl, of course not!" scolded Mrs. Huff. "His lordship has saved her!"

His lordship nearly killed her, but Dane didn't waste breath correcting the woman. He ran up the stairs, snapping orders all the way. "Petty, you must help me bathe her and put her in a clean shift—"

Lady Reardon stepped into his path. *"I'll* help Petty. You've done quite enough."

"My lady," Dane growled. "Get out of my way."

She stepped back but followed him to the mistress's bedchamber. He gently deposited Olivia on the bed, then knelt beside her.

"Oh, dear God," Lady Reardon breathed. "She must have crawled a mile. She went after the traitor herself, didn't she?"

Dane closed his eyes. His insides burned with shame. He'd abandoned his breathtaking Olivia out there, bleeding and broken, to die like a carriage-struck dog.

Lady Reardon knelt on the other side of the bed to take one of Olivia's filthy, bleeding hands tenderly in hers. "Oh, you poor creature." She turned to look at Dane. "Is that a bullethole in her skirt?"

Dane nodded, his vision filled with what he'd found when he'd inspected her unconscious form in the wood. "The bullet is still—" Her thigh had been discolored and swollen, already beginning to flush with fever. He swallowed and took a breath. "It must be dug out."

Lady Reardon forced back her sympathy and began inspecting Olivia all over. "She has a head wound as well. Concussion. I'll check her out thoroughly in the bath. Do you think whoever it was—" She turned dark eyes to Dane. "Do you think they—"

He shook his head quickly. Not that, at least. Sumner had been in a great hurry to escape, he imagined.

Of course, when Lady Reardon undressed Olivia, she would see the marks that he himself had left on her last night. Not so bad, except for those places where his teeth scraped her breast. . . .

Oh God. His Olivia was right. He was such a bastard. He started to rub his hands over his face, then stopped. He had her blood all over his shirt and weskit—

All over his hands.

He stripped off his coat and weskit, rubbing at the stains on his hands with the expensive superfine wool.

Only then did he touch her again. He picked up her poor, battered hand and held it over his heart.

Uncaring that Lady Reardon watched, he dropped his

head to roll his brow on Olivia's shoulder. "Do not die, my lady," he whispered. "Who will laugh at me if you die?"

Petty rushed into the bedchamber, followed by an army of footmen carrying enough steaming water to bathe all of the elephants in the Royal Menagerie. Lady Reardon stood up and clapped her hands. "Men, out! Huff, Petty, to me!"

Dane watched as his loyal staff offered instant obedience to Reardon's little tyrant. Olivia ought to have taken charge like that, Dane thought dully. Instead, she had tried to win them over with her sweetness and caring, wanting his army of servants to be her new family.

He could have told her how it was done, if he'd cared to. He could have eased her way in so many avenues.

Instead, he'd plugged her into the slot designated "Lady Greenleigh" in the vast Greenleigh machine and left her there to fly or flounder, judging her performance more harshly with every passing day.

Lady Reardon put her hands on his chest and pushed, but nothing happened. He turned his gaze down at her. "I'm staying."

"Then you're staying out of the way." She pointed to the chair that had been pulled aside to make room for the copper bathing tub. He followed her direction, but he did not sit. Instead, he stayed where he could see everything over the heads of the women.

They held Olivia gently in the warm water and stroked the bloodstains away with soft sponges. Petty worked her fingers through Olivia's matted hair, removing the clotted blood and woody filth. "Do you think the physician will make us cut her hair? We mustn't cut her hair," he heard Petty whisper to Lady Reardon. "She says it is her only good feature."

Dane's eyes began to burn. So strong and lovely and generous, yet she thought only her hair was passable. He stared unblinking at the figured wallpaper until he had the engulfing remorse under control.

Bastard.

Finally, the three women had Olivia bathed. Dane stepped forward without a word to lift her from the tub, letting the now-brownish bathwater stream down his clothing without care.

Once Olivia was dried and clothed in a brief shift that would allow the physician to tend to her leg, Dane laid her on the clean bed linens, then tucked the bed-clothes gently beneath her chin.

She murmured something and rolled her head. Dane pressed a hand to her forehead. "She's hot."

Mrs. Huff nodded. "It's a blessing, really. If she'd lost overmuch blood, she'd not be able to run a fever." Mrs. Huff wiped her hands on her ruined apron. "I'll have Cook send up broth and brandy. She may wake up and it'll go easier on her if we can spoon the brandy down before the physician comes."

The doctor would be digging out the bullet. The agony would be excruciating. Dane felt sick. She was so damaged already, but it was necessary.

There was a tap on the door. Dane opened it to see Marcus in the hall.

"Dane, we found the carriage. It was abandoned just outside of Gretna Green."

Dane stared at him. "You continued the search, against my orders."

Marcus gazed back evenly. "You weren't thinking clearly. You were too close to the case."

It was true. In fact, if he wasn't much mistaken, he *was* the case. Or at least the target.

It was all over, at any rate. Sumner and whoever he was working with would have crossed this venture off as a failure. Dane was on to their plan to manipulate him, the Prince Regent was safe, and the Cheltenhams had been exposed. The game was up.

All that was left was for Dane to see to the Prince Regent's safety, now and always.

Dane turned to look at the door to Olivia's bedchamber, now closed against him. She was still as much of a problem as she'd been this morning before Marcus had pounded on the cottage door . . .

The door opened. Petty stuck her head out. "My lord, she's awake!"

29

Olivia found herself safe and warm and clean—blessedly clean. Her thigh still throbbed horribly under the bandage Mrs. Huff had hastily wrapped about it—"No need for you to see that, my lady!"—and Olivia's head felt as though a knife was repeatedly slicing through her brain.

Her bandaged hands were wrapped about a mug of broth that stung her sore throat when she swallowed. Other than that, she was quite thoroughly a mess.

Over the bandages that covered her hands to her wrists, her arms were scraped and bruised. Her unbandaged leg looked much the same. Her back muscles ached horribly, and she was fairly sure her nose was running.

Petty wiped it for her matter-of-factly. "Picked up a bit of a chill while you were out there, my lady. Doctor will put you right, straightaway." Petty was obviously very happy to see Olivia awake, which made her wonder if there'd been some doubt about that event.

"Look, my lady! His Lordship's here to see you!"

Obviously Petty wasn't nearly as glad to see Dane, although the lady's maid put up a good front. "See, my lord, she's right as rain."

Olivia kept her gaze on her broth. Lord Gargoyle could go rot in the stable dung heap for all she cared. She'd been drifting in and out over the last hour, but she'd heard a few things when people had thought her unconscious.

She wasn't sure what was true and what was fever dream, but she knew that Dane hadn't bothered to search for her.

She heard Dane say something quietly to Petty, then heard the rustle of skirts as Petty bustled from the room. The door closed and blessed silence reigned. Olivia adored Petty, but the girl did not understand how to be silent.

Dane, however, was bloody good at it. He was trying to outwait her; she could tell. She could see his boots at the edge of her vision, planted sturdily and stubbornly on her carpet.

Bloody Dane and his bloody boots could bloody wait.

She slowly sipped her broth. Her inclination to hang on his every word, her puppyish—and undeserved—loyalty, her tendency to dissolve when he was about . . . well, that was yesterday.

She gave the last swallow of broth a little swirl in the bottom of the mug. She was probably hungry, for it had been more than a day since she had eaten and she'd lost most of that on the ground. She'd not touched a thing since before the Hunt Ball—

Good heavens, was that only last evening? It seemed a month past.

Dane cleared his throat. Olivia shot him a sour glance. If he was waiting for her to speak, he was going to have a long wait. She'd spent her voice screaming for him. She had nothing left, in more ways than one.

Petty came back in carrying a fresh cup of broth and a flask. "Mrs. Huff thought you might need the brandy, my lady. For when the doctor comes."

Olivia finally turned to look at Dane with alarm in her eyes.

"You've a bullet still in you, Olivia," he said quietly. "The physician must dig it out."

Oh . . . oh . . . she didn't know a word bad enough for that. She took the flask from Petty's tray between her two cloth paws and upended it, tossing back a mighty swallow of brandy.

It hit her sore throat like fire, but she clapped a bandaged hand over her mouth and coughed it down. She was about to do it again when Dane's big hand wrapped about both of hers.

"You might want to go easy on that," he said mildly. "You wouldn't want to see it again."

It was the one thing he might have said that could stop her. She let him take the flask and relaxed back against the pillows. The single swallow of spirits was already beginning to vague away the pain.

He eased his big body onto the mattress at her side. He was clad in stained shirtsleeves and filthy trousers. His hair had fallen around his shoulders and his face was lined with strain.

He looked absolutely beautiful.

Olivia's eyes began to fill with irrational tears. The world was so unfair when he could be such a mess and such a bastard and look so wonderful, while she was clean and truehearted and she knew she looked just putrid.

Go away, she mouthed at him.

He clasped his hands over his bent knee and leaned back. "I cannot. I must know what happened."

"You left me out there." She wished she could scream it instead of whispering soundlessly.

He nodded. "I did. I offer my apologies for under-estimating you, not that I expect you'll accept them right now."

She raised a brow at him. *If ever.*

He caught that, too, for he nodded again. "That is your prerogative, of course." He tilted his head slightly and his gaze warmed. "I don't know how to tell you how glad I am that you were not leaving—"

One of her pillows struck him in the face. He thrust it away and frowned at her.

"What—"

Olivia gestured to Petty, pointing at her writing desk with an urgent hand. Bless Petty, for she understood instantly. "Oh! Yes, my lady!"

In a moment, she was back with paper and a pencil. "I thought that might do better, my lady."

Olivia held out her right hand and Petty unwound some of the ridiculous muffling bandages. Finally, Olivia's individually bandaged fingers were partially released. She pulled away, trailing a long banner of white from her wrist, and began to write furiously, large and clumsy and with great pressure.

She thrust the sheet at Dane. He took it and read aloud. " 'You'd rather I be injured and lost and nearly dead than safe and sound and with another man?' " He looked up, confused. "Well . . . yes . . . I mean, no, of course not! But . . ."

She was writing again. She threw it at him.

" 'But yes,' " he read aloud, although he needn't have. " 'Go away. I don't fancy you anymore.' "

Dimly Dane heard Petty turn and leave the room. Looking at Olivia's bleak expression, he couldn't blame the maid. He felt desperation rising within him. He'd done everything wrong with his sweet Olivia, from the very beginning.

And now he was losing her. He knew it, felt it as she gazed at him, her eyes more than sad, more than grieving. Her eyes said that she was done. Done with him, done with any chance they had.

Words threatened to choke him, words he knew he could never say. The truth stood between them, a secret that could never be told, knowledge that would only endanger them all . . .

And yet he spoke.

"Olivia . . . there is something you must understand. There is a reason why I have been so unwilling to trust you. . . . I cannot trust anyone outside a select few. . . . I should not tell you this—"

She scrawled something.

" 'Then don't. If you have so little faith in me, then don't.' "

He looked up at her, startled. She met his gaze and he went very still. Those were not Olivia's eyes looking back at him. Those were the eyes of a woman who believed in nothing and no one. His shock must have shown on his face, for she laughed sharply, a gasping, bitter sound.

" 'Everyone has their secrets, everyone has their uses for me, everyone has their hoops for me to leap through like a circus animal.' " She seemed to have no trouble putting her thoughts to paper. " 'Yet you had no faith in me. Now I am supposed to have faith in you?' "

She was going to leave him and he deserved to be left. Even now, with all that he knew, he could not quite dismiss his reservations.

" 'You made a mistake, my lord. I am tired of paying for it. All I have ever tried to do is please you, yet I am never enough. It is an impossible task. Frankly, I'm weary of trying. So please, tell me nothing. Do not burden me with more of your insurmountable requirements.' "

Dane sat there, inches from her, holding pages and pages of her pain in his hands, unable to meet her eyes again. What had he done to her?

He'd drained her, devoured her generosity and heart and sweetness, then turned around and asked for more. More proof, more evidence, more security that she was good enough for him. She'd taken her anguish to Marcus and Dane had blamed her for it. She'd made a friend in the Prince Regent and Dane had thought the worst of her.

She'd done for him what no other woman had ever dared, and he'd suspected her of treason.

She'd even tried to bring back his traitor and he'd thrown her away, discarding her pitilessly.

Her parents have admitted to the plot. She was meant to win you over. You must question her.

He closed his eyes against the voice of suspicion that still lived within him. Yet it was possible that everything she'd done was meant to make him throw everything he was away, all for love.

Love.

He stood as if he'd been burned by her nearness. "I shall disturb you no longer, my lady." Was that his voice, so strained and tight? He forced himself to look at her. Her head was dropped back on the pillows and her eyes were closed, but the tension within her told him she was not sleeping. She was only waiting for him to go.

He obliged, quietly closing the door on his own silent damnation.

Olivia slumped wearily when she heard the door latch click. Then she rolled carefully over, reaching beneath her mattress for her diary.

The pencil was making her fingers ache, but she forced her eyes to focus on the blank page before her.

> *Every moment he was in the room, a part of me longed to throw myself on him and weep away my fears and longing. I love him so. . . .*

The pencil faltered. The problem was, she was beginning to believe that the man she'd fallen in love with had never truly existed. She'd dreamed him into being, fooling herself with her own fantasy of some valiant lord of old, a man who would love and treasure her forever, a man who would never hurt her.

What a ridiculous idea. The world was full of pain. There was no such thing as love that lasted forever.

She'd been a silly child. Silly children believed in magical tales. Olivia felt solid, cold reality filling her, hardening her former wispy dreams into strength and resolve.

She snapped the diary shut and flung it across the bedchamber, the pages fluttering with the force of her rejection. She missed the fire, but the book hit the mantel with a satisfying thud and fell out of her sight.

I am not powerless. I am not a princess locked in a tower. I am Lady Greenleigh.

Then the door opened and the doctor entered, his bag of instruments in his hand.

And Dane had taken the flask.

Dane paced the hall outside Olivia's bedchamber. Her hoarse, broken cries of pain had barely been loud enough to penetrate the solid door, yet each one had stabbed through him like a sword.

He stopped and pressed his forehead to the cool wood. He couldn't bear another, he thought, then scoffed at his self-absorption. He wasn't the one with the knife digging in his leg, was he?

Yet no more cries came. That made him more worried than ever. Why had she stopped? Was the doctor done? Or had she—?

The door opened before him. The physician stood there, coat on, hat in hand, bag strapped up, and ready to leave. "The bullet is out and her concussion is becoming less serious. Her ladyship will be fine," he said cheerfully. "Provided she does not develop more fever and die."

Dane stared at the man, who nodded briskly and passed him by. Physicians existed on a separate plane of Society, it seemed. Well aware of their necessity, they rarely paid due respect to high birth.

Then Dane's weary brain took in the man's words. Olivia was going to be fine.

Fever.

Fear of that mysterious ailment filled him. He ran through the sitting room to Olivia's bedchamber, bursting through the door.

30

Lady Reardon was there, bathing perspiration from Olivia's pale face. "Shh," she ordered without turning. "She finally passed out, thank heaven. Bloody damned ham-handed doctor." Her voice was tight. "I feared he was going to take forever."

"What of fever?"

Lady Reardon shook her head. "She's very strong, not like I expected at all. There's a bit of heat in her, but nothing that won't pass now that we've the bullet out."

Dane sank to the chair that had been pulled up on the other side of the bed. "Oh, thank God."

Lady Reardon shot him a disbelieving glare. "Hmph. Nathaniel told me you still have her mother and father locked up. You haven't even allowed them to visit her."

Dane didn't back down. "Lord and Lady Cheltenham have been in the employ of a very dangerous French intelligence agent—"

"Who coerced them into this." Willa put down the damp cloth and tucked the covers more tightly around

Olivia. "Have you never been at someone else's mercy, my lord?"

I love you, you phenomenal ass. All I ever wanted was to be your lady.

"Once," Dane said, his voice a thread. "Just once."

Lady Reardon stood. "I think it's safe to let her sleep," she said. "I'll send one of the 'Etty sisters in to watch her."

"I'll stay," Dane said quietly.

"If you swear you won't tie her up or arrest her, or something else ridiculous."

Dane slid his gaze her way. "Not tonight, at any rate."

Lady Reardon folded her arms. "I don't like you, Lord Greenleigh. Nathaniel thinks I'm being an idiot, of course. It is our first real argument, in fact. I think you're hard. He thinks you're well aware of your duty." She turned to go but stopped at the door. "I want to ask you one question."

Dane didn't turn. Olivia looked so very pale. "What is that?"

"Why did you marry in the first place if you were never going to put your faith in a woman?"

Dane shook his head. "Good night, Lady Reardon."

She left, and the room fell silent. Dane moved his chair closer to reach for a strand of Olivia's hair that clung to her damp cheek.

"Your hair is always a mess," he whispered to her. He let the silky strand trail through his fingers and drop to the pillow. "I dream about your hair."

The doctor had rewrapped her hands. Dane carefully picked one up and brought it to his lips. "What am I going to do with you, my lady?" he said softly.

"You make me understand how my father could have done what he did."

He let out a breath and closed his eyes. "I never told you about my father, did I? Of course not. I never told you about anything."

He leaned back in the chair wearily, keeping her bandaged hand gently in his. "You must understand, he was a demanding man, but I was proud of that. I felt such high expectations were the sign of superior standards and ethics. When I was able to please him, I knew I'd done better than 'well enough,' better than 'quite good.' I knew I'd done just a bit beyond what he'd expected me to, that I'd reached a level somewhere just short of perfection."

Dane sighed, remembering. "Yet he was only human, after all." All too human. That scene in the study came back to him in full clarity. "I was so proud to be . . . who I was, so damned sure that I knew everything. I disdained him, accused him, renounced him to his face. There wasn't a drop of sympathy or compassion in me. I appointed myself judge, jury, and executioner."

She didn't comment of course, but Dane could well imagine what Olivia would tell him, the same as Marcus had.

Suicide was your father's choice.

Dane shook his head against that fact. "Suicide was the only option I left him. I was so angry, so betrayed . . . I told him I had sent a letter to the Prime Minister, informing him of everything. But I hadn't."

He rubbed his other hand over his face, trying to wipe away weariness and that suspicious moisture leaking from his closed lids. "I'd written it. It was still on my dressing table because I couldn't bring myself to post it. But I wanted to hurt him, strike out at him, shake him like he'd shaken me."

Old anger surfaced. "He should have seen it through. He could have faced the consequences and served his sentence." Dane made a dark noise, contradicting himself. "Of course, his sentence might have been hanging. He'd given vital plans to her, battles that we lost, *men* that we lost. Then again, perhaps it wasn't because of me. Perhaps he simply couldn't live with himself."

He opened his eyes and gazed at his sleeping wife. "Or live without her. She disappeared just then, doubtless running back to France. He loved her, you see. He loved her above everything. Above his country, above his duty, above even . . ."

Above even me.

Dane stood abruptly. "Well, this is just ridiculous," he muttered to himself. "Sitting in the dark talking to no one." He turned to leave the room. He ought to have one of the 'Ettys take over the watch.

A piece of paper crackled under his shoe. He automatically bent to pick it up and kept going. He had important matters to see to, after all.

Then he left, closing the door on the woman who watched him from the bed with wide-open eyes.

He was in the library before he recalled the scrap of paper in his hand. He opened it and examined it idly. It was a fragment of a page, a corner torn away, filled with tiny cramped writing.

Frowning, he moved closer to the candles.

Only three lines remained.

> *. . . mistaken adoration honestly / so that it*
> *might not leave me when he finds out the*
> *truth?*
>
> *Might he then be tricked into loving me?*

Ah, his suspicious inner voice rejoiced darkly, *I knew it.*

Dane gazed at the torn bit of paper, forcing himself to face the truth.

She was not a victim of her parents' plotting. She'd known the entire time.

And he didn't care. He wanted her anyway.

Black fear threatened to choke him. *He wanted her anyway.*

His emotions chased one another madly though him, leaving cuts that bled out anguish. She was going to be fine. She was part of the plot. She'd given him the gift of passion. She had said she loved him. She had been tricking him into loving her. She'd tried to stop Sumner. He'd left her out there, alone and injured.

She was a liar.

She was Olivia.

Guilt. Passion. Shame. Suspicion.

Duty. *Olivia.*

He turned and strode from the library. There was only one person who could help him with this, only one who could understand.

The study door was locked, the key gone. Dane kicked it open without a pause. The room was icy and cobwebbed, the furniture shrouded in dust cloths. Dane ripped them all away, tossing them into a corner.

He dropped to his knees on the floor where a

jewel-toned carpet had once lain, one that had been burned because of the blood and brains that covered it.

"Father, help me." His hoarse whisper filled the dead room. "What am I to do?"

He knelt there until his limbs were cold, until the dust had settled, until the moon set and the room went entirely dark.

His father wasn't here. The study wasn't full of Henry Calwell, who had loved and lost himself. It was only a room, cold and unused.

Dane bowed his head. And he was only a man, no better or worse than his father. He was weak and inconsistent and subject to all the vagaries of other men.

Yet he was the Lion.

Therefore, he knew what he must do.

Early in the morning, two days after Olivia had been shot, she found herself on the road again.

Dane had explained that she need not go immediately.

"But I must go," she'd pointed out to him. "So I should like to go as soon as possible."

He'd only nodded. "I shall ride with you to Greenleigh—"

"Cheltenham," she'd said, her head high. "I will go to Cheltenham."

I am not powerless. I will decide where I will live. And I will live at Cheltenham.

Since she doubted Dane would like the world to see her in rags, she was fairly sure she would be receiving an allowance. An allowance she would pour into Cheltenham. Her parents were still young enough to enjoy many years there, but then it would be hers and hers alone.

She would never be Dane's lady, but she would be mistress of Cheltenham.

He'd agreed easily enough. And why not, when his sole purpose was to dispose of her as soon as possible?

She allowed a footman to carry her to the bottom of the stairs, but then she insisted on walking. She would not heal properly if she never used her leg.

"You are a most durable woman," Lady Reardon said with a sad smile. "You make me feel rather puny."

Olivia shook her head. "Not nearly durable enough."

They walked past a room that was having a much-needed clearing out, by the look of it. "That is where the former Lord Greenleigh died while cleaning his pistol," Lady Reardon said softly.

"Ah." Olivia willed herself not to feel a thing for Dane's loss. He didn't want her empathy. "Think you the weather will hold?"

Lady Reardon glanced at her. "It seems as if you will have good travel," she answered easily. "I pray our journey will go as well in a week."

Lord and Lady Reardon were staying out the entire week, as were the Prince Regent and the Duke and Duchess of Halswick. The other guests had cleared out sometime after Olivia had been brought back bloody and gun-shot, apparently, including Miss Absentia Hackerman. *Imagine that.*

Fled back to the rest of Society with a mouthful about the new Lady Greenleigh, no doubt. Olivia found it rather difficult to care. She couldn't even remember being the girl who'd been so desperate to please the world with her Hunt Ball entertainment.

Outside in the drive, organized chaos reigned once again. Dane was going to ride Galahad, leaving Olivia the carriage. Petty popped up at her elbow. "Are you sure you won't need me with you, my lady?"

Olivia shook her head, forcing a small smile. "I'm only going to rest, Petty. Cheltenham is not far over the border. We'll be there by nightfall. I shall be perfectly well on my own." She was panting to be alone, to tell the truth. Constant nursing did bring one's health back, but it also drove one mad when all one wanted was a good howling cry.

She looked down to see her lockbox in the maid's hands. It reminded her. . . .

"Petty, did you pack my diary?"

Petty swallowed. "Oh, my lady, I—you threw it in the fire, my lady. I thought you didn't want it."

Olivia sighed. "No, that's fine. As long as it's gone." God forbid someone should read her childish dreams and scribbling about Dane.

Running hoofbeats down the drive caught her attention. She stepped back warily. The last thing she needed at the moment was another fall. Horses had the oddest tendency to run into her.

Lord Wyndham leaped down, covered in road dust.

Dane strode out of the house to greet him. "Hellfire man, did you gallop from London?"

Wyndham shrugged. "I changed horses on the way." He flicked his sharp-eyed gaze at where Marcus and Lord Reardon stood. Dane watched as both

Nate and Marcus turned instantly. The Royal Four had that instinct about them, didn't they?

The four of them strode inside. Dane led them to the newly opened study. It was only a room after all. A room with a newly repaired door and most of the books and items cleared to make way for fresh decor. Only the big desk remained. Dane leaned one hip on the edge and nodded to Wyndham. "You have the floor."

"Barrowby died last night," Stanton said shortly. "Without heir."

"Damn." Marcus and Nate made similar noises. It wasn't the legal heir they cared about. The Four didn't give a damn what happened to the old lord's estate— but to die without naming a new Fox?

"Liverpool wants us all at Barrowby. Now."

The Prime Minister had no real ability to call an emergency session, but the fact remained that without a Fox, the very fabric of the Royal Four was weakened.

Marcus shrugged. "I can stay to guard the Prince Regent. We have more than enough men, and we're on our guard now."

Dane nodded. "I don't think he's in as much danger now. They had the element of surprise before and they failed."

Nathaniel nodded slowly and looked at Marcus. "If I may leave my lady in your care?"

"Of course."

They looked at Dane. He hesitated. It would take the entire day to reach Cheltenham at the convoy's speed, and it would take him away from the road to Barrowby.

You are the Lion. Are you going to let her rule your every decision?

"I am ready to go now."

Reardon nodded and left to pack a bag. Wyndham threw himself down on a nearby sofa for a catnap, for he'd left just after midnight. Dane and Marcus discussed any additional precautions to be taken now that Marcus would be on his own.

"Dane, go. I'm more than able for this."

Dane grinned at his friend. "I know. You do realize that if there truly is no Fox heir, you are the logical choice to become the Fox."

Marcus shrugged. "I live to serve."

Dane wasn't fooled. He knew what it meant to Marcus. Dane clapped his friend on the back, then turned to leave. There was one more thing to do.

31

"I see," Olivia said quietly when Dane told her she would be traveling without him. He'd sent Lady Reardon to her husband, and they stood alone on the front apron of Kirkall Hall.

"You'll be perfectly safe," Dane assured her. "I'm sending some extra footmen along as well." Armed footmen, but he needn't tell her that.

She raised her chin, meeting his gaze. "Then I have one thing to ask of you. I shall send you word in a few weeks if my courses do not come. If they do . . . well, I'm aware that it is still my duty to bear you an heir. I only beg of you to leave me be for a while. It—it will be easier to see you after some time has passed."

His heir. He'd completely lost sight of that possibility somewhere in all this madness. Even now she could be carrying his heir.

Torn again. He could have sworn that he showed no expression, but she evidently read him too well. Her eyes went blank and cold, like the frozen surface of a lake.

She turned and limped away from him, taking a

footman's help to climb into her carriage. She didn't look at him again, nor wave as the vehicle smoothly rolled into motion. But then, Errol wouldn't jar his lady if his life depended on it.

Dane watched the convoy roll down the long drive, finally losing sight of them around a curve.

Nate and Stanton came up behind him, toting a change of clothes. "Shall we be off?"

Dane nodded. His own things had already been moved from the carriage to behind his saddle. He silently took Galahad's reins and mounted, then joined the others as they trotted down the drive.

Being without her would clear his head and give peace to his mind. He was sure it would.

In due course.

Physical pain was an astounding tool for clarifying the mind.

Every jolt of the carriage on the road sent a fresh bolt of angry pain up Olivia's thigh. The suspension was the finest money could buy and Errol had sworn to carry her carefully, but she now realized she'd been a fool to think she was ready to travel. The past several hours had been hellish. She would never survive another three or four to Cheltenham.

Stupid pride and desperation had prompted her to claim herself more healed than she was. To lie in that bed for several more days, with Petty doting and Dane there, somewhere in the house, feeling him there but never seeing him, knowing what she knew now—

She'd heard every word he'd said about his father and she had known then that there was no hope. Dane thought love was a weakness, an illness, a stain on the soul to be washed out.

She'd lain there, listening, and realized that she didn't want Dane's sort of love.

She'd told herself that she would be fine alone. She'd been alone for a very long time, even when Walter was alive. Alone was a familiar place to be.

But cold.

She wrapped her arms about her middle, thinking of the possibilities. She might be carrying now. If Dane didn't want her child, then she would raise it herself, at Cheltenham.

She didn't allow herself to think about if he did want her child. If she bore a boy, Dane would surely want him. What would happen if a powerful lord wanted her child but not her?

Once she would have declared Dane incapable of that sort of heartlessness. Now she wondered.

Another jolt reminded her of a more practical, immediate problem than her possible offspring.

She needed to use the chamber pot. Not a wise move when in motion.

Bracing herself on the opposite seat and stretching high, she struck the ceiling of the carriage with the heel of her hand. Errol popped open the small trap there.

"Yes, my lady?"

"I think it's time we had a rest, Errol."

"Yes, my lady. Will you be wanting your maid?"

The thought of Petty fluttering over her made Olivia nearly shudder. "No, I wish a bit of quiet. I—I might have a nap."

Unlikely, with her leg throbbing that way, but it

would keep the overly solicitous Greenleigh staff away. Olivia longed to go home to her silly pottering old butler and housekeeper, dependent and sweet and needing her to care for them.

The carriage slowed and rolled to a most perfect stop. "Errol, you're a marvel," she called out. She might keep Errol. There was much to be said for skillful driving.

She heard him jump down, followed by a rain of footmen leaping down from her carriage. Heavens, she felt like a dog with too many fleas.

Well, they would all take their time eating, thinking her napping quietly.

Olivia bent to drag the unused chamber pot from beneath the seat. Unfortunately, she found it impossible to use. Unable to truly bend her wounded leg, there was no way to do it without—er, missing.

The thought of riding for hours in a urine-stained coach was nearly as bad as the prospect of explaining it later.

She could call for Petty, who had helped her often in the last two days—but she'd never get rid of her again.

Her leg throbbed, her bladder ached, and her head was beginning to pound as the carriage grew stuffier now that it wasn't moving.

Air was what she needed. Air and a careful stretch of her legs and a chance to . . . well, she was country bred, after all.

She slipped out of the far door of the carriage, away from where the servants were gathered with their hampers. She had her own dinner packed in the carriage, which she would eat when she returned.

The day was warmish, considering the season. She

spent a few moments limping up and down alongside the carriage, until her thigh cramp eased.

Then she carefully stepped down the slight slope—nothing like the road at Kirkall, thank heavens—to the brushy area beside the road. She'd go in a bit to find a nice thicket. She wasn't completely shameless, after all.

She found one straightaway, and quite a relief it was. Done, she awkwardly bent to wash her hands in a tiny streamlet. A stick cracked nearby. She carefully straightened. "Now, don't carry on, Petty. I was only—"

Sumner stood before her, filthy and wild looking, his blue eyes desperate.

Olivia took a hurried step back, forgetting her wound. With a cry, she felt her leg give out beneath her. In a flash, Sumner was on her, his hand covering her mouth.

"I didn't want you hurt," he gasped. "I did my best, but you would go and make him fall in love with you."

Olivia felt herself being dragged, back and away from the road and help. She struggled wildly, but he had her from behind now with his other arm about her waist. Her limbs flailed uselessly. Finally, he picked her up off the ground entirely and lurched off into the wood with her.

Olivia awoke in the dark. "I am entirely weary of waking up on the ground," she murmured tightly, or at least she tried to around the cloth strip tied over her mouth. This time at least, she was on a floor made of wide splintery planks.

Her head pounded, but that was because of hanging head down over the withers of blasted Sumner's blasted bony nag. Her thigh was a beaten bruise now, pushed beyond any healing she'd managed by the struggling she'd done.

Her hands didn't hurt much, it was true, but that was likely because they were numb from being tied behind her back. She was still bound, but not for long. She'd not had a brother mad for playacting for nothing. This was hardly the first time in her life she'd been tied up.

"I've been bound by pirates and Red Indians," she muttered around her gag. "All better men than you, Sumner."

She took a breath, for this was going to hurt in the condition she was in, then bent nearly double and slid her bound hands down over her buttocks, over the backs of her thighs—*breathe deep; do it anyway*—the backs of her calves, and finally up and over her bound feet.

Pull the gag out first. Then use one's teeth to figure out the knot. *Hmph. Sumner obviously did* not *have a brother.* The knot was a simple double one and not all that tight. She managed to worry it free, though her jaw ached mightily by the time she was done. *I never thought I'd thank you for that, Walter.*

The bindings on her feet were simple enough. Finally, she stood, free.

To be stuck in a dark room. With a sigh, she began to explore. There was the splintery floor. That told her she wasn't in a house, or at least not a very nice house. She moved carefully, sliding her feet just in case there were rotted places, for she smelled rot, clearly. Her outstretched hands touched wall. More splintery planks.

All right, that meant some sort of utilitarian building. A stable? A springhouse?

She became aware of the sound of rushing water. And that smell—she knew that smell. It was a compound of damp rot, dry wood—

And ancient flour.

She was in the abandoned Cheltenham flour mill.

She laughed out loud. "Sumner, you idiot. I know this place upside and down." She'd even been tied up here before, come to think of it, before she and Walter had been forbidden to play in the rotting building.

She followed the wall and found the crude door. Locked. "I thought so." She turned from the door and walked confidently toward the center of the room. The giant millstone would still be here, far too heavy for anyone to steal. "One, two, three—"

She stumbled and fell over something unpleasantly soft and giving. She reached out, patting carefully, then drew her hand back sharply at the feel of cold flesh.

She was locked in the old mill with a dead body.

Then her mood lightened when it occurred to her that it might be Sumner who was dead. "I've never been bloodthirsty before," she explained to the body. "But I've come to believe that some people deserve to die."

She reached out carefully, letting her fingers lightly look for some sort of identifying characteristic. Sumner was tall. So was the body. Sumner had big hands. So did the body. Sumner had longish dirty hair. So did the body.

"Well, things are looking up," she murmured. She took a breath and reached for the face, hoping it wouldn't be too icky. She ran her hands lightly over the forehead. High brow. Could be Sumner.

Straight nose. Could be Sumner.

Half-inch-long crescent-shaped scar just below the left eye. Could be—

"*Walter?*"

32

Nate's horse threw a shoe mere hours into the journey. When the three riders met a crossroad that showed high traffic, Stanton suggested they follow it to the nearest village and change out horses. They'd pushed a fast pace, although Galahad was barely winded.

Dane knew Galahad could make it, and it was un-likely they'd find a horse that could carry him at some coaching-inn hostelry. There was a fine tree at the cross-ing and a small grass-lined stream.

"I'll wait here and rest Galahad. Fetch me back a meat pie and a flask of wine."

The other two eyed him curiously but nodded. Dane didn't want to explain his need to be alone.

As they rode on, Dane dismounted and removed Gala-had's bridle, letting the stallion graze. Dane reached into his satchel for a hoof pick to make sure Galahad didn't come up lame.

His hand encountered something that ought not to be in there. He pulled out a small book bound in blue leather that he'd never seen before. He flipped a few

pages and froze, recognizing the cramped tiny letter-
ing.

This was Olivia's. He marveled at page after page
filled with the tiny printing. Who knew she had so
much to say?

Suddenly he noticed the smile spread across his
face. He snapped the diary shut and stuffed it back
in the bag. With swift efficiency he tended the stallion's hooves, then hesitated as he deposited the pick
back in the satchel. A blue corner stuck up out of the
opening.

He shoved it back down, hard, then strode to the tree
and threw himself down in the shade. It was far too
warm for this time of year. He rotated his shoulders uneasily. Such weather made him restless, itchy.

He gazed sightlessly down the white chalk roads
crossing the moor. Barrowby used to talk about the
moor, going on about how a man could think with so
much sky above him.

The last thing Dane wanted was to think.

If he thought, he would have to ponder why he'd felt
something break inside him when he'd watched Olivia's
carriage disappear around the curve.

He'd have to wonder why it was he couldn't go three
minutes without thinking of her, despite the urgency of
his mission.

He'd have to wonder why he was perishing to read
her diary.

He rubbed a hand across his cheek. Her diary would
be full of her. It would bring her close again, just when
he'd managed a bit of distance.

There might be some interesting intelligence inside.

For once, Dane welcomed the suspicious voice of the Lion. Of course! He must read the diary. He sprang to his feet, startling Galahad.

Soothing the horse, Dane finally reached for the satchel. Thrusting his hand inside, he felt about for the book.

He couldn't find it. Impatiently he yanked the ties that held the satchel to the saddle and dumped the damn thing out on the ground.

The book plopped out onto the pile of clothing he was apparently not going to be wearing without a good cleaning.

Dane picked it up and went back to his spot under the tree. He was a fast reader, despite Olivia's odd writing, and it wasn't long before he was thoroughly engrossed in her thoughts.

The first half must have covered the last year or more, for she talked of holidays with Walter and her parents, of the state of Cheltenham, of her worries about her sickly staff and the last remaining cottagers.

"Cow suppositories?" Had he read that correctly?

Then he encountered the hurried, careless scribbling telling of Walter's death.

> *Drowning? Walter? It doesn't seem possible*
> *when he swam better than I!*

Dane frowned. Now that he thought on it, it did seem unlikely. Olivia was a superior swimmer; he'd seen it for himself. It might behoove him to look further into Walter's death after all.

Then there was the entry about the day on the

bridge. "Viking god?" he muttered, smiling slightly. Then, "I am *not* a dandy!"

His eyes flew over the pages, reading faster and faster. Her confusion about his lack of courtship. Her frustration with her mother's insistence that the family forgo mourning. Her fears about wedding a stranger.

He could have eased those fears so easily—but then again, most of them had come true, hadn't they? She'd been abused, neglected, and ultimately sent away.

Then he found the torn page.

He dug the scrap of paper from his weskit pocket and matched it to the other half. It was a poem of sorts. A very bad one, but then he didn't think she'd ever meant anyone else to read it.

> *If one gathered together the finest of men / If one took the broad shoulders of this one fellow / And the fair hair of that one. / The blue eyes of another / And the chiseled features of that one over there.*
>
> *The intelligence of the scholar / The sensitivity of the poet / The humor of the rogue / The wealth of the king / The virility of the stallion / Then you might have a man like mine.*
>
> *The mystery is . . . Why is he mine? / What do I have that would attract / A man such as that?*
>
> *I am not beautiful, nor particularly good. / I am not wise, nor am I always clever. / I am not elegant, nor poised, nor even witty.*
>
> *If there is some strange attraction, then*

dare I think that answer to the mystery be
love?/And though I might not be worthy, it is
possible that he does not yet know that./
Might I make myself worthy somehow? Might
I become a woman who is loved?/Might I
earn that mistaken adoration honestly/So
that it might not leave me when he finds out
the truth?

Might he then be tricked into loving me?

Dane put the diary down and blew out a breath. And she'd been worried about living up to *his* expectations? He was no paragon, no poet, no king.

The stallion bit, well . . .

So the scrap of betraying evidence was simply part of a—a love poem. He tipped the book up and peered at the date of that entry. It was the day after they had wed.

Well, he had done rather well that night . . . not that she would have known the difference. These weren't the musings of a seductress. These were the thoughts of a young woman, innocent yet wise beyond her years.

Read the entire thing. You shall see.

He did, and he had to admit that he thoroughly enjoyed it, even dropping his head back and laughing helplessly at parts.

He saw his life and his household as he'd never seen it before. She was wry and ridiculous and she never missed a single thing, showing him his life through Olivia-tinted lenses that made him miss her smile with a deep, sudden stab of loss.

Then he read the last lines, dated two days before, scrawled in pencil with wounded hands.

Every moment he was in the room, a part of
me longed to throw myself on him and weep
away my fears and longing. I love him so. . . .

Dane was finding it hard to breathe. He couldn't go
on; he couldn't hide it from himself any longer.

He loved her. He loved his sweet, droll, spirited
Lady Greenleigh with all his heart, and more so with
every breath he took.

What a fool he was.

Not for loving her, but for doubting himself. How
could he ever think loving her was a weakness?

Lady Reardon's words came back to him. *Why did*
you marry in the first place if you were never going to
put your faith in a woman?

Faith. His faith in other fragile humans—and in
himself, to recognize wicked from decent—had died
with his father.

Until Lady Olivia pulled him from the mud.

In the mill, Olivia was still in the dark, waiting for Walter to awaken. She'd pressed her ear to his cool mouth
and felt his breath and rejoiced that he was not dead after all—but he was so still and cold.

She lay down behind him, wrapping her arms around
his waist and hoping her warmth would help him.

And she waited.

Now that she thought on it, she hated waiting, and
she ought to know. She'd done more than her share of it.

She been waiting away the years in Cheltenham.
Waiting for her parents to care if she existed, waiting
for her life to begin, waiting for her dreams—dreams

she had never admitted to anyone as she went about her life—to come true.

And for a little while, they had.

Rather, she had convinced herself they had. She'd placed her heart on a plate and served it to the world along with a knife and fork. She had never believed in anyone or anything the way she had believed in Dane.

How could she have been so naive that she thought her knight would ride in on his white horse and save her from her life?

Instead, she'd pulled a Viking god from the mud.

Perhaps she ought to have known right then that things were not going to go as planned.

Yet who could have predicted matters would go so badly, so quickly? As instantly as their passion for each other had ignited, it had burned away every possibility they had of being happy.

She'd done everything she knew to do. She'd tried so hard to be who he wanted her to be, until she scarcely recognized herself anymore.

He'd left her anyway.

No. You left him first.

Olivia pressed a hand to her throat. Oh no.

She *had* left him first. When he'd failed to rescue her in the wood, she'd given up on him. She'd listed him with her parents and Miss Hackerman and the Greenleigh servants—all the people who had never been there for her. Just like that, she'd thrown him back like an unsatisfactory fish. Because he wasn't as perfect as she'd wanted to believe he was, she'd rejected him.

Just like every other woman had.

The ache in her heart was no longer for herself alone now. What she'd done—it was the same as she'd accused him of.

She'd had no faith in him. No faith that he could join her in hammering out something wonderful in the fire they had begun together. Just because she'd fallen in love very nearly immediately didn't mean that he would, too. She'd not bothered giving second chances or third chances or fourth if required for him to see what they could become.

He'd failed her once, so she'd given up on him.

And now he was gone, heading away from her, and heaven knew when she'd see him again.

Next to her, Walter stirred.

"Walt?" She rose to her knees and put her hands on his shoulders. "Walt, please wake up."

"Livvie?" His voice was a rasp. "That tears it. I've gone barking mad."

Olivia laughed, tears of happiness forming in her eyes. She wrapped her arms about her brother. "Walt, you aren't dead!"

He coughed. "No, but apparently I'm mad," he croaked. "Bugger it all. I tried so hard to hang on."

Olivia only laughed and laughed, hanging on to the only person in the world she was sure loved her.

"Livvie, for a hallucination, you certainly do cut off a bloke's air."

"Oh!" She released him, giggling madly as she cried. "I'm sorry. . . . I'm simply so—"

"Bloody hell," Walt breathed. "You're *real*."

"Indeed." She fought to get hold of herself. "As happy as I am to see you alive and well—"

Walt coughed again. "Scratch the 'well,' I'm afraid. I've been sick for—I don't really know how long, but I'm bloody weak."

"You drowned more than a month ago," Olivia told him.

Walter scoffed. "I did not! Can you imagine—" His indignation was cut off by coughing. Olivia pounded him helpfully until he was done.

"It was that bloody valet."

"Yes," agreed Olivia. "Bloody Sumner."

"Damn right, bloody—hold on; how do you know Sumner?"

Olivia sighed. "To make a short story of it . . ." She counted on her fingers. "I hired him. He made the Duchess of Halswick vomit. He made a fool of me at the Hunt Ball. He tried to kill George. He made my husband reject me. He shot me. He kidnapped me. . . ." She thought for a moment. "Yes, that covers it fairly well."

Walt whistled. "Bloody Sumner."

Olivia nodded sadly. "Bloody Sumner indeed."

"Hmm. Husband?"

"Lord Greenleigh. Very handsome."

" 'The Dane.' Not bad. This George bloke?"

Olivia sighed. "The Prince Regent. Very sweet."

"My, you have been busy. The Duchess of Halswick, eh? Must have been the kippers."

Olivia nodded. "Under her eggs. Ruined a number of fine carpets."

"Bloody Sumner."

They sat in companionable silence for a bit. Then Walter shifted. "How's Mum?"

"Under arrest. Father, too."

Walter sighed. "I tried to get them out of it, Livvie. A few more weeks and I would have wed Miss Hackerman."

"I know." Olivia leaned back on her hands. "Although if I were you, I'd rather be trapped in this mill."

Walt fell back, snickering helplessly, with an intermittent cough. Olivia listened with a smile on her lips.

"Walter, we know this mill better than anyone. How was it that you haven't been able to escape?"

Walter caught his breath. "Ah, then you missed the leash." He did something and Olivia heard a chain rattle on the floor. "Tight around my ankle. Tied up like a bloody dog."

"Is it very long?" If they could climb up the millstone's machinery to the miller's chamber upstairs, there might be something—

"I can walk this chamber," he said, "but only just. The bloody thing gets wrapped around the millstone."

The millstone. Two hundred stone of . . . well, *stone*!

"Walt, if I can engage the gears . . . do you think the millstone can crush the chain?"

"That's my favorite plan," he said agreeably. "There are two issues, however. One, I couldn't get upstairs to throw the lever."

"That's where I come in," Olivia said excitedly.

"Two, if the chain gets caught up, I could get dragged into the millstone myself."

Olivia deflated. "Oh. That isn't good."

"My second-favorite plan was to surprise Sumner when he enters, strangle him with the chain, divest him of his key, and walk out the front door."

"I like that. Especially the strangling-Sumner part. Why isn't that your favorite plan?"

"It was. But then he left and never came back. Until today, apparently."

Olivia gaped. "He left you chained here while he went to work for me? How did you survive?"

"There's a lovely drip of water there in the corner that never dries up. As far as food, I simply stopped thinking about it a while ago."

Olivia reached out. "Give me your hand." He placed his cold hand in hers. She slid her fingers up his wrist and under his tattered sleeve.

His arm was nothing but bone and stringy muscle. "Oh, Walter!"

He pulled away. "Well, you know, bloody Sumner and all."

She felt icy with fury. "Let me strangle him. Please?"

"Be my guest. If he ever comes back."

At that moment, the door opened, flooding the room with light.

33

When the light swept the room, Walter went limp. Olivia threw her arm before her eyes, blinded.

"Forgot to tell you about that part," Walter whispered from where he lay like the dead. "That's why it never worked out."

Olivia blinked back the blindness quickly, but then she hadn't been in here for weeks like Walter. What had seemed like a brilliant sunbeam was merely the light from a cheap lantern.

Sumner stood in the circle of light, holding the lantern high. "Who untied you?"

Olivia spread her hands. "The ghost, of course."

Apparently Sumner wasn't the superstitious sort, for his expression became derisive. "Ballocks. You wormed out of the bindings, didn't you?"

It had been worth a try. Olivia folded her arms. "You must release us. Walter is very ill."

To her amazement, Sumner actually looked worried. "I know he is. That's one reason why I brought you here."

"What did you do to him?"

"He drowned—or almost."

Olivia narrowed her eyes. " 'Ballocks,' " she quoted.

"I did it for the same reason I kidnapped you. To protect you both!"

He knelt next to Walter, putting his hand over Walter's brow. "We were on the pleasure barge, Wallingford and us and *him*."

Olivia didn't think he meant Walter.

Sumner went on. "They were going to kill your brother when he refused to cooperate. I followed him up on deck and I conked him on the head, planning to carry him off the barge in one of the small boats. He fell left instead of right and hit the water. It was a close call, trying to get him out." He shook his head. "The water was terribly dark."

Did he expect her to feel sorry for him? He could have killed Walter—and still might if she couldn't get her brother to a physician!

Sumner went on, spilling everything in a shaky, desperate manner. He was the unwilling minion of a French spy, who had a hold over him because of his criminal past. He was being forced to act against them but couldn't bring himself to kill people who had been so kind to him.

As he went on—and on and bloody on—it became apparent to Olivia that Sumner was a weak man but not an evil one.

He explained that he did his best to foil his master's plan to manipulate Dane by keeping Olivia and Dane from succeeding in their marriage. Unfortunately, when Dane sent Olivia away, Sumner's master decided that she must be eliminated to make room for another attempt.

Sumner had been ordered to kill her just as he was ordered to kill her brother.

Olivia took a breath as Sumner's story wound down. She had to be careful here. He was obviously in a very unbalanced state.

She slapped him across the top of his head. "You bloody idiot!" she shrieked at him. "Don't you realize who my husband is? Who I am? If you had come to me, I could have helped you! I could have gone to the Prince Regent himself on your behalf! You didn't have to kidnap us!"

Sumner held up both hands against her tirade. "Rescued! Not kidnapped—rescued!"

Olivia planted both fists on her hips. "Don't be stupid. We're obviously your prisoners. Walter is very ill and very thin. In a few more days he might die." She swallowed back panic. She must convince Sumner.

"Please listen, Sumner." She forced her voice to a soothing level. "It's not too late. If you take us to Cheltenham House, I will send for my husband and tell him only what he needs to know. You'll be a hero, Sumner, not a criminal. A richly rewarded hero," she said warmly. "Very richly rewarded."

But Sumner only shook his head urgently. "No. No, *he* will find out. I'll be too dead to be rewarded."

Olivia held out her hands to calm him. "I see. Of course not. We must work that out then, how to protect you. But we can't do that until we get to Cheltenham House. We'll all be safe there. It's only a half—" She wasn't any too quick these days. "It's only an hour's walk from here."

Sumner nodded. "I know. That's why I chose this place. No one ever looks under their very nose."

It was true. To think she may have driven right past the captive Walter when she'd first left Cheltenham for London!

"Walter used to tell me stories about the two of you as children," Sumner added fondly. "How you used to play here. I thought he might like it."

Olivia blinked. Bloody Sumner was bloody well out of his mind. "Sumner, Walter doesn't like it here anymore. Walter likes Cheltenham House."

Sumner looked down at Walter, then back up at her. "I don't know what to do. He won't like it if I disobey."

"Sumner," Olivia softened her voice with great care. "Sumner, haven't you already disobeyed him when you refused to kill us?" She had to step cautiously. She wouldn't want Sumner to suddenly regret keeping them alive.

Sumner blinked. "You're right," he said slowly. "You're right. It's already too late, isn't it?" He reached into his pocket.

Olivia froze. What was it? A pistol? A knife?

A key. Sumner bent next to Walter's ankle manacle. Olivia closed her eyes and let her breath out softly.

"How perfectly accurate, Sumner," came a voice from the doorway. Olivia jerked her head up to see a small, dapper, round-faced man standing there, with two taller men behind.

"It is much, much too late." The small man smiled kindly at Olivia over his pistol. "Lady Greenleigh, I assume? Forgive my informality, but I already feel I know you so well, having shot you myself." He bowed.

"Let me introduce myself. I am the Chimera or, as your parents know me, the Debt Collector."

Dane was bridling Galahad when Stanton and Nate rode up.

"Excellent," Stanton said. "We've a good part of the day left. We'll make it tonight."

"But you will make it without me," Dane said as he mounted. "I'm going to Cheltenham."

"Good for you," Nate said with a grin.

Stanton wasn't as pleased. "But what of Barrowby? With the Chimera on the loose, it is imperative that we straighten this mess out immediately."

Dane gazed at the Falcon evenly. "Stanton, is Barrowby dead at this moment?"

Stanton blinked. "You know he is. I told you so hours ago."

"Right. And will he still be dead tomorrow?"

Catching on, Stanton gave Dane a sour look. "Of course he will."

"Then I will be at Barrowby tomorrow." Dane smiled, thinking of being in Olivia's arms again. "Probably, anyway."

Nate was grinning widely, but the Falcon was eyeing Dane with dark intensity. Dane had always suspected that Stanton mistrusted him.

Well, who bloody cared? The Falcon didn't outrank the Lion, after all. Dane blinked innocently at the Falcon. "Oh, and Stanton? You know that saying, 'Blood will tell'?"

"Yes."

"Well, it's a great lot of ballocks."

With that, Dane turned his mount's head toward Cheltenham and his heart—his amazing, delightful, and, he hoped, forgiving Olivia.

Back at the mill, the Chimera promptly disposed of Sumner with a blow to the head and advanced on Olivia. "Lady Greenleigh, I was so hoping we would have a chance to chat before you die. Tell me, what is it about Lord Greenleigh that makes me want to kill him so thoroughly?"

Olivia took a step back. "Ah, his height?"

The man flinched slightly. A direct hit, apparently.

"Tell me about him."

"He's very, very tall."

The small man pursed his lips. "I was thinking more along the lines of secret societies, powerful partnerships between lords, the power behind the Crown . . . that sort of thing."

Oh, Dane, I fear I'm in a mess here. "I think my husband likes to shoot grouse. And work on his investments. And sleep with me."

The small man smiled. "I imagine he does. What else does he do?"

Olivia licked her lips. "I . . . I've only been married for little more than a week—"

"Eleven days," the Chimera corrected her gently.

The man's chill soul seemed to emanate from him. Olivia found herself very much afraid of him. "Eleven days. Yes. I don't really know him all that well. He doesn't even like me. He sent me away."

She backed right into Walter, who continued to play dead. Luckily she didn't step on anything vital. The small man stepped forward again. The two men behind him moved into the light.

"Wallingford," Olivia gasped. She felt Walter twitch in response.

The Chimera smiled happily. "There, you see, Wallingford? Your reputation precedes you. Even the wife of the powerful Lord Greenleigh fears you."

Wallingford let his eyes travel disrespectfully over Olivia. She immediately felt the need to bathe.

"I'm a married man now," Wallingford said with a lascivious smile. "My bride is back in Gretna Green right this moment, crying her eyes out for joy after the wedding night of her dreams. Perhaps you know her? Miss Absentia Hackerman?"

Oh, Abbie, you title-hungry little fool. Olivia had the terrible feeling that Abbie now knew precisely how foolish she'd been.

Then Wallingford's gaze dropped to the form at her feet. "Is that Walt?"

The Chimera nodded. "It is indeed. It seemed our Sumner had a mind of his own, more's the pity. A small mind, it's true, but an independent one for all that."

Behind the three men, Olivia saw the fallen Sumner stir. She quickly looked away, hope blooming within her. Heaven bless men with hard heads!

Olivia saw Sumner's hand moving slowly toward his pistol on the floor. She nudged Walter with her toe, twice. *Ready, steady.* He grunted faintly so she knew he remembered the old signal.

Sumner leaped to his feet behind Wallingford and coshed the man on the head with the pistol. Then he reached into his pocket and tossed something small and glimmering at Olivia. She caught it even as the Chimera was turning to point his pistol at Sumner. The key.

She dropped it next to Walter's hand, then flung herself on the Chimera's back. She wasn't accustomed to fighting, so she used her weight to bear him to the floor. She took an elbow to her belly and fell from his back to the floor, breathless. The Chimera's pistol went spinning into the darkness.

Walter was up, standing unchained before her. "Up the mill axle!"

Together they scrambled up the rod that ran vertically from the wheel gears to the millstone. It was dark and they were both injured, but the way was familiar from years of play. Once there, Walter's strength failed and he collapsed.

Above, Olivia made her way around the catwalk to the giant lever that engaged the water wheel gears.

She closed her eyes and prayed, hoping that the neglected waterwheel still had enough teeth to move the millstone. Then she threw the lever to engage the waterwheel and sent the mill into loud, creaking operation.

Under the cover of this distraction, she aided Walter to his feet and helped him hide in the stone grain reservoir above. As she pulled the trap closed, she kept it open a tiny slit to watch for pursuit. Please, let the noise have concealed their passage!

The small man appeared at the top of the still slowly rotating millstone machinery. He looked very, very angry.

34

Galahad's pounding hooves ate up the miles now that he wasn't being held back by the smaller mounts. In only a few hours, Dane found himself on the road to Cheltenham. He ought to catch up to the caravan just as they made it to the manor, in another hour or so—

He rounded a turn and pulled Galahad to a dust-raising stop. Olivia's caravan was heading right toward him. They pulled to a hurried stop as well.

"What is the meaning of this?" he bellowed.

The entire coterie stared at him, blank terror on their faces. Dane felt something black and frightening skitter up his spine. He trotted Galahad to the foremost, luxurious carriage and peered inside.

It was empty.

He twisted to look up at Errol. "Where is her ladyship?" His voice was flat and lethal. If they had let her come to harm—

"We don't know, my lord. She was napping in her carriage over the rest time, or so we thought, so we didn't wake her when we started off again." Errol shook his head. "It wasn't until an hour later that I lifted the trap to check on her. I should have known there was no one aboard. She don't weigh much, but the carriage ought to have felt lighter."

Not with all her baggage above. And knowing Errol, he'd kept the bouncing to a minimum, making the lightness very hard to detect.

"Where was the rest time?"

"Well . . ." Errol looked about at the others. "We think right about here, my lord, just the far side of this curve."

Dane swung down from Galahad without another word. Now that he was looking, he saw clearly where the convoy had parked. The heaviest wagon with the wider wheels. The servants' carriage with the less expensive wheels. Finally, Olivia's luxurious coach and four, parked alongside the wooded side.

He found where she'd slid slightly leaving the carriage. Her wound must have been bothering her. She'd moved deeper into the wood. Why?

She couldn't use the chamber pot in the carriage, he realized. Too confined and awkward for her just now.

So she'd taken herself off for a little walk in the wood. If he wasn't feeling so panicked, he'd smile.

Then he found true reason to panic. A man's boot prints and signs of a struggle. Great rents in the soft earth where she'd been dragged.

He must have given up and carried her, for there were only the boot prints after that, leading to a path that ran alongside the road and hoofprints, one of which had a cracked shoe.

Something bright lay in the dirt. He knelt to pick up

a broken Chinese comb he recognized all too well. Olivia's hair couldn't hold on to a thing.

His fist tightened around the fragment of cloisonné. This path was doubtless used for no good, hidden from the road as it was. Used by smugglers and thieves, no doubt. Dane called for Galahad to be brought.

Dane mounted, following the distinctive hoofprints. He wouldn't think about anything but following the trail.

He couldn't bear to.

He hadn't been following the trail for long, but it felt like hours, panicked hours, leaning far over to make out the marks in the growing dimness.

He heard the sound of rushing water ahead of him. A river. He hoped he wouldn't lose the tracks in the water—

A woman's scream rose above the river's murmur. *Olivia*. Dane bent low over Galahad's neck and kicked the stallion into a gallop.

Olivia stood, frozen with fear, unable to scream again. The Chimera had a pistol pressed to Walter's temple. The mill creaked and shivered around them. High as they were, she could feel the entire structure sway as the power of the millwheel ripped the rotten planks asunder.

"We must get down," she cried out to the cold little man. "We're all going to die!"

"No," he said patiently, loudly enough to be heard over the shrieking of snapping wood. "You're going to die. I'm going to win."

"Win what?" she cried desperately. "Why are you doing this?"

"Because I want to know," he answered reasonably. "I have a theory and I want it proven." He ground the barrel of the pistol into Walter's temple. Even more frightening, Walter didn't respond at all. The Chimera went on. "I want to know if your husband is part of a secret society."

"I don't know!" Olivia couldn't bear it. Walter was dying and no one was coming and she was very much afraid she was going to tell the malevolent little bastard everything he wanted to know and he was going to kill them anyway!

The mill was beginning to crumble around them from the stress of the malfunctioning waterwheel. As if in answer to her prayers, a great timber fell on the little man, knocking him away from Walter. His dapper-clad legs were the only part of him she could see, protruding out from under part of an old hand-hewn rafter.

Olivia dived to her knees and wrapped her arms about her brother. "Walter?" she shouted over the madness. "Walter, we must get out! You must help me!"

Walter stirred and blinked up at her. He smiled. "You got him, Livvie."

Then the roof fell in on them all.

From atop Galahad, Dane watched in horror as the rickety mill began to collapse in on itself and Olivia. He knew she was in there, for he'd heard her cry out for her dead brother.

Dane leaped from his horse and charged into the building, dodging falling timbers and stones while bellowing her name. He saw Wallingford dead, his skull burst by a falling stone.

He heard a wordless muffled cry coming from be-neath a pile of debris. She was buried beneath what seemed to be half the roof. There was no time to go for help. The rest of the mill could come down on them at any moment.

He was the only one who could save her. He put his shoulder to the largest portion and felt it give only slightly. Dear God, even his extreme brawn was not go-ing to be enough. For the first time in his life, he wished he were even larger than he was. He'd become a giant and run off to live in a cave if only he could be strong enough to dig her from this rubble!

He strained mightily, giving a wordless roar as he put his heart into it. She would *not* die here!

The buckled piece of roof slid aside. He felt the lower floor sway beneath them. He hadn't much time.

The rest were large but not so stubborn. At last, he lifted the final plank away from her. She had her arms wrapped around a thin man with sandy hair.

It seemed Walter wasn't dead. Yet. Dane knelt beside Olivia, brushing the hair out of her eyes. "My lady, you must awake."

She finally drew in a great breath, then coughed. "It hurts. . . ."

He cupped her face, making her look at him. "You likely have some broken ribs, my love." Please, let that be all. "Can you stand?"

She did with some help, staggering as the mill shud-dered violently beneath them. "The mill! Dane, you must help Walter—"

Dane already had the fellow flung over his shoulder. He held out his hand to her and led her to the broken edge of the floor. "I don't think we can get out by going down!" he shouted as the groaning mill protested louder. "We'll have to jump in the river!"

"Not here!" She gestured to the waterwheel. "We're too close—"

Something hit Dane from behind, knocking him and his unconscious burden off the broken wall and into the river below.

"Dane!"

35

Olivia watched in horror as the two men she loved most in the world fell into the suction of the waterwheel. She fell to her knees, unaware of her own danger, unable to tear her eyes off the disaster below her.

Dane surfaced first and whipped his long hair away from his face. He looked around wildly. Olivia saw his lips move. He was calling for her brother.

Her heart swelled with love and fear for him. Then she saw Walter bob briefly to the surface, his arm reaching, trying to swim, even weak as he was. Dane struck out strongly toward him, reached him, and began towing him away from the base of the wheel.

Suddenly something pulled Dane down, ducking him violently from beneath. Another head emerged from the water behind Dane.

It was only then that Olivia realized what had caused Dane and Walter to fall. The Chimera was in the water with them!

Dane let go of Walter rather than pull him under as well. Walter tried to swim back to help him, but Dane shoved him away, then turned to dive beneath the surface looking for the Chimera, who had slid beneath the surface again like a crocodile.

Walter began to drift. It looked as though he was losing consciousness again!

The mill swayed beneath Olivia as she knelt on all fours. She cast one last look at Walter, then began to crawl toward the safer side, away from the great wheel.

Once there, she stood shakily, then reached behind her to undo her gown. It wrenched her sore ribs horribly and her hands were clumsy, but she got enough undone to rip the gown over her head. She let it flutter to the river below.

Then she jumped.

Under the water, Dane's battle against the elusive Chimera wasn't going as well as he'd hoped. He didn't only want to stop the bastard from drowning him; he wanted to catch the Chimera. Failing that, Dane would truly like to kill him.

Alas, Dane's superior size and strength were not doing well by him in the churning water. The smaller man was faster and Dane's strength did little in this world where he could gain no purchase.

After a few moments, he was stunned to find that he was fighting for his life. The fight was also moving too close to the mill wheel.

At last, he had his hands wrapped about the bastard's throat. Dane's own sight began to dim suddenly. He needed air immediately, but not until he'd rid the world of the bloody damned ubiquitous Chimera.

Struggling against his own lungs' demands, Dane pressed the Chimera back, back—

Dane felt an enormous tug against his grip and immediately let the man go. Go to his death beneath the broken, howling waterwheel.

Dane struggled for the surface, toward air and life and Olivia. Then the wheel snagged his trousers and pulled him under and away.

Olivia dragged Walter up the gravelly embankment downstream of the mill. "Walter," she gasped. "Breathe, Walter!"

"Yes, Mummy," he groaned. He rolled onto his side and spit up water in a heaving retch. Then he rolled onto his back. "Is the Dane all right?"

Olivia was watching the water. "I don't see him." Her fear was quiet and complete.

"Well, go get him," Walter said, waving his arm. "You can do it, Livvie. You're the most amazing woman I know."

Olivia pushed him back down. "Stay here. If you see that nasty little man—"

Walter nodded. "I'll play dead. It's what I do best these days."

Olivia left him to run upstream. Without giving it a thought, she took a deep breath and dived beneath the millwheel.

The water was murky and cloudy with disturbed earth. She cautiously grabbed the side of the wheel and let it carry her deeper. There was a trick to riding the wheel. If she could avoid getting caught in the graveyard of dead limbs and rubble that had been swept and entangled beneath the wheel over the decades, the wheel would carry her right out again. It was something she and Walter had learned when they were too naive to realize their danger.

There wasn't enough light coming from the dusky sky above. She wasn't going to be able to find Dane—

She saw his white shirt ballooning below her in the water. He was caught, tangled in the black grasping branches of a sunken limb.

She left him there and let go of the wheel to rise back up to the surface. It hurt her to leave him, but she needed more air if she was going to free him.

Her head broke the surface. She gave Walter a reassuring wave, then filled her lungs deeply again and again. It made the air last longer; she wasn't sure why.

Then she dived, straight down, following her memory and her heart. She saw Dane's shirt again in the bluing light and swam strongly toward him. She felt the pull of the wheel's turning, but she didn't care how close she had to go. Dane was almost within reach.

His long hair floated around his head, wrapping silky strands about her fingers when she reached for him. She followed his body down, sliding her hands over him, searching for where he was caught.

He burst into wild struggles, roused by her touch. His eyes were wide with alarm as he tried to push her back toward the surface.

She fought his hands away and caught his face between her palms. She glared at him through the murky water and their twining, floating hair.

He blinked, then raised both his hands. *I surrender*.

Bringing her mouth down to his, she pressed her lips tightly to his—and breathed half her air into his mouth. Then he took her shoulders in his hands and pushed her away.

She hovered, keeping her position with her arms

and legs, until she saw him free his snagged trousers. Then she shot upward to the sapphire-tinted surface to await him there.

He was right behind her, rising from the deep like a rather soggy Viking god. She let herself drift downstream as she panted for breath, smiling as he shook his head like a dog, flinging back the wet hair over his eyes.

He took her into his arms, right there in the middle of the millstream, and kissed her deeply. When he released her she frowned at him.

"There's a great deal I need to tell you," she began. "It was that Chimera fellow all along. I never knew—"

He pulled her close and kissed her again. Olivia was barely aware when they floated right past Walter where he lay on the bank. Dane began to steer them both toward the bank. "You're cold. I can tell by your lips."

"But I must tell you—"

He towed her with him. "No, you mustn't. I don't believe you had a thing to do with anything."

She let him pull her, surprise nearly overwhelming the delight. "You don't? Why not?"

He stood in water that was still too deep for her. Careful of her sore ribs, he lifted her and walked toward the bank. "I knew you could save me," he said. "Just like I know that you love me and that you would never, ever betray me."

"How can you know that?" she asked, not quite believing his change of heart. "How can anyone truly know that?"

Dane simply grinned at her as he carried her easily from the river.

"There's this little thing called 'faith.' "

Epilogue

Olivia and Dane cuddled before the fire in the now nearly deserted Kirkall Hall. All the guests were gone except for the Prince Regent, who was passing his time with the Duchess of Halswick.

Olivia lay her head on Dane's chest. "You know, I'm still worried that the Chimera's body wasn't found."

Dane stroked one hand down her hair. "Don't worry, my lady. If he is still alive, there are people in place who will take care of him."

She tilted her head to look up at him. "More of your 'friends,' my love?"

Dane smiled. "I'm a very popular fellow."

Olivia lay her head back onto his chest. "Sumner walked today. Petty is ecstatic."

Dane grunted. "That's good news. I thought I was going to have to carry the bloke about the house forever."

"Thank you for having the Prince Regent pardon him."

Dane nodded. "You're welcome. As long as he stays

in our employ, he will be safe. If he ever leaves us, I won't be able to help him."

Olivia nodded. "If he leaves us after what he's done, I'll hunt him down myself."

Dane chuckled. "Bloodthirsty wench."

There came a knock on the door of the bedchamber. Dane grudgingly allowed Olivia to leave his lap to answer it.

The Prince Regent stood in the doorway. "What kind of bloody idiot left this on my bloody bed pillow?" He help up the long-lost fifth Rod of the Rajah.

Olivia clapped a hand over her mouth, unable to stifle a giggle. Dane came up behind her and wrapped both arms about her waist.

"You can keep that, if you like, Your Highness. We don't need it any longer."